Praise for

Seven Nights of Sin

"Lacey ——————————————————————————— rl in all
of us. Unforge————— —— ——, ye ——————————— e' sort
of way."   —Michelle Buonfiglio, MyLifetime.com

"Thoroughly tantalizing, with magnetic characters, a sizzling
plot, and raw sensuality, this book will have you fanning yourself
long after the last page!"   —*Romantic Times*

Praise for

Lacey Alexander

"Ms. Alexander is an exceptionally talented author who, time
after time, takes us on extremely erotic journeys that leave us
breathless with every turn of the page. . . . This author pens the
most arousing sexual scenes that you could never imagine.
Lacey Alexander is a truly gifted storyteller."

—Fallen Angel Reviews

"Lacey Alexander has given readers . . . hot, erotic romance with
no holds barred."   —Romance Junkies

"Ms. Alexander is probably one of the most talented, straight-
forward, imaginative writers in erotic romance today."

—The Road to Romance

continued . . .

ALSO BY

LACEY ALEXANDER

Voyeur

Seven Nights of Sin

The Bikini Diaries

Lacey Alexander

HEAT

HEAT
Published by New American Library, a division of
Penguin Group (USA) Inc., 375 Hudson Street,
New York, New York 10014, USA

Penguin Group (Canada), 90 Eglinton Avenue East, Suite 700, Toronto,
Ontario M4P 2Y3, Canada (a division of Pearson Penguin Canada Inc.)
Penguin Books Ltd., 80 Strand, London WC2R 0RL, England
Penguin Ireland, 25 St. Stephen's Green, Dublin 2,
Ireland (a division of Penguin Books Ltd.)
Penguin Group (Australia), 250 Camberwell Road, Camberwell, Victoria 3124,
Australia (a division of Pearson Australia Group Pty. Ltd.)
Penguin Books India Pvt. Ltd., 11 Community Centre,
Panchsheel Park, New Delhi–110 017, India
Penguin Group (NZ), 67 Apollo Drive, Rosedale, North Shore 0632,
New Zealand (a division of Pearson New Zealand Ltd.)
Penguin Books (South Africa) (Pty.) Ltd., 24 Sturdee Avenue,
Rosebank, Johannesburg 2196, South Africa

Penguin Books Ltd., Registered Offices:
80 Strand, London WC2R 0RL, England

First published by Heat, an imprint of New American Library,
a division of Penguin Group (USA) Inc.

First Printing, February 2009
1   3   5   7   9   10   8   6   4   2

HEAT is a trademark of Penguin Group (USA) Inc.

LIBRARY OF CONGRESS CATALOGING-IN-PUBLICATION DATA:

Alexander, Lacey.
The bikini diaries/Lacey Alexander.
p. cm.
ISBN 978-0-451-22590-0
I. Title.
PS3601.L3539B54 2009
813'.6—dc22   2008028607

Set in Dante

Printed in the United States of America

*Y*ou always see those girls at the beach—the ones who some-how make you feel inferior even when you're usually a fairly confident person, happy with who you are. Killer tan, killer boobs, and those long, silky, to-die-for legs, all strapped into some sinfully tiny bikini that has Fuck Me written all over it.

I'm watching one of those sex goddess types approach even as I write this. God, she's beautiful. I kind of hate her—for making every other woman on this beach look so dreadfully normal, for making married men and dads stop talking with their wives or building sand castles with their kids in order to stare.

What is it like to be her?

Is this really who she is—a woman who's so comfortable with her sexuality that she wants to advertise it, a hot chick looking for a good lay and that's all? Or does she work so hard to look perfect because she secretly harbors low self-esteem and tries to cover that with physical beauty? And is it sex she wants, or is that just a trap and she's really looking for love?

I prefer to think the former, I suppose, since even though I'm intimidated by her, I also envy her. The sexually comfort-able her. The her who wants to get laid and nothing more. And even though I like myself just the way I am most days—right now, just for a moment, just a brief little second, I want to _be_ her.

Chapter 1

Wendy Carnes closed her journal and dropped it inside the beach bag next to her lounge chair, along with the pen. She couldn't help resenting the fact that she wanted to be that woman—the one she'd just watched walking up the shoreline, all tan and perfect, hard nipples jutting through the two white triangles covering her breasts, long blond hair blowing behind her in the sea breeze. She couldn't help resenting it, but she could accept it. It was only natural—everyone wanted to be beautiful and desirable.

And maybe . . . maybe everyone secretly wanted to know that sort of power. Because that was what the bikini woman possessed—power. Over all the men on the beach. And some of the women, too.

Of course, she couldn't forget to factor in pleasure. One glance had told Wendy that the blond bikini babe *knew* pleasure—how to give it and how to take it. Her eyes had nearly sparkled with it.

Beauty, power, and pleasure. What was there *not* to envy?

But then Wendy shook it off. Because she was here for *business*, not pleasure. In fact, she was surprised she'd let Miss Bikini Babe distract her so much. To think she'd even started writing about it in her work journal—that wasn't like her.

Then again, her work seldom led her to places so intoxicating as the Emerald Shores Beach Resort, edging three miles of pristine white sand along Florida's panhandle, also known as the Emerald Coast. The word "emerald" got tossed around a lot here with good reason—when the sun hit this particular edge of the Gulf of Mexico, the pale sand beneath turned the water a nearly electric shade of green.

No, her job usually led her to a downtown Chicago office building, where she served as administrative assistant to Walter Carlisle, a wealthy real estate investor with holdings all over the country and a genuinely pleasant guy to work for. Walter was serious and stalwart when it came to business, but he was also a fair and friendly employer who liked to go boating, play Texas hold 'em, and spend time with his wife and their young grandchildren.

Wendy had been stunned when Walter asked her to go to Emerald Shores on what, in the office, they called a "scouting mission." Even when Walter had chosen to permanently relocate his usual "scout," Marie Hill, in Seattle to oversee his large collection of property there, Wendy had assumed he'd hire someone new for her position. And who knew? Maybe he still would. But at least for now, he'd elected Wendy to take on the task of traveling to Emerald Shores to determine if Walter should sink significant money into the place.

And maybe the job wouldn't be so daunting if Emerald Shores was your run-of-the-mill beach resort. But it was far from it—it was, in fact, an enormous upscale self-contained community. In addition to thousands of high-rise condo units stretching both along the beach and the adjacent bay area, Emerald Shores boasted abundant shopping, nightlife, restaurants, and even a full-scale grocery and pharmacy—along with biking, golf, tennis, and a free shuttle to get you wherever you needed to go. It was a world of luxury that also came with all the conveniences of home, and that was the charm of the vast property—for vacationers, for full-time residents, and for Walter Carlisle.

When one of the resort's largest investors had pulled out, the Emerald Shores executives had begun vigorously courting Carlisle Enterprises. As a result, Wendy found herself sitting on an immaculate white beach, digging her bare toes into soft, warm sand, and . . . well, now, wondering what it was like to be sex on a stick.

Because even though White Bikini Babe had disappeared out of sight, she remained in Wendy's thoughts. She'd felt both . . . intimidated and rebuffed by the woman's very presence.

So why again did Wendy envy her?

Did she secretly long to be intimidating, to make other women feel bad about themselves? No—she was a nicer person than that.

But White Bikini Babe was one of the "beautiful people," the type who had it easy in life, or at least easier than most. And Wendy couldn't stop wondering what it was like to be an object of pure sexual desire, plain and simple.

Focus, she told herself. She wasn't here to watch girls, or guys—she was here to check out every aspect of Emerald Shores from both a tourist and investor perspective, talk with the resort executives about what she felt needed to be changed or updated, and then, based on their response, she would share her findings with Walter when she went home next week and make a recommendation that he invest—or not.

After taking a sip of the frozen mango daiquiri, complete

with umbrella, that a Hawaiian-shirt-clad waiter had just delivered, she lowered the drink to the sand and took up her journal and pen again—this time making notes that mattered.

Umbrella drinks—too expensive. People may be willing to pay $12 for a drink, but I'm sure they resent it. Lower the price by 25% and you still make a profit, people will likely drink more, and they won't feel ripped off.

She'd examine later if that was actually an issue worth presenting to the Emerald Shores execs, but she'd decided to bring a journal, keep it with her as often as possible, record anything that occurred to her, and then sort through it all later.

As for why she'd written down her thoughts about White Bikini Babe—she supposed she'd been venting. And no one would ever see the journal but her, so she could use it however she wished.

It was when she abandoned the journal once more, taking another sip of the mango-and-rum concoction, that she noticed a vision in white in her peripheral vision. She looked up to see that—lo and behold—White Bikini Babe now glided back down the shoreline in the opposite direction. This time her hair blew around her face a bit, making her look more windblown-and-sexy than sleek-and-hot, but the effect remained the same. As those lithe tan legs moved smoothly over the sand, Wendy could feel every guy in the vicinity watching—just as *she* was. Like before: dads, husbands; young men and old.

But this time a group of twentysomething guys who had just arrived to start tossing around a football all stopped to gape, too, and something about *that* got to Wendy on a deeper level. Because the guys were cute—hot, even. And now two of them had abandoned the game completely to boldly approach White Bikini, and Wendy watched as they spoke, visibly flirting. Suddenly, *Wendy* wanted to know how to flirt like that. Because she suddenly wanted such cute beach guys to notice *her*, to want *her*.

And as the conversation ended—maybe with plans for later?—and the white bikini sashayed on up the beach still looking enviably hot, Wendy finally understood her strange fixation with the woman. In fact, it hit her like a ton of bricks.

Wendy was thirty-four years old. And if there was a window of time in her life to ever look that good or act that way—to openly advertise herself sexually—it was probably past. And that meant she would never know what it felt like to fuck a drop-dead gorgeous guy for no other reason than pure physical pleasure.

Unless . . . unless she grabbed the opportunity right now.

She bit her lip, stunned at her last thought.

She wasn't normally a sexually aggressive person—she saw herself as mild-mannered and pretty-in-an-ordinary-way, and she hadn't dated since getting her job with Carlisle Enterprises two years ago.

It hadn't been a conscious decision, but . . . well, she'd been through a number of relationships with dreadfully average guys who were crazier about her than she'd been about them, and she supposed at some point she'd decided they just weren't worth her time. Given that her job came with long hours. And that the guys she seemed to attract just weren't very exciting to her.

Of course, at night, in bed, she occasionally allowed herself some pretty wild fantasies about fabulously hot guys—and in them, she was always stunningly sexy. Which, now that she analyzed it, probably meant she had desires she was shoving under the rug, bored and irritated with the offerings in her life.

And now, suddenly, for the first time ever, as she glanced at the round tan ass of the girl moving away from her up the beach, she wondered—was it even conceivable? Could she, Wendy Carnes, ever *pull off* stunningly sexy? Could she wear a skimpy bikini like that one? Other sexy clothes?

She didn't see herself as overly prim, but she generally tried to be *appropriate*. When she went to Myrtle Beach in South Carolina with her sister and three nieces every summer, she always wore a conservative two-piece suit—the same she wore right now. She wasn't twenty-one anymore, nor did she have the body she'd had then. What a crime that when she *had* been twenty-one, she hadn't the guts to wear something skimpy and would have feared sending the wrong message. Now that she *wanted* to wear it, *wanted* to send a different message than ever before—just once, just for this week—she suspected her body was probably too imperfect. A classic catch-22.

Still, it was a pretty decent body for her age. God had blessed her with good boobs and, so far, only one small spot of cellulite on the back of her right thigh. She worked out regularly, so that helped. And she'd just gotten a new hair color, which everyone said looked sexy, although that hadn't been the goal—she'd gone from her regular medium brown to a coppery hue with a few blond streaks.

She stared out at the ocean, pondering the unthinkable.

Except that, to her surprise, it had suddenly become thinkable.

Could she pull it off? Could she become like that woman? Could she become . . . someone else?

. . .

That hot May afternoon, Wendy made her way up the scenic, winding "beachwalk"—the path dotted with small palm trees and brightly blooming shrubbery—and back to her room in one of three tall, lavish pink buildings situated along the ocean and called the Shellside Towers. It was her first day at Emerald Shores after arriving late last night, and though the beach was a large part of the place's appeal, she couldn't squander all her time there—she had to start checking out other aspects of the resort.

So she'd decided she would do a little shopping this afternoon, and tonight she'd shuttle over to the Bayside Village—the area of the resort where most of the eateries and nightlife were located.

Thus her mind was back on work—kind of.

Since as she prepared to step into the shower, she found her mind also back on . . . her body. Which was odd. She'd taken countless showers in her life without necessarily being turned on by the mere fact that she was naked. But today, she found her glance flitting to the large mirror stretched across the bathroom vanity.

She supposed she still had sex on the brain. She supposed she was still wondering if she could ever pull off the sexy-and-ready look, if she could wear a skimpy bikini without feeling ridiculous.

God *had* given her good boobs. They weren't perky, but they were large and round, D cups, and just now, her nipples were hard and she couldn't help thinking they were fairly gorgeous. Not *Playboy* gorgeous, and not boob job gorgeous, but gorgeous in a *real woman* sort of way. And the tan lines she'd picked up today seemed to emphasize them, outline them.

Additionally, her hips seemed thinner than the last time she'd really looked at them. Was that even possible—for hips to shrink? But maybe the elliptical machine at the gym was paying off.

That thought urged her to turn her butt toward the mirror and view it over her shoulder. Biting her lip, she stood up straight and stuck her ass out a little—and liked what she saw. The elliptical *was* working. Of course, her particular posture at the moment was helping, too—but her bottom looked rounder than she ever remembered.

Although . . . maybe she'd never actually taken the time to study her own ass before. Boobs were easier—they were in front and ended up in the mirror all the time; the ass it took a concerted effort to see.

She surprised herself when she bent over then, arching higher, still peering over her shoulder, until she could see her pussy from behind. The view looked like porn. Of course, most porn chicks shaved. But still, she found herself titillated by the very idea that she could look even *remotely* pornlike.

"Stop this," she scolded herself then, glad no one could see her. Then she finally stepped into the cool shower, letting the water sluice over her and begin to wash away the shine and scent of sunscreen and sweat.

Reaching for a bar of the aromatic soap the resort provided, she ran it over her skin, making suds—and realized she was concentrating on her chest, stomach, and breasts more than usual. She glanced down to see . . . more porn. Soapy, sudsy tits. She bit her lip, unable to deny liking the way they looked—and wondering if those cute guys on the beach would like them, too. The very thought made her surge with moisture below.

Wendy stayed in the shower for a long while, leisurely glid-ing the soap over her curves again and again before finally wash-ing her hair and letting the water sweep away the sparkling white bubbles to leave her soft and clean. Upon getting out, she let her gaze drift back to the mirror, watching herself reach for a towel and dry off, then watching herself comb out her long hair and blow it dry without even putting on underwear first. She sup-posed it had just been a long time since she'd really studied her body, and she was surprised at how attractive she found it.

The real question, though? Was she deluding herself? Did she just look . . . "pretty good" for her age? Was she *too* curvy? Were her breasts too heavy, her butt too round? And how notice-able *was* that cellulite anyway?

Exiting the bathroom, she donned a white bra and white cotton panties. Ugh—they suddenly seemed boring, making her wish she had something sexier. "Not that it actually mat-ters," she mumbled. It wasn't like anyone was going to be seeing them, seeing *her*.

She might think she looked good—but sanity had just kicked back in to remind her who she was. She was sane, hardworking, middle-of-the-road Wendy Carnes—not White Bikini Babe. You couldn't just decide you wanted to be someone else and magi-cally have it happen.

It was with that sobering thought that she donned a casual summer skirt and tank, slipped on sandals, and set out to ex-plore more of Emerald Shores. Getting away from the beach had probably been a good idea—shopping and dinner, around people who were fully clothed, would get her back in her right mind.

· · ·

Wendy couldn't help being impressed with the shopping options, even before entering any of the stores. A grand boulevard divided by a parklike strip of land complete with a fountain was lined on both sides by everything from Banana Republic to Victoria's Secret, with nonchain specialty shops tucked in between.

She knew, of course, what the brand name stores offered, so when she reached a boutique called the Beach Bazaar, she stepped in, wind chimes on the door announcing her arrival. And coming inside had nothing to do with the sexy bikinis in the window, either. Or at least not much, she insisted to herself.

"Hi," said a beautiful Asian girl standing behind a circular counter.

"Hello."

The dark-haired girl smiled, the gesture making her even prettier. "We've got a lot of great sales going on. Fashion watches are twenty-five percent off, and clearance dresses," she said, pointing to a round rack, "are half price. That table of cute panties is reduced, too."

Wendy's gaze dropped to the table next to her, spread with lacy thongs and sexy boy-short panties. "I'll check it all out," she assured the girl.

And silly as it was, she found herself wishing she'd worn something trendier than her simple skirt. The salesgirl was hip and stylish and confident without trying in low-rider jeans and a lace cami of baby blue that accentuated her generous cleavage. Wendy knew it was insane to compare herself to the girl—who couldn't have been a day over twenty-five—yet apparently White Bikini Babe had her feeling sexually inferior to every attractive woman she encountered now. Great.

Perusing the panties closer, Wendy picked up a few pairs.

She'd never worn the boy-short kind before and wondered how she'd look in them. A couple of thongs couldn't hurt, either. Not that she ever wore thongs. But hadn't she just lamented her boring undies? Maybe it was time for a change.

Heading to the dress rack, she found a sexy tangerine-colored halter dress with a built-in bra for only thirty bucks. The question of the day flitted through her mind: *Could I pull this off? Or would I be one of those women who looks tacky because she dresses too young?*

"That dress is fabulous," the salesgirl said, coming up from behind.

Without planning it, Wendy was completely honest. "Do you think it's too . . . young for me?"

The Asian girl's gaze widened in surprise. "Not at all! It's sexy, sure, but classy, too. Which fits you to a tee."

Wendy's eyebrows shot up. The salesgirl thought she was sexy? And classy. Hmm.

Then again, maybe the girl just needed to move these dresses.

"I'll try it on," Wendy said, still unsure.

"Great—I'll start a dressing room for you." With that, the pretty girl extracted the hanger from Wendy's hand and took the panties from her, as well, a sweep of her long, straight hair brushing over Wendy's bent arm and making her shiver a little for reasons unknown.

"Where can I find bikinis?" Wendy heard herself inquire as the girl walked away. Her eyes automatically dropped to the salesgirl's swaying ass as she departed.

"Up front on the left," the girl answered over her shoulder.

Taking a deep breath, Wendy headed that way. Odd, perhaps, that looking through bathing suits should make her nervous—but she knew she wasn't seeking just *any* bathing suit, and she knew why. Having the salesgirl refer to her as sexy had just imbued her with a strange new sort of confidence.

Of course, the problem with bikinis was—it was hard to know what you were getting until you tried them on. So Wendy ended up pulling a lot off the rack, trying to make bolder choices than usual.

Twenty minutes later, she'd tried them all, finding fault with most of them . . . until finally, upon slipping into the last, she discovered herself standing before the long mirror, gazing at her body in pure awe.

The suit wasn't as skimpy as White Bikini Babe's, but it was more revealing than any she'd ever worn before. She'd never even attempted a triangle top given the size of her boobs, but this one possessed subtle foam half moon shaping under the breasts, giving them a little lift and support while leaving an ample amount of both inner and outer curves on display. The simple black bottoms were also more sparse than any she'd sported, featuring small gold buckle-like rectangles at either hip to connect the fabric.

She studied herself for a long time, noting the outline of her hardened nipples through the thin black top and realizing this suit would give her an entirely new set of tan lines. *If* she bought it. And *if* she wore it. Because *she* thought it looked good—almost *scary* good—but what if she was delusional?

So, swallowing back her pride, she finally did what she felt she had to—sought a second opinion. Opening the dressing room door just a crack to find the boutique still blessedly empty but for the pretty salesclerk, she called lightly, "Um, excuse me."

The girl appeared cheerfully before her a few seconds later. "Need another size?"

Wendy couldn't help being a little embarrassed, but . . . "Actually, I was wondering if I could ask your opinion on a bikini. Your *honest* opinion. Because it won't hurt my feelings to find out it doesn't look good, and I'd rather know the truth than risk it."

Casting an empathetic expression, the girl used her index finger to draw an invisible X across her ample chest. "Cross my heart. I'll be completely honest."

"You won't let me buy something that's too skimpy for my shape?" she asked, just to clarify.

"Promise," the pretty girl said, sounding sincere.

And then it hit Wendy that if she really looked awful in this, she didn't even want the attractive salesgirl to see her in it. But better one person than a whole beach full.

So she bit her lip, hesitating, but finally said, "All right then. Can I pull this off?" She opened the door—and even struck a bit of a pose, because she felt she had to do *something* rather than just stand there looking afraid of herself.

She watched as the Asian girl's jaw dropped, her eyes going wide. "Oh my *God*." Her gaze swept over Wendy's body from head to toe. "Hell *yes*, you can pull it off."

Wendy hadn't even *imagined* such an enthusiastic reaction. "Really?"

The girl's eyes perused her shape again, before rising back to her face. "Of course, really. With those curves, I can't even believe you have to ask!"

"Well, I . . ." *I guess I keep them fairly covered a lot. I guess I haven't actually let enough people see me to even* know *if my body is gorgeous—except for all the Mr. Averages in my life.* "I wasn't sure.

I . . . just don't want to look silly or tacky or like I'm trying to compete with college girls, you know?"

Her new friend was nodding as if she understood completely. "Look, you don't have to be twenty-one to be hot. I can't imagine *anyone* seeing you in that and not thinking you're *totally* hot, babe. Trust me." Her gaze still drank in Wendy's body, seeming to focus on her breasts now, and just like in the shower, Wendy's pussy went warm and moist.

She decided to take the dress, too, and all the panties.

"I bet you look amazing in *all* this stuff," the salesgirl said as she rung up the purchase a few minutes later, and Wendy, oddly, found she liked watching the girl's slender, manicured hands run over the lace and other fabric as she handled it.

"I hope so," she replied quietly as she passed her credit card across the counter.

"Getting it to wear for a special guy? Your husband?" The girl completed the transaction, passing a slip for Wendy to sign as she packed her new items in a peach-colored shopping bag with the store's logo on the side.

"No," Wendy replied, and still feeling unduly honest, added, "Just the opposite, actually."

The salesclerk looked up with a conspiratorial smile, clearly understanding what Wendy meant. "Happy hunting," she said. And Wendy returned the smile and picked up her bag to go, the girl stopped her with a "Hey."

Wendy looked back from the door.

"If by some miracle you don't find anyone who appreciates your charms, come back and see me."

Wendy blinked, forced a last smile and hoped it looked natural, then walked out into the bright, hot sunlight.

Whoa. Was her pretty salesgirl coming on to her? Or had she meant something else entirely—like she knew some guy she could fix Wendy up with? Wendy didn't know, but she felt flushed, nervous—and surprisingly aroused.

She'd never even *thought about* liking girls that way before, but she knew in some circles it was definitely chic to explore the same gender thing these days. And as she strolled up the street, she couldn't stop wondering if the girl had truly been attracted to her—and what might have happened if she'd responded in kind.

Not that she ever would.

She couldn't imagine it.

But her pussy still fluttered with curiosity beneath her skirt as she walked.

Of course, maybe it wasn't fluttering just because of the Asian girl. Maybe it was fluttering because of the sexy panties she'd bought—the boy shorts had looked shockingly hot. Or the sexy dress—which she supposed *was* classy, but still definitely said she wasn't shy. Or that tight, revealing bikini. Was she *really* going to wear them all? Was she *really* going out to look for a man—in the clubs, on the beach?

She bit her lip as the tingle in her crotch skimmed its way up her spine. She couldn't quite believe it, but the answer, she realized, was yes. Yes, yes, yes. She *was.*

Happy hunting, indeed.

I can't believe I'm really doing this. But I'm wearing the dress now—cut lower than anything I've ever worn. And I'm starting to feel . . . braver. When I look in the mirror I see . . . well, I guess I'm starting to see what my new little "girlfriend" at the boutique saw. No, I'm not twenty-one, not by a long shot. But I look pretty damn hot. The truth is, I hardly recognize myself. Maybe that's a <u>good</u> thing. Because if I am to actually do this—go out and catch myself a man, a gorgeous, sexy one-night stand—I can't be my normal self. I have to keep seeing what <u>she</u> saw. I have to be the girl on the beach. I have to toss my fears aside.

I even shaved my pussy before getting dressed. I've never done that before, and it was surprisingly . . . titillating. I guess because I knew why I was doing it, because I suddenly want to reveal that part of myself to a stranger. And because I've never actually had occasion to be quite so intimate, visually, with myself. I expected to be nervous with a razor so close to such sensitive skin, but my arousal—and anticipation— totally outweighed that.

I shaved away all but a little oval swath of hair just above my slit, and it was strange—enlightening—to really see myself there. And to think of someone <u>else</u> seeing me there, <u>that</u> way. I couldn't believe how smooth and silky it felt to my fingertips, and added to my new tan lines, it makes me feel un-believably . . . exotic.

And even though part of me is scared to death to walk out the door in this dress, wearing a new black lace thong underneath—and beneath that being <u>completely</u> bare in a way I never have before—another part of me can't wait to put myself out there and see what happens.

I've decided to think of this as sort of an . . . experiment. Was the girl at the shop right? Am I sexy? Amazing? Can a dress or a bikini really change who you are, who you can <u>be</u>?

I don't know the answer, but just for one night, I want to be someone I've never been before—I want some hot man to make me feel like the white bikini girl, like the personification of sex, like nothing else matters, like sensible Wendy Carnes doesn't even exist. I want to be the hunter, the one who takes, the one who feels nothing but pleasure and walks away satis-fied in the end.

Take <u>that</u>, White Bikini Babe.

Chapter 2

*I*t felt weird eating alone. She hadn't expected that because, as a busy single woman, she ate alone in restaurants at home all the time—but this was different. Because of how she was dressed. Because she was in the entertainment district of a busy resort teeming with people. So as she sat dining on the veranda of a Southern-plantation-themed restaurant, appropriately called Tara, she couldn't help being aware that people stared.

They wondered, she supposed, if she'd been stood up on a date. Or maybe they wondered if she was . . . well, exactly what she was: a woman on the prowl for sex. And both ideas embarrassed her at first, until she noticed how many of the inquisitive looks came from *guys*. Inquisitive and *admiring* looks.

It wasn't like when White Bikini Babe had gone gliding up the beach—she didn't capture every male eye. But enough. More than usual. And slowly but surely it began to make her feel warm in her new thong panties. It began to remind her that she wasn't sensible Wendy tonight. She was wild Wendy. Wanton Wendy. And she was doing this, *really* doing it.

And though it felt odd at first to be the object of so much male attention, it was also a quiet way to get used to those eyes on her, a quiet way to learn to like it. She sat eating, keeping her gaze to herself but fully aware of the ones that studied her. She could have easily continued to feel embarrassed, but instead, she grew to *like* the question she knew her solitary presence created in the minds of her observers.

And by the time she descended the front steps of Tara on the sexy new heels she'd paid too much money for today, she realized those eyes had given her the confidence it would take to walk into a club now, to *truly* put herself out there.

Even so, she found herself bypassing the swank, trendy-looking dance clubs she found—the people heading inside were too young, college age, and she didn't want some young boy. She wanted a man. Someone who'd been around enough to know what he was doing in bed.

Then, just as she noticed that the crowd in the village was changing—that families must be going in for the evening as darkness fell, since mostly couples and singles strolled around her now—she spotted an establishment that instantly felt a little friendlier, more mature, and less intimidating. She might be overdressed for it, but she didn't care—it would only make her more eye-catching. She made her way to what sounded from outside like a piano bar—called Volcano's.

As she'd sensed, the mood inside was festive—two dueling pianos played rollicking tunes as the pianists tried to engage the crowd. Wendy smelled beer, popcorn, nachos. And she felt herself instantly immersed in more men's stares. To the degree that it normally would have made her very uncomfortable. But she was too elated inside to feel unsettled. Because, God, this meant her salesgirl friend *was* right—she was hot! Not tacky. Not silly. Just hot.

She moved through the crowded club as if she had someplace to go. Of course, she *would* start to look silly if she kept circling the place like a land shark, so after a few minutes, she slowed down and tried to act cool.

"Buy you a drink?"

She looked up to find a guy in a cowboy hat standing near her.

She bit her lip and attempted to look like she wasn't sizing him up—even though she was. And he was okay—right age bracket, decent body. But he wasn't what she'd come here looking for—he wasn't a stud, a hunk.

"No thanks—I'm meeting a friend." Wow, that lie had rolled off her tongue so smoothly you'd have thought she'd actually planned it.

"I'd be happy to buy one for her, too."

She smiled kindly. "Thanks. But no." Then she turned to move on, squeezing through a particularly tight crush of patrons without looking back.

She stopped when she found herself with a clear shot of the stage, listening as both pianos joined in on a request someone had shouted from the crowd, an old seventies song with a good beat called "I Hear You Knockin'." That was when a hand touched her bare arm.

She turned her head to see—oh, yuck—a guy old enough to be her father, and then some. Despite the tropical temperatures, he sported a leather blazer and wore his hair too long for his age. "Hello there," he said, clearly putting the make on her.

Seriously? she wanted to say. *You really think this is gonna go your way?* But even wanton Wendy couldn't be quite *that* cold, even if she thought this goofball deserved it. Instead, she gave a slight nod, trying to appear bored, and turned her attention back to the pianos.

"You look like you need a drink. What's your pleasure?"

She didn't bother to look at him again. "No thanks—I'm not thirsty."

He leaned closer in response. "Then what say we get out of here, go someplace where we can talk."

Okay, come on now. If he were thirty-five and attractive, that would be overly bold at this point, but from this guy, it was *ridiculous*. And this time, Wendy couldn't help it—without weighing it, she let out her natural response, rolling her eyes at him.

Then she saw him flinch and realized what she'd done.

Wow, wanton Wendy was a whole new animal!

"Some advice," she said to her suitor then. "Try approaching women born in the same decade as you. And don't be so smarmy about it."

"Fuck you," the man said, then stalked away.

Now it was Wendy who flinched, but it was softened when two girls on the other side of her laughed. One of them said, "Way to go. That creep kept hitting on us, too. What on earth is he *thinking*?"

Good question, since these girls were even younger than her—although not dressed so provocatively. The second girl said, "*We* should buy you a drink—for getting him out of here."

Wendy smiled, feeling as if she'd performed a public service, then took the opportunity to move on through the crowd, thinking it was time for greener pastures.

Soon, though, she understood the fatal flaw in her plan: Most men simply weren't hot enough for what she had in mind. She was approached by several guys who were pleasant, kind of cute, and on most nights of her life, she'd have been happy to get acquainted with them. But this was about more than getting laid. About more than being desired. This was also about what *she* desired, deep down. She'd come out tonight to "live the fantasy" and nothing else would do.

She wanted a guy she could be dirty with. Dirty and nasty. She wanted a guy who would inspire her to let her inhibitions run free. It had been building in her all day—the powerful need to be a sex goddess, to do and say and be as wild as in her nighttime fantasies with nothing at risk, because it would only be for a night. And sadly, for that, no simply "pleasant" guy would do. To be a sex goddess, she needed a sex *god*.

And that was when—oh God—she spotted him.

He wore a summery button-down shirt with stylish khaki cargo shorts and stood leaning with his back against the bar, a bottle of beer in his hand. His pale hair dusted his collar, and the darker stubble on his chin said he hadn't shaved today, but she was pretty sure in "real life," away from the resort, he was the professional type—which appealed, given that *she* was the professional type, and that it probably meant he had brains as well as looks. As his blue eyes sparkled on her and her heartbeat kicked up, she thought: *This is it. This is really it!*

She tried to flash her best come-hither look—and only hoped she could pull *that* off. She tilted her head to the right, just slightly, touching her tongue to her upper lip, easing it slowly across. She cast a sexy little smile at the same time, aware of the fluttering sensation between her thighs.

But . . . nothing in his expression changed. She saw no recognition of her gesture whatsoever.

And then—oh no—she realized where she stood. Between him and the stage. He was looking past her, to the piano player now pounding out a solo rendition of "Stuck in the Middle with You." *Oh. God.*

She shut her eyes, trying to block out her humiliation, then moved on quickly, praying no one else had seen the one-sided exchange. Spotting the bathroom, she ducked inside, since she was starting to feel like *she* was on a stage.

In the stall, she sat down to rest her feet and began to wonder if she was really cut out for this. The "attracting guys" part was working like a charm, so she knew now—it was confirmed—she could pull off the sexy dress. But there just weren't all that many truly hot guys *here*. Hell, maybe she should go to one of the trendier clubs, after all. Or . . . maybe she should just catch the shuttle back to the Shellside Towers and call it a day and return that bikini tomorrow and consider this an experiment that had failed with a capital F.

Taking a deep breath, she exited the bathroom, not even bothering to check her look in the mirror. It was too crowded and she was bummed out. The flutter in her panties had long since waned.

"Want a ride? I'm driving."

The deep voice caught her off guard and drew her gaze to the right. She found herself staring into a small, open elevator she hadn't even noticed before. And into . . . sparkling blue eyes that made her weak at a mere glance.

Good God, it was her hot, sexy guy from the bar!

Without even considering it, she stepped inside the elevator and heard herself begin to flirt. "But have you been *drinking*?"

He shrugged and cast a gorgeous smile. "A little, but I'll be careful and try not to get a ticket." The fluttering in her panties promptly resumed.

Only after the doors slid shut, though, did she inquire, "Um, where does this go?"

He let out a deep, good-natured laugh. "You should be more careful about taking rides with strangers. That's the first thing you should have asked." Then he explained that the elevator led to a quieter bar on the second floor—an idea that immediately appealed, under the circumstances.

"I had no idea there was another bar here."

"Most people don't. But it's nice."

When the elevator opened, Wendy heard a Phil Collins song and shifted her gaze to a small band in one corner of the room. Indeed, the mood was more serene here—most of the tables were occupied, but there was plenty of walking and standing room as compared to Volcano's first floor. A carved sign near the stage declared this the Lava Room.

"What are you drinking?" he asked, and she realized they were walking to the bar together as if it were the natural thing to do.

"Nothing, yet. What do you recommend?"

"For you?" He drew back and gave her a once-over, which she was pretty sure turned her nipples hard. "Sex on the beach," he said. Which made her pussy moist, too.

She bit her lip playfully, and grew bolder still. "The drink—or the activity?"

His eyes went warm, wholly sexual. "I definitely advocate both, but I was talking about the drink."

Advocate. She was right. Her hot man was smart, and intelligence turned her on as much as anything else. She leaned her head back with a slight smile. "And exactly why is that the drink for me?"

"Well, it's fruity and light, so girls usually like it. Plus its name allows me to bring up sex mere seconds after meeting you without getting slapped."

She laughed and thought, *You I wouldn't slap for bringing up sex.* But she liked his sense of humor, along with the fact that he was taking the time to flirt with her.

When the bartender arrived, her guy ordered two sex-on-the-beaches. And as they talked more, Wendy couldn't quite believe *this* guy was in to her. He was everything she'd come out looking for tonight—handsome, sexy as hell, gorgeous eyes, thick hair, and he clearly hid some muscles under that shirt, judging from the way it stretched across his chest. Plus there was that added perk of brains. That quickly, she wanted to be under him so badly that she could taste it, just as strongly as the fruity—and quickly intoxicating—drink.

She learned that her hot guy actually lived at the resort full-time—he owned one of the condos and worked locally. "I grew up in Alabama, a few hours north of here, but my family came down to the beach every summer, and I always hated going back home." Now that he mentioned it, at moments she could hear just a hint of a Southern accent hidden under his usually clear and direct enunciation, and it somehow made him all the more sexy. "So I worked down here on summer break through college, and it only made sense to come back to stay."

In reply, Wendy explained that she was here on business, but left it at that. Despite that she'd liked hearing a bit about *his* life, it seemed simpler that way.

"Hope you're not adverse to mixing your business with a little pleasure," he said with a soft, seductive grin.

Which prompted her to motion down at her dress and be completely blunt. "What does this dress tell you?"

His gaze swept appreciatively over her breasts and downward, then he gave her another scintillating smile as he leaned closer. "I hope it says you're a woman who likes pleasure as much as I do."

"*Very* much," she assured him, a frisson of it scurrying down her inner thighs.

A moment later, the band began playing a slow song, inviting people to dance. When several couples moved onto the small dance floor, her man motioned toward it. "Shall we?"

Oh God, this was fun. Just to be with a guy so smooth and sexy. To know he wanted her just like she wanted him. To know she was good enough, hot enough, to snag him, even if only for a night. She answered by putting her hand into his as she set her drink on the bar.

The band played Marvin Gaye's "Sexual Healing" as her man pulled her close and molded his hands over her hips. She didn't back away, but instead let her breasts press into his chest as they began to sway together. Part of her had wondered if, when it came to this part—actual physical contact with a stranger—she'd find it too weird or difficult in some way. But her hot, perfect man with the blue eyes made it incredibly easy. Her whole body tingled with delight.

"I'm embarrassed," he said deeply, "that I haven't even asked your name yet."

And for some reason, she thought fleetingly about going with her given name—Gwendolyn. She used it on her business cards and résumé because she thought it made her sound more mature and serious. But then it hit her—why on earth would she want to sound mature and serious right *now*? This was a one-night thing and she was White Bikini Babe. That was what *he* wanted her to be. And that was what *she* wanted to be, too. "I'm Wendy," she said, thanking her lucky stars for a name frivolous enough to belong to any garden-variety stripper or porn star.

"Brandon," he returned easily.

When she skittered off her heel once during the dance, she quickly *chose* not to be embarrassed. Wanton Wendy the stripper/porn star *wouldn't* be. "New shoes," she said instead, managing a giggle.

He glanced down, so she turned her foot sideways to show off her brand-new peek-toe pumps. "Very hot," he informed her with a heated grin, "and well worth a little stumble."

Together they moved then, the dance creating just enough friction between their bodies that Wendy found herself beginning to grind slowly against him. She didn't plan it, but she also didn't stop the urge. And—oh my, Brandon began to grow wonderfully hard in front, his arousal brushing across her hip, her mound, and making her want to sigh with the heat it built inside her. She forgot all about her shoes and didn't stumble again.

When the song ended, he leaned to whisper in her ear. "More sex on the beach?"

Biting her lip, and feeling still more daring, she rose on her tiptoes to whisper silkily back into his. "The drink? Or the activity?"

He drew back slightly, parting their bodies just enough to glance lustfully down at her cleavage. "Why don't we take a walk and see where it goes?"

Oh God. It's really, really happening now.

"I might be a little overdressed for the beach," she said, the words coming out saucy, sexy.

He grinned. "It'll be dark—no one will know and your secret's safe with me."

And she knew she was probably crazy to actually be doing this, going off with a total stranger to have meaningless sex, but she reminded herself again: This could be her one shot ever at fucking a truly hot guy who made her wet at a glance, and she wanted to know how that felt—to just drink in the physical sensations, to simply be fucked purely for the sake of fucking.

As they walked through Bayside Village hand in hand, Wendy felt like a queen. A sex queen. And she fully expected them to proceed to the shuttle stop since the beach was at least a mile away, but to her surprise, Brandon led her to a group of golf carts, motioning to one. "Your chariot, milady."

She'd forgotten that for an exorbitant price you could rent a golf cart to traverse the resort as well, bypassing the shuttle system. So her hot-man-for-a-night possessed not only brains, but money. It hardly mattered, given the "a-night" part, but it still pleased her and made for a fun ride across the palm-tree-laden resort in the dark.

Parking near the beach, Brandon led her by the hand to a boardwalk that crossed the dunes, and when they reached steps leading down to the sand, he motioned to her shoes. "Might want to leave those here. Sand and heels don't mix."

Good point, and she was glad he'd mentioned it—the vodka and schnapps in her drink had her feeling giddy and not thinking as clearly as usual. But as she leaned against the wood railing to remove them, Brandon said, "Allow me," stooping down before her.

"Oh . . ." she heard herself breathe when he lifted one foot in his hand and gently slid the shoe off, brushing his fingertips across the bottom arch of her foot, a simple move that sent a fluttery ribbon of heat up her leg.

He removed the other pump as well, this time running his index finger lightly over the top of her foot. She felt *that* caress in her pussy and hoped he didn't notice the lustful sigh she released, even letting her eyes fall shut for a second.

As her bare feet sank into the sand, she noticed the beach was surprisingly empty, and dark. Bayside Village must provide enough distractions, she decided, to lure away people who might normally enjoy combing the beach after the sun set. A warm sea breeze blew her hair back from her face as she walked with Brandon over the wide expanse of cool sand toward the shore.

Moonlight gleamed across the calm waves, which broke only lightly before rolling up onto the sand, and the June temperatures made the water cool but comfortable as it rushed over Wendy's feet. She immediately liked being alone with Brandon in the dark and it turned the silk between her thighs even wetter.

He held her hand as they waded into the surf, although it surprised her when she realized he was leading her gradually deeper into the water. When one of the incoming waves splashed up around her knees, she laughed and said, "Where are on earth are you taking me?" She might not be opposed to a midnight swim, but not in her dress.

"There," Brandon replied. "A sandbar. See?" He pointed out an area slightly offshore where the water flowed smooth in the scant moonlight, no waves breaking at all.

But she only gave another laugh. "Afraid you're on your own." Even as aroused as she'd been all day, she didn't mind if he wanted to have a little beach fun before sex—but she had no intention of wading out to a hidden sandbar in a brand-new dress that probably wouldn't like salt water very much.

Her "date" shrugged playfully. "Suit yourself—you don't know what you're missing." And, releasing her hand, he moved deeper into the surf, stopping to roll up the legs on his long cargo shorts as the water rose higher around him.

"What am I missing?" she couldn't help calling after him with a smile as the distance between them grew. She'd never actually had occasion to wade out to a sandbar before, so she didn't know what the great appeal was.

"I used to do this when I was a kid," he called back over his shoulder. "It was fun to confuse the hell out of people because it looked like I was walking on water."

Just then, he emerged up out of the waves, suddenly standing only ankle deep, even though he was at least twenty yards off the beach. Indeed, it gave the impression he was standing on the ocean's surface. He flashed an unmistakably boyish grin, confiding, "It's kind of cool even when no one's around. Come on," he added, motioning her toward him from where she still stood watching at the water's edge. "I'm lonely out here."

Ah, hell. Even with his shorts rolled up and acting like a little boy, he was beyond tempting. And she couldn't resist. If Brandon wanted to hang out on a sandbar with her for a little while, who was she to argue? Besides, she wanted to be fun, lighthearted— not sensible. If the dress got ruined, the dress got ruined. The memory would last much longer than the dress anyway.

"You don't have to get in too deep," he assured her as she took the first tentative steps toward him in the surf. "Just go where you see the smoothest water—that's the shallowest path."

Wendy followed his instructions, using both hands to raise

her dress around her thighs as she waded deeper. For some reason, as the water rose higher on her legs, she got wetter in her
panties.

When she realized she'd made a bad move at some point
and, even though she was nearing the sandbar was also officially
going deeper into the water rather than higher, she looked up at
Brandon and said, "What now?"

And as he studied her in the moonlight, his eyes changed,
his expression going suddenly darker. She couldn't help imagining what she looked like holding the skirt of her slinky dress up
nearly to her crotch.

His smile had faded completely. "What's now is—you wait
there and don't move a muscle because here I come."

His answer confused her. "What?"

But now Brandon was easing toward her through the shallow water, trying to find the easiest path himself without going
deeper, and by walking in a sort of half-circle through the ocean
he reached her without getting any more immersed. Peering
into her eyes as he finally reached her and stepped up close, he
said, "I must be fucking crazy, screwing around with sandbars
when maybe . . . I can be screwing you instead."

Any other time, any other guy, and Wendy would have found
the sentiment crude, but Brandon's lustful expression turned the
words hot and increased her arousal tenfold. Her nipples rubbed
against the fabric of her dress, hard as granite, and her swollen
cunt felt oh-so-ready for attention.

"Follow me, honey," he said, his voice still deep and seductive, and she let him take one of her hands, still using the other
to keep her dress hiked high, as he led her back to shore.

At the water's edge, he turned toward her, bringing their

bodies agonizingly close without touching. Then his hands rose to her face and he brought his mouth down on hers. It wasn't a hard kiss, yet it was firm and controlling—*mmm, yes*, he was clearly a man who knew how to seduce.

The second his tongue pressed at her lips, she parted them and met it with her own. Her arms circled his neck as his palms curved over her hips, pulling her to him. Oh God, he was completely erect now, his erection pressing intently at her clit—and she felt it *everywhere*, her whole body tensing with a thrill of hot, rigid pleasure. She kissed him harder, instinctively, and his hands dropped to her ass, molding, squeezing.

And just like back on the dance floor, she waited for something to happen, some odd feeling of revulsion, or just plain wrongness, because she'd never slept with a stranger before— she'd never even made out with a stranger at a party or anything like that; her life simply hadn't gone that way. Hell, she'd never *thought* of herself as prim, but maybe her actions didn't always reflect the woman she was inside. Maybe she'd let fear or propriety or appearances rule her life in some ways up to now.

But tonight, right now, she was completely ready for this, completely ready for *him*, her hot stranger. And she heard herself whispering up into his ear as his kisses spanned her neck, as his cock pressed into the juncture of her thighs. "I'm so glad you like bad girls." Because that was what she was, at least tonight, for him. She'd never felt hungrier, nastier, or more ready for down-and-dirty sex.

So it surprised the hell out of her when Brandon pulled back slightly to cast a sexy yet scolding grin. "You're not a bad girl, honey—you're a sweetheart."

Damn it, she was *so* a bad girl. How, after the way she'd

flirted and come to the beach with the clear intention of having sex, could he think she was *sweet*? She drew back a little more and looked down at herself. "Since when do sweet girls dress like *this*?" The inner slopes of her breasts were displayed and the dress hugged her every curve. "Since when do they meet a guy and leave a bar with him fifteen minutes later?"

But Brandon just chuckled, his hands still resting on her hips. "It's not about what you're wearing. It's in your eyes, your voice, the way you talk." He gave his head a challenging tilt. "If you want to convince me you're a bad girl, you'll have prove it."

Wendy drew in her breath, prepared to do just that. She hadn't come this far, taken this many daring personal risks, to let her dream lover tell her she was *sweet*. "What if I said, 'Fuck me—now'?" She tried her damnedest to put a bite in the words.

His eyes glazed with lust as he answered, low and deep. "I'd say that your wish is my command—but that even sweet girls like to fuck."

So he was going to be insufferable about the sweet issue. But her pussy was too engorged with lust to keep worrying about that part. So she moved on to what was more important at the moment and, again, tried to sound as naughty and demanding as possible as she said, "Then *fuck me. Now*."

I didn't know until that moment that it was about more than just fucking a hot guy. I didn't know that there was so much inside me dying to come out. But Brandon was the perfect guy to let it all come out <u>with</u>, because he was everything I'd ever wanted in a fantasy lover. And I knew that before the night was through, I <u>would</u> prove it. If not to him, then at least to myself.

I <u>am</u> a bad girl.

I am a <u>very</u> bad girl.

Chapter 3

$\mathcal{B}$randon led her up through the soft white sand to the beach cabanas directly in front of the building where he occupied the twenty-second-floor penthouse condo. Convenient because he happened to know these particular cabanas came with large wooden lounge chairs covered with thick, upholstered mats. He chose the cabana on the end—a half-tent-like structure with two chairs jutting from inside—because it was the easiest to reach, and with his little sandbar trip, he'd managed to turn himself impatient. He loved this beach like he loved little else, and he simply enjoyed "playing" here, along with the opportunity to share it with someone new, but he'd been a damn fool to waste time in the water—time he could have spent in *her*.

It had hit him when he'd looked up to see those shapely, slender thighs, her sexy dress flirting with the very tops of her legs. She was beautiful and willing, so what the hell was he waiting for?

Turning to face her, he kissed her again, tasted those sweet, moist lips, let his tongue ease inside. Neither of them wanted to go slow here—he knew that—so he curled his hands over her sweet round ass and pressed his hard cock directly to her slit. He could feel it, even through her clothes, that slight indentation he knew led to heaven.

When he began to grind against her, she moaned into his mouth and made his chest contract. Still kissing her, warm, their tongues mating, he let his palms glide up her back, the top bared by her sexy dress—then drew one hand around to her breast. They both moaned as he molded his hand to the soft, pliable flesh—so big in his hand—and raked his thumb across the pebble-hard nipple.

Without quite planning it, he found himself pinching it then, just lightly, because he liked how damn hard it felt already and had the urge to make it harder still. She whimpered and sighed against his mouth—until she was leaning her head back, until his kisses drifted down over her neck, onto the silky skin of her chest. Ah, shit, he loved her cleavage and quickly found himself kissing his way down the inner curve of one soft, ample breast, listening to her breath grow labored—and wanting more of her.

He could have reached behind her neck and untied the dress to let the top part drop down, but he was suddenly too impatient—so he used his hand to push the fabric aside, baring one lovely tit in the moonlight. He instantly massaged and caressed, studying the large pink areola, the beautifully long, turgid nipple at its center. He lasted only a few seconds before taking it in his mouth to suck.

Above him, her whimpery moans increased as he licked and sucked that gorgeous tit. He ran his tongue around it, simply liking how rigid and pearllike it felt—then he drew it in deep, wanting to make it still longer and harder. Her fingers were in his hair, her breath warmed the back of his neck. He pushed his hand beneath the fabric covering her other breast and massaged the flesh firmly in rhythm with his suckling.

The truth was—Brandon, like most guys, loved breasts, and he could have stood there enjoying hers for a long while without complaint. But he sensed that Wendy wanted to go faster—not only from the 'Fuck me now,' but from the way her body moved, the desperate little cries coming from her throat—and he wanted to give her what she needed.

Not *too* fast, though. No, a woman this hot was something to savor, something to be enjoyed.

So, with some effort, he released her stiffened nipple from his mouth and forced himself to let go of her body and back away a few feet.

She looked surprised until he said, "Untie it. Let it fall."

Slowly, without ever taking her eyes from him, she reached up beneath her hair and pulled at the fabric. A second later, the top of the dress dropped to her waist.

The groan he emitted rose from his gut. He had no idea why, given that, at thirty-six, he'd seen plenty of topless women in his life. But something about her . . . she just looked so gorgeous, so vulnerable, so sexual, so many things at once. Her tits were not the kind you saw in *Playboy*—but they were real. Round. Big. And beautiful. *She* was beautiful.

"Lie down," he finally said, firmly, pointing to the lounge chair a few feet away.

She didn't hesitate, but padded across the sand to recline on the thick padding. She propped on her elbows to look at him, fire in her eyes.

"Now pull up your dress. Slowly," he warned, thinking of the view he'd had of her in the ocean when she'd been wading out to meet him.

She obeyed the instruction silently, reaching down to pinch

a bit of fabric near the hem and delicately beginning to ease it higher, higher.

"That's right," he said, low, his heart beating so hard that his chest ached. "Keep going."

She did, lifting the orangy fabric higher still—until revealing her panties. A strip of dark lace circled her hips and a tiny swatch of black descended over her pussy. She looked beautifully erotic wearing only the tiny scrap of underwear, her dress in a heap at her waist.

"Now spread your legs for me."

Again, she obeyed, spreading wide, planting her feet on either side of the chair. And even in the dark, even through black panties, he thought she looked swollen with excitement. At the end of the chair, he dropped to his knees in the sand, intent on having more of her.

Wendy tried to control her breathing, but it was hard. She'd never been so aroused in her life. And she'd never been with a man who told her to spread her legs before, either. Something about the command, and her acquiescence, had her nearly orgasmic already. Her pussy felt so needy, drenched with want.

She watched as Brandon bent down to kiss her through her thong, and her whole body shivered at the mouth-to-cunt contact.

Her uncontrolled response made him wild—he opened his mouth and gently bit down on as much of her as he seemed able to get in his mouth, making her cry out.

His eyes on her shone glassy with lust in the moonlight, and when they drifted to her breasts, she realized she'd absently started teasing her nipples between her thumbs and forefingers for added sensation. "That's *so* hot," he growled.

"I *told* you I was a bad girl."

He only grinned, even if a bit wickedly, and when Brandon curled the fingers of both hands into the lacy strip just above her pussy, her stomach contracted, her whole body seizing with pleasure. "Lift," he said, somehow making even that one tiny word among the sexiest commands she'd ever heard.

Bringing her feet back up onto the chair, she raised her ass and waited as he gently peeled the tiny panties away. As soon as they were gone, she didn't hesitate to dig her toes back in the sand where they had been, spreading for him again, boldly putting her freshly shaven cunt on full, open display.

His low moan said he liked the move. And as a salty breeze washed over her most sensitive flesh, as she watched Brandon lean closer, closer, she knew without doubt that her experiment was *not* a failure, that her experiment had truly turned her into what she'd wanted to be: a very bad girl.

When his tongue raked upward through her slit, she trembled once more, a loud moan escaping her. And then the breeze was back, wafting across where he'd left her even wetter than she'd been, to send a delightful, oh-so-sensual chill through her whole body.

His mouth returned then, licking—through her parted pussy lips and up over her engorged clit, making her sob, again, again. The stubble on his chin moving across the smooth skin she'd shaved only hours earlier created still more sensation.

"You taste so good, baby," he rasped against her mound. "Such a hot, sweet little pussy."

"*I want you in it,*" she said through lightly clenched teeth. Then raised back to her elbows to look at his handsome face. "Do you have . . . ?"

"Of course."

"Give it to me."

Wendy wasn't usually very aggressive during sex. But she wasn't usually having sex with a guy as insanely hot as Brandon, either. As he rose to reach into his back pocket, she sat upright on the lounge chair and pressed the flat of her palm to the front of his shorts.

Again, they both moaned. She'd never felt anything so incredibly hard in her life. And he felt *big*, too. She couldn't help starting to work at his zipper, anxious to get to his cock. Beneath his shorts she found silk boxers and didn't hesitate to reach through the opening in front to extract what waited inside.

Glancing down, she found her hand wrapped around the most magnificent male appendage she'd ever had the pleasure of beholding. Rock solid and arrow straight, it had to be eight inches long. The width filled her hand so well that she couldn't even come close to making her fingertips meet her thumb. She gasped with pure awe as she watched a dot of pre-come gather at the end and her chest seemed to stretch with raw desire.

"Here," he breathed, thrusting a condom into her free hand. She released him, but found herself shaky trying to get it open.

God—calm down. Don't freak out and ruin this.

But she was so excited that she could barely stand waiting another second.

Be like White Bikini Babe. Be cool. Seductive. Smooth. Be his fantasy lover, too.

Okay, that helped. At least she slowed down and managed to grip the condom between her fingers without dropping it in the sand. She took a deep breath, positioned it at the tip of his hard-on, and began to roll it tightly down. And in that moment, she

discovered that as much as she'd liked feeling his sense of control over her a few minutes ago, now *she* wanted some control,
too. And he made her a confident-enough woman to take it.

Now that he was sheathed, she pressed her palms to the
shirt covering his chest and shoved him flat onto his back in the
sand. He went down with a small groan, clearly not expecting
the move, but she didn't apologize. Instead, she straddled his
hips on the beach and yanked his shirt open hard, actually sending buttons flying. "Shit," he muttered, but in a way that meant
he liked it. She liked surprising him.

Without another second's delay, Wendy curled her hand
back around his cock and this time sheathed it with her cunt,
sliding down, warm and wet, taking him deep, to the hilt.

Oh Lord. At first, she feared it was a mistake—he was too big
to put her weight on; he filled her too deeply.

But then both his hands closed over her breasts, squeezing, massaging—and pain became pleasure. *Deep, invasive* pleasure. His full length was still challenging to take, but she eased
her body slightly forward, then back a little, finding the best
position.

Beneath her, he breathed deeply. "Okay?"

Her voice came out sounding thready. "So big."

"*Too* big?"

Clearly, she wasn't the first girl to have slowed down at this
point. "No way," she assured him. "You fill me so full. I just have
to . . . ease into this."

"Take your time, honey," he whispered, speaking slowly.
"I want to make you feel *so* fucking good. I want to make you
come."

Oh my. His dirty talk instantly made her pussy somehow

expand and deepen. As she let out a hot little "Oooh . . ." in response, her body sank more easily against his, accepting the whole length of his erection.

"Yeah, baby, ride me. Ride that big cock." His voice was still smooth, low, deep, gently prodding—and only then did she realize she'd begun to move on him in small, rhythmic circles, fucking him. Fucking him like the bad girl she was. Loving his dirty talk all the more because she was dirty, too.

And, oh—it felt *so* damn good! Suddenly, quickly. The deep pleasure radiated all through her, echoing outward in every limb even as her clit connected with his body just above his penis, her every sensual undulation rubbing it exactly the right way. "Oh God," she moaned, the words seeming to come from someplace deep. "Oh God, *yeah*." This wasn't going to take long.

And apparently he knew it. "Come for me, honey. Come hard."

And that fast, she exploded into ecstasy. "Oh! Oh . . . God! God!" Then she heard her own orgasmic cries spring forth, loud sobs of ultimate delight echoing across the beach as the sensations pumped through her body—until finally they faded and she came back down to earth.

And this would have been another key time when it all could have changed, when she could suffer regret, or emptiness, or even a little doubt—but nothing like that occurred. All she felt was replete with pleasure and as if she were a more fully realized woman in this moment than ever before. She'd never felt more strangely . . . feminine.

Although as she slumped to his now-bared chest in exhaustion to feel his arms close over her naked back, she also couldn't help being thankful that the man she'd done this with was such a *nice* lover, someone happy to hold her after her climax, someone patient and skilled and concerned with her pleasure as much as his own.

Raising her head from where she'd nestled against his chest, she lifted one hand to his stubbled jaw and kissed him. Soft at first, but then harder. And at some point as they made out, she realized he was still inside her and how used to it she'd become in such an amazingly short stretch of time.

"I want you," he breathed between short, hot kisses, "on your hands and knees."

Mmm, God—it was *his* turn to be in control again. And that suited her fine since she was more than willing to give it up and see where else he would take her.

Rising off him, she felt that initial emptiness as his cock left her, but wasted no time in "assuming the position" he'd just demanded. She crawled back onto the padded lounge chair, arched her ass for him, remembered the similar view of herself in the mirror, and said over her shoulder, "Please fuck me hard."

The request earned a deep, lusty sigh from her man, and the next thing she felt were his hands molding to her bare hips, then his stiff cock, seeking entry where she was still wet and ready. She lifted her ass a little higher, trying to accommodate, more eager than she could have imagined to have his length back inside her.

As he began to slide inward, she had to grit her teeth against the incredible pressure, but then, like before, her body seemed to open to him, letting him glide all the way in. A low moan rose from her throat. Oh *God*, he was big. Almost overwhelmingly so. The mere sensation of having him inside her made her feel impaled—in a good way.

"How's that?" he rasped in the darkness.

"Amazing," she nearly purred. This was everything. Everything she'd wanted. A hot guy. A sea breeze. Great sex. Astounding pleasure.

Then he began to fuck her, delivering short, hot thrusts she felt all the way to the tips of her fingers and toes. "Unh! Unh! Unh!" she cried out at each jolting stroke. She could feel nothing else. Think of nothing else. Only the hard sensations that buffeted her body. She'd never had sex in this exact position before and was poleaxed by how much she felt it *everywhere*.

"Fuck me," she heard herself begging. Even though he already was, and quite well. "Harder. Faster." She supposed she just wanted more of this, all she could take—she didn't want to miss a single sensation her beach lover could give her.

He responded with increased strokes that she feared might split her apart at her very core but at the same time delivered still more mind-numbing pleasure. Her sobs echoed through the night air until she felt a vague wonder that they'd not attracted an audience by now, but she was too drunk on sensation to even care. If she'd looked up to see a large crowd watching them, it wouldn't have doused an ounce of her joy. Behind her, Brandon grunted with each hard drive of his cock, filling her with still more dirty delight.

"Oh!" she cried out when he brought the flat of his hand down on her ass, hard. It stung—and shocked her.

But it also moved through her in a pleasing way, since it added yet one more feeling to everything she was experiencing.

He smacked her ass again—and once more, even as it delivered a hot, stinging pain, it heightened her pleasure. The very idea that he was actually *spanking* her excited her for reasons she couldn't understand. She drank it in, every nasty little slap of his hand, relishing the way it vibrated through her body like the pluck of a harp string. A really *hard* pluck, of course. It was like the perfect little cherry on top of a very naughty sundae, and before she knew it, she could barely discern between the pleasure and pain of it, just wanting more and more sensation—of any kind.

She gasped when his hand touched her face from behind, his fingertips running across her lips. She felt herself part them, felt herself draw his middle finger inside. She sucked on it, using tongue and teeth, everything at her disposal, unduly aroused to have yet another small part of him inside her body. She even turned her head to meet his gaze and soon realized he was pushing his finger into her mouth, then pulling it back out, same as his cock in her pussy.

What stunned the hell out of her, though, wasn't when he took his finger away, but when a second later he used it to rub wetly against her anus in a tight little circle that instantly drove her mad! Oh! Oh God, she'd never . . . she'd had no idea . . . how that could feel . . . so very, very good!

When he thrust the tip of his finger into her ass, she sucked in her breath, then let out a mewling cry of pure, unadulterated pleasure. Just when she'd thought he couldn't make her feel anything more—oh God, it was overwhelming. And then his finger slid deeper, deeper, making her whimper as she broke out into a sweat, every pore of her body reacting to this new, unexpected way of being fucked.

At some point her arms gave out, curling beneath her on the chair, but she kept her bottom raised high as he continued giving her the most glorious fuck of her life. The pleasure was so strange and new and intense that she began to fear she would lose her mind. She wanted to touch herself, in front, but she simply hadn't the strength—he'd drained it all from her.

"Please," she begged him without considering it, "rub me. Rub my pussy."

"Ah, Jesus," he murmured behind her, and she knew he liked the request. A moment later, the hand that had held steady at her hip all this time snaked around her thigh and between her legs, his fingertips stroking, stroking, where she needed it most.

"Oh yes, yes, yes!" That was all it took, all she needed, that last little bit of sensation in just the right spot. And she was tumbling, screaming, into an orgasm so intense that it jolted her body almost violently—once, twice, three hard times before the pulses of pleasure felt more like normal ones. She heard herself sobbing, nearly crying with the release, not quite able to make sense of what had just happened to her body. She'd never experienced anything like this—she felt drunk, crazed, pleasured, replete, all at once.

Behind her, Brandon's thrusts grew harder, even harder, but she met them enthusiastically—the very desire to please him as much as he'd pleased her delivered a burst of energy when she least expected it. "Yes!" she told him through clenched teeth. "Fuck me! Fuck me!" There was no pain now, only a profound and pounding pleasure deep inside her as she took all he had to give.

His hands were back on her ass now, and he lifted one to spank her some more, the stinging smacks coming precisely as he rammed himself into her deep. He began to groan, to curse below his breath, "Ah, damn . . . fuck . . . yes . . ." And then he thrust deeper than he ever had before, nearly pushing her knees

out from under her, but she struggled to hold her position, and
he rasped, "Ah, yeah, *now*," and drove deep, again, again, again,
until finally they collapsed together in a heap on the lounge
chair.

They lay that way a minute or two, long enough that Wendy
began to wonder if he was falling asleep. Long enough to start
feeling regret—if she were going to feel it. She didn't, though. At
all. Elation was more like it.

"Hey," he finally whispered near her ear. "You okay?"

She turned, rolling onto her back and into his arms. "Way
more than okay," she assured him.

He grinned down at her, looking amused and maybe a little
pleased with himself, until finally she said, "What?"

"Sorry. I'm just thinking about when we first got here, how
concerned you seemed with not getting the bottom of your
dress wet. And look at it now." He raised enough for Wendy to
spy the tangerine-colored garment in a twisted jumble around
her waist. Bits of sand stuck to the fabric, and to their skin, from
when she'd pushed him down onto the beach. They were a sexy,
sticky, erotic mess.

She couldn't help smiling wickedly up into his eyes. "Some
things are worth ruining a dress for."

The glimpse she'd taken between them—her body naked
but for the bunched dress, his cock still impressively erect, his
chest as broad and strong as she'd suspected, also dotted with
grains of sand—reminded her. "Do you believe I'm a bad girl
now?" she asked, peering up at him.

"Mmm, maybe," he said with a shrug.

"You must, since you gave me such a nasty little spanking."

At this, he let out a loud laugh, then brought his gaze back to hers, lowering his voice. "What can I say? I'm a little kinky sometimes."

She simply smiled, thinking: *Maybe I am, too.*

"Working tomorrow?" Brandon heard himself ask as Wendy made the last tug involved in pulling her dress back into place.

"Some meetings in the morning," she said, brushing sand off her arm. Her long coppery hair was totally mussed, like that of a woman who'd just been well fucked—a look he definitely liked on her.

He took her hand as they began heading back toward the boardwalk. "Will you be by the Shellside pool in the afternoon?" She'd told him which building she was staying in. "Or on the beach?"

She tilted her head, the ocean breeze blowing strands of hair across her face. "Um, I'm not sure."

He'd found himself watching the sand as they walked, not entirely comfortable with his own pursuit of her, but at this answer, he glanced up with a grin. "Are you being indecisive or coy?"

"The former. Mostly," she added, then laughed prettily.

"Well . . ." he said, not quite sure where to go from there. "Maybe I'll see you. At the pool. Or on the beach." The truth was, he wasn't used to seeking out a woman a second time. And he sure as hell wasn't used to having a woman leave him uncertain as to whether she wanted to see him again. This was the exact opposite of how his trysts generally ended.

She smiled at him in the moonlight as she grabbed her shoes from where they'd left them. "At least *these* survived the night unscathed," she said.

Shit—changing the subject. Not a good sign.

And he liked her. He'd liked fucking her, of course, but beyond that, he just *liked* her. He liked everything from her willingness to be so up front about sex to the way she kept insisting she was a bad girl—which he thought proved she probably really wasn't deep down inside. He liked that she was both smart and sexy. He'd liked dancing with her. He'd liked spanking her. He'd liked everything in between.

And damn, the girl had a gorgeous body. It *wasn't* a girl's body, though—but a woman's, rife with grown-up curves.

He wanted more. Both of the body and the brain. Which wasn't his usual way. He liked one-night stands. They were easy to find in a world filled with tourists—girls' getaways, bachelorette trips, spring break. His work was his life—his work and this beach that had drawn him since his boyhood—and he had no room in it for a woman who would *need* him, for a relationship that would require *effort*. He loved his life as it was and had no desire to change it. And for that reason he purposefully sought out one-night liaisons. He didn't see it as tawdry; he simply saw it as two people having fun, fulfilling physical desires.

So it had surprised the hell out of him to hear himself ask her what her plans were tomorrow. And it had surprised him even more to realize maybe he was being turned down. After sex like *that*. Panting, heaving, screaming sex. But he didn't let his surprise show. It hardly mattered. After all, he *did* like one-nighters. Why should he mind if she did, too?

Maybe this was about his business troubles. She'd kept his mind off them, all night—maybe he wanted her to *keep* his mind elsewhere. Since the outcome was pretty much out of his control now—a game of wait and see. While he was waiting, it would be nice to let Wendy keep right on distracting him.

"Think the dress will recover?" he asked as they traversed the wooden walkway, her feet still bare and sandy.

His heartbeat picked up when she took his hand back into hers; her smile remained laced with sex. "Doesn't matter. I told you, there are some things worth ruining a dress for."

Without discussing it, they took the path that led toward the Shellside Towers, even though his building lay in the other direction. They walked in silence—he was tired, happy enough just to bask in the memory of their hot beach sex, and he supposed she felt the same.

When they reached the Shellside entryway, he eased his arms around her waist and pulled her close, glad it had gotten late enough that no one else was anywhere in sight. "Tonight was . . . fucking phenomenal," he told her softly.

"I agree," she said. "Glad I took that ride you offered."

He chuckled softly, having forgotten about that. At the time it had just been his natural inclination to flirt with a pretty woman. He'd had no idea how things would turn out.

Something about it made him decide to take another stab at this. Still holding her, their bodies pressed together from chest to thigh, he whispered in her ear, "Remember when I slipped my finger into your ass?"

She flinched reflexively in his embrace, and he *felt* her remember. She didn't look up at him as she said, "Yeah."

"You, uh . . . seemed to like that."

She hesitated slightly, maybe a little embarrassed, then he felt her smile bashfully into his chest. "*Yeah.*"

"Well, I want to do it again," he murmured against her ear.

"I want to do *everything* to you again. And more." With that, he released her, stepped away—and said with just a hint of arrogance, "I'll look for you at the beach tomorrow." He concluded with a wink, then turned and walked away.

Maybe he'd never see her again. But *damn*, he wanted to. Maybe she *was* just like him—someone who enjoyed one-night stands because they kept her life practical. But he hoped that naughty little tease would be enough for her to make an exception and go for two.

I have spent thirty-four years living in a box. A box with straight walls and a low ceiling. And inside that box with me was the idea of what sex is supposed to be. It's not a <u>bad</u> box—don't get me wrong. I've always liked sex. I've had some <u>good</u> sex. I've been comfortable with who I was sexually.

But the sex I had last night was . . . not in that box. It was like the walls had fallen down, like I'd discovered this whole new sexual world outside of what I already thought was a pretty <u>good</u> sexual world. It was like living in a really nice house your whole life, but then one day getting brave enough to walk out the door and see what's outside. And once you're out, nothing is ever the same again. You might go back inside the house, but you won't stay there. Not all the time. You can't. Once you see the sun and feel the wind, you need it. You need it like you need to breathe.

The truth is . . . I think part of me wanted to feel <u>empty</u>, to be that intimate with a total stranger. Maybe on some level I wanted to find out that sex meant more to me than just the physical pleasure of it. I wanted, deep down, to discover it was about the connection, the emotion. But that's not what happened—that's not what happened at all. I have found a brand-new and utterly startling part of myself. And I just don't think I can go back in the box.

Chapter 4

The next morning at nine a.m., Wendy met with Emerald Shore's top two accountants in the corporate offices, which were at once professional but beachy, the decor consisting of much teak, bamboo, potted palms, and sand-colored tile.

It had felt positively strange to sit there in a pale yellow suit with other professionally attired people discussing profit-and-loss statements, listening to projected earnings, and looking at complicated financial reports—after last night. At moments, she almost began to wonder if last night had really even happened. But then she'd feel the tingle between her legs that reminded her it had been *very* real. Not just a tingle of desire, but a sense of having had a man inside her recently, having had her body opened that way.

So it had been hard to concentrate. She kept seeing Brandon's handsome face when she should have been seeing numbers. Big numbers. That represented big money. That meant she had to snap out of it and pay attention here.

Mostly, she did. But her own reveries also reminded her that it had been downright foolish to indulge in what she'd indulged in while technically on the job. After all, what if someone in this office had seen her swaying with Brandon in her sexy dress on the dance floor last night? Worse yet, what if someone in this office had come upon them on the beach when she'd been yowling her pleasure like a deranged animal?

Even now, as she warmly shook hands with Marian Kinders and Jay Anderson as they parted ways after lunch at a stylish resort café, she shivered—both at the memories and the mere thought of how devastating it could have been to be seen by the wrong people.

"Thanks so much for lunch," she said, smiling at the accountants on the windswept porch of the Sea Bistro. "I appreciate your time and preparation for this morning, and it was a pleasure meeting you both. And, Marian," she added, alluding to a conversation they'd had over lunch, "I hope your trip to Hawaii is fabulous. I'm serious about wanting you to e-mail me some pictures, okay?"

As she walked away, her low heels clicking on the winding path that would lead back to her building, it occurred to her that maybe last night she *hadn't* been at risk. Because no one here had known what she looked like yet. But then again, maybe they would have remembered her upon being introduced to her today. She'd started and ended her Emerald Shores meetings with Marian and Jay, but while in the offices, she'd been introduced to at least a dozen other people who worked in accounting and investments and new developments. Which meant maybe someone *had* recognized her. She had no way of knowing, after all. The very thought made her stomach shrivel.

But don't do that to yourself. The chances were incredibly slim, after all. The people who worked here probably didn't live here or play here. *You had an amazing night, you lived your wildest fantasy, you came away with no regrets—only a sense of hedonistic free-*

dom you've never experienced before—so just bask in it, appreciate it,
be glad and proud you did it.

Because the truth was—she felt different than she had yesterday. She had no idea if the feeling would last—for all she knew,
maybe it would fade over time—but right now, today, she felt
confident, powerful, in control of herself and her life. In control of her pleasure. She felt beautiful. Desirable. *Hot.* She felt
as feminine as she did professional—adjectives she wasn't used
to combining when thinking of herself, generally feeling as if
she were one way or the other at any given time. And recently,
professional had outweighed feminine by a landslide, so it was
more heady than she could have imagined to suddenly feel like
a real woman again.

The further truth was, she felt *so* feminine, and *so* desirable,
that each and every time she'd encountered a new male today
who could be considered even remotely attractive, she'd wondered if he could in some way see in her what Brandon had
seen. Someone sexy. Someone sensual. Someone with a hidden
passion that was just seething to get out. She'd found herself
looking more directly in the eyes of the suit-and-tie guys at the
Emerald Shores offices. For no particular reason than impulse,
she'd smiled almost flirtatiously at the cute twentysomething
waiter in the café. She'd done nothing inappropriate, but she'd
simply felt more aware of her own sensuality in every breath
she'd taken today, and maybe, she thought now as she neared
the Shellside Towers, her own self-awareness had made her
more aware of *other* people today, too.

And not just guys, and not just sexually, either. With everyone she met, she'd simply made more contact than she normally
would, taken a more sincere interest in people. She'd noticed

what they were wearing; she'd caught a whiff of Marian's perfume; she'd taken note of Jay's tie clip and found out it was a gift from his kids last Christmas.

But the even *further* truth was—as much as she thought all of her revelations made last night seem *healthy* and *positive*, how healthy and positive was it *really* if she found herself wanting to do it *again*?

Her heart beat faster as she stepped inside the cool lobby of her building and rode the elevator to her studio condo. She was thinking about that bikini she'd bought. And she was thinking about Brandon's last words to her.

Don't do it, a voice inside her said. *No matter how slim the risk is, some people here know you now.* And tomorrow she was supposed to meet with Mr. Worth and Mr. Penny, Emerald Shores' CEOs. She imagined stepping into some lavish office and facing two dignified old men who would announce to her that their employees had seen her having sex on the beach—and not just the drink—and that they felt obliged to report this behavior to her boss. She had no idea if being seen doing something like that *would* automatically result in such a report, but she certainly didn't want to find out. And couldn't afford to, either—it was her *job*, her job where she appeared to be *climbing the corporate ladder*, her job that she *loved*. She couldn't risk messing that up.

But if she couldn't risk messing that up, why was she walking over toward the cute little Beach Bazaar shopping bag still sitting on a chair in her room and plucking out the two pieces of the swimsuit?

Why was she holding them up, remembering the way they'd molded to her body?

Why was she dying to put it on?

Simple. Because Brandon's words still rang in her ears. *I want to do it again. I want to do everything to you again. And more.*

Despite herself, she couldn't help thinking: *more?* What more could there be?

And how could she bear not finding out? After all, this was her one time away from home by herself. This was the one time she'd already started something brazen and hedonistic with a man, so maybe continuing it to see where it led only made sense.

If you can block out the "what if someone with the resort sees me?" part.

And realistically, she decided, she could.

Because this place was *huge*, with literally thousands of occupants.

Because the people who worked here were working *now*, not hanging at the beach or poolside during business hours.

This was a playground. It only made sense to play. And no one from the corporate offices would see her. It was nearly a mathematical impossibility. She'd have a better chance of winning the lottery.

And the fact was—the temptation of getting more of what Brandon had given her last night was simply too great to resist.

Thus it was ten minutes later when she found herself stepping down into the soft white sand in her sexy new black bikini and the short, equally sexy black sarong she'd bought to go with it. She toted a straw bag on her shoulder containing a towel, sunscreen, and her work journal.

Although she'd felt a bit nervous upon first leaving her room so scantily clad, already now, she felt sleek and svelte and sensuous as she padded across the beach toward her reserved umbrella and chair—and she felt the eyes on her, just like last night in the entertainment village. Again, it was nothing so extreme as the way people had stared at White Bikini Babe, but Wendy knew she was being noticed, and she'd never felt more desirable.

Her original questions, hopes, came back to her in a glorious sense of success as she strolled up the shoreline. She *could* pull this off! The dress, the bikini, being a woman who sought pleasure, *everything*. It was a revelation. It was like waking up after a very long sleep. It was like looking in the mirror and suddenly realizing you were beautiful.

Of course, as she neared her umbrella, fresh new doubts crept in. Not about her new self-confidence, but about Brandon. Would he really find her here? The resort was enormous, after all, the beach was long, and her reserved umbrella sat several building lengths away from where they'd "played" last night.

And as she spread out her towel on the beach chair and sat down, she began to feel like an idiot to have had him practically begging to see her again and not being more precise about it. At the time, she'd *liked* being coy, as he'd put it. She'd never been coy in her life, and she'd been toying with the power of it. Plus she'd been stuck on her plan of "one night" and about it being solely sexual and, therefore, *not* about seeing each other again. She could only chalk up her actions to orgasmic euphoria.

But now that all seemed stupid. She'd had the best freaking sex of her life—crazy, riotous, no-inhibitions sex like she'd never even dreamed of—so why *shouldn't* she want it again? Just like she'd written after getting back to her room last night, she couldn't go back in the box.

Maybe a part of her had been a little let down in a weird way to find out that, really and truly, she *could* have meaningless sex.

But now that she knew how good it could be—just the pleasure, just the fun—she craved more of it. *Please let him look for me.*

As she watched the tide rushing in, kids playing in the surf, she began to relax a little. Whatever happened here happened. If Brandon didn't find her, no biggie. Hell, maybe his own orgasmic euphoria had worn off by now and he wouldn't even look. And if that was the case . . . she'd live. She'd miss exploring her new sexual freedom with him some more, but she'd still go away with a new sense of herself, new sensual secrets, a new confidence no one could take away.

"Hi there. Can I get you a drink?"

Her eyes rose to a beach waiter in a flowered shirt—the same one from yesterday. Only he was looking at her differently now. She felt his admiration; she felt how much of her body, her breasts, was on display. Her pussy tingled as she smiled boldly up at him. "I'd love a mango daiquiri."

He smiled back, raising his gaze from her chest to her face. "Coming right up."

Power. She suddenly had power with men. Amazing.

But, of course, she still found herself looking up and down the beach for her lover from last night. Until her drink arrived. Until she'd made a few practical notes in her journal about the resort, then stuffed it back in her bag. Until the daiquiri was half gone and there was still no sign of him.

Maybe he really wasn't going to show.

She ignored the silly lump of disappointment gathering in her stomach and pushed it aside. She didn't need him. She didn't need anything.

Except maybe more sex. After last night, she was feeling more aroused than she had in . . . years. Which was exciting even as it felt a little scary. Because where was she going to get sex without Brandon? How was she going to go back in the box?

Just then, a darkly tanned guy with messy black windblown hair came strolling easily up the beach. He wore long swim trunks and a T-shirt; his longish hair was pulled mostly back into a low ponytail, but some had escaped in the breeze. Muscles stretched his tee—he was tall and broad and didn't smile.

Wendy's first thought was that he looked vaguely famil- iar, and she was just thankful that his appearance made it fairly impossible for him to be someone from the corporate office. Her second was that he was *hot*. In an unconventional, messy, slightly scary way. He was, quite simply, the sort of man whose very stance and expression would have intimidated her before yesterday—he looked so confident and comfortable that she was sure he could get any sexy beach babe he desired; he looked like the kind of guy who probably hung out with swimsuit models or starred in porn movies or something.

But when he glanced up at her, then stopped and did a double take, it *didn't* intimidate her. It only felt like the next strange, heady occurrence in her daring little experiment. She met his eyes, saw that they were blue like Brandon's and pretty enough to soften his expression just a little, and she wasn't even tempted to look away as he veered from the shore to come nearer.

His small smile, coupled with the inquisitive tilt of his head, was sexy as hell. "You . . . look familiar. Have we met?"

Her new boldness came almost naturally as she smiled back, instinctively thrusting her chest out slightly. "I was just wonder- ing the same thing. I've only been here a day, though, so . . ."

He playfully scratched at his darkly stubbled chin. "Well, I don't know where I know you from, but I wouldn't mind knowing you *better*."

Maybe it was all a line—maybe he was just *pretending* to think she looked familiar. But if so, she didn't mind at all. "Likewise," she offered up flirtatiously, taking a sip of her drink and wondering if her nipples were visible through the thin black fabric.

"You parasail?" he asked.

She glanced past him to the big, colorful parachute-type thing currently floating across the sky out over the ocean, being pulled by a boat. "Um, I never have."

Seeing her look, he pointed to the boat. "I own that boat and two more. I run the parasail operation here on the beach." That explained the logo on his shirt, Sky Pirate, and she couldn't help thinking the whole pirate image suited him well. "You should come parasail. I won't even charge you."

She raised her eyebrows. "Why not?"

He gave her a wink. "Consider it one of the perks of being hot. I'll have guys lined up a mile behind you, wanting a ride."

Hmm. The truth was, despite liking his flirtation—a lot— parasailing didn't sound like such a great idea. It would probably make her nervous, and she didn't want to be nervous in front of this guy. But that very knowledge reminded her again—*Be bold. Be the new, bold, aggressive you.* "I'll consider it," she said, "but . . . where's the part about wanting to know me better?"

A sensual smile unfurled on her beach pirate's face. "Well, when you put it like that, screw parasailing. What do you have in mind, pretty lady?"

And that was when the question hit her hard: *Could I fuck another guy on this trip? Could I be that brazen? Could I possibly have sex with more than one stranger in just a couple of days?*

Before she could answer, though—him or herself—he tilted his head the other way, eyes narrowing. "Wait. I think I know where I saw you. Hot, orange dress? Piano bar?"

Oh boy. She lowered her chin a bit flirtatiously, wondering exactly *what* he'd seen. "Guilty as charged, officer."

He chuckled slightly, then pointed a finger at her, shaking it slightly as he kept deducing more. "You were hanging with my buddy Brandon last night."

Holy crap. She remembered him now, too. He'd been one of a group of guys near the downstairs bar the very first time she'd spotted Brandon. His hair had been down then, so he'd looked different.

"You're a friend of Brandon's, huh?" Stunned, she couldn't think of anything else to say.

"Since college," he replied, nodding, and she felt oddly as if she'd been caught at something—but the beach pirate didn't look remotely bothered by the coincidence.

"Trying to steal my beach bunny, Faber?"

Wendy flinched at the sound of Brandon's deep voice, then turned her head to see him approaching from the other side of the umbrella. Her heart nearly stopped at the sight of her handsome lover in only a pair of stylish navy blue trunks with a white design running down the outside of each leg. It was really him! He *had* found her! Their hedonism wasn't over!

She caught her breath and tried to appear cool, acting playfully affronted. *"Beach bunny?"*

Brandon looked her over from head to toe, making her breasts ache and the juncture of her thighs feel heavy. "If the bikini fits, honey. And the bikini definitely fits."

Her whole body warmed, and she decided she didn't mind

the moniker at all. In fact, it fit quite well with her little game here. "Honey? Shouldn't that be *bunny*?"

Both guys laughed, and Wendy thoroughly enjoyed feeling like the center of their attention. Who'd have imagined? *Her*, flirting with *two* hunky beach guys!

"So, I see you two have met," Brandon said.

"Well, not formally," Wendy pointed out. "We were just figuring out that we . . . uh, had you in common."

Brandon's slightly possessive smile moved all through her, reminding her anew of all the crazed heat they'd shared last night. "Let me do the honors," he said then. "Pete Faber, this is Wendy . . ."

Even when Brandon hesitated, she didn't offer up her last name. Just closed it off by switching her glance to Pirate Pete to hold out her hand. "Nice to meet you, Pete."

He took it, but instead of shaking it, bent to kiss it, then said, "The pleasure's all mine," in a way that curled seductively through her, even as she saw Brandon rolling his eyes with a slight laugh.

After that, Pete informed Brandon that he'd invited Wendy parasailing, but Brandon just grinned and said, "Maybe another day. She's got other plans right now."

Shifting in her chair, and enjoying the rush of sexual adrenaline, she raised her eyebrows. "Oh, do I now?"

But her tone didn't quell him at all. He simply said, "Yes, bunny. You're spending the afternoon with *me*."

Brandon couldn't resist wrapping around her from behind in the water, glad the surf was calm today, letting him play with her in the ocean without having to worry about them getting crushed by a wave. Damn, she felt good in his arms. And damn, she looked fine in that bikini. He was still basking in the masculine arrogance of finding her on the beach—just where he'd told her he'd look for her.

Beneath the clear water's surface, he splayed the fingers of both hands across her smooth stomach, letting one thumb flirt with the underside of her breast. He wondered if she could feel him getting hard against her ass, just from touching her.

"Mmm," she sighed, leaning back against him as he rained a few soft, openmouthed kisses across her neck, shoulder.

"I'm glad you decided to come to the beach today," he rasped in her ear.

Still in his embrace, she turned toward him with a smile. "I guess you think that's because of you."

He shrugged easily. "I think it's because you want what I promised you last night."

"What if I do?" She still sounded as cool and aloof as she had walking back to her room after fucking him.

He leaned near her ear once more, tightened his grip around her waist to lift her slightly as a small wave rolled past, and whispered, "Then you won't be disappointed."

Glancing down over her shoulder, he couldn't help appreciating the view. Her nipples were prettily hard, jutting against the black Lycra of her sexy top, which bared nearly as much of her breasts as it covered. "You have amazing tits," he growled in her ear, pleased to have found out last night that she liked talking dirty just as much as he did.

She answered by turning her head toward him once more and lifting one hand to his cheek to pull him into a warm, lingering tongue kiss that made his cock even stiffer.

Without thought, he followed the instinct to let his palm glide downward over her stomach until it snaked onto the fabric between her legs. She sucked in her breath at the touch, and he began to rub his fingers in little circles over her clit, his middle finger sinking into the valley of her slit even through her bikini bottom.

"Ohhh . . ." she purred, moving against his touch in front, his erection in back. "Oh . . . God."

"Does my hot little beach bunny like that?" he said low in her ear.

"Brandon," she began, sounding short of breath. "I . . . we . . . there are people around."

Ah. He *knew* she wasn't really a bad girl, deep down. A truly bad-to-the-core girl wouldn't give a damn. "But they're all far away."

She looked to the nearest swimmers—a teenage couple about thirty yards to their right and, probably more troubling to her, a family complete with two kids slightly closer to shore than the couple. "Far is a relative term."

He chuckled softly to himself, still stroking her sweet pussy under the water. "No one's watching, trust me."

She looked at him over her shoulder. "You've clearly done this before."

He couldn't help giving another light shrug. "Jealous, bunny?"

She blinked. "How could I be jealous? We just met. In fact, I'm glad."

Brandon raised his eyebrows. "Glad?"

"I like a guy who knows what he's doing." With that, she turned back around, facing away from him, as he continued to rub her.

"Well, you're in luck," he said. "Because I *definitely* know what I'm doing." Just then, another low wave rolled in, and he lifted her lightly to carry them both across it, watching as the water lapped at the soft curves of her breasts.

"It shows," she breathed, leaning back into him harder—and he knew for sure she could feel his cock now.

He didn't fight the urge to withdraw his fingers from her cunt just long enough to ease them down inside the front of her suit, directly into the folds of her pussy. They both expelled soft moans at the touch and she said, "Brandon, I can't," even as she moved against him, fucking his fingers.

"It *feels* like you can," he teased her, rubbing deeper, finding her rhythm, and making her moan again. He was getting hotter, too, feeling it in his gut and, of course, lower. He rasped in her ear once more. "Ah, damn, bunny, I want to fuck you so bad. I want to pull down your sexy little bottoms and fuck you right here and now."

He loved the sound when she sucked in her breath, even harder this time, and began to emit naughty little panting noises. He nibbled at her neck, found himself sliding his cock in the valley of her ass. He rubbed her harder in front, harder, harder, feeling the nub of her clit slide beneath his fingertips. His breath came rougher, too, and he began to wonder if he could really do it—fuck her right here, right now, in the water. What he'd said was true—no one was paying any attention to them. But they'd have to do it slow, soft—not like last night. They'd have to calm down a little.

He stopped moving, stopped caressing her. "Turn around," he said softly instead.

"What?" she murmured, even as she rotated to face him in the chest-high water. His arms slid around her waist; hers circled his neck.

And when he looked into her eyes, saw her lust, and was reminded again how pretty she was, her arousal clearly mingling with uncertainty, he knew—knew more than ever before—that Wendy *wasn't* the bad girl she claimed. She might *want* to be, but there was more to her than that, and something about *that* was sexy as hell.

He spoke soft and low, his voice gravelly. "I want to take off your bottoms and then I'm going to pick you up and you're going to wrap around me—and ride me."

She looked breathless—at once frightened but ready. Then she swallowed and glanced down at herself in the water. "We can't lose my—"

He cut her off, knowing what she was going to say. "No worries—I'll loop them over my wrist." Then he leaned close, so close that he could feel her heat even in the salty water, and whispered in her ear, "Are you ready for this, Wendy? Are you ready to have me inside you again?"

She still looked nervous, doubtful—but she nodded.

And just as he let his hands drop to her ass, slipping his thumbs inside her bikini, a huge burst of kids' laughter drew both their gazes toward the beach.

Ah, hell. A group of about ten or twelve people—most of them under the *age* of twelve—were coming into the water, carrying colored floats and wave boards and looking as if they planned to stay awhile.

Both he and Wendy stayed silent until they finally turned to look back in each other's eyes. "I'm going to kill you," she said very calmly and resolutely.

He was so surprised by the words that he laughed. "What did *I* do? Besides pleasure you, I mean."

"Precisely that. You got me all . . . you know. And now we can't."

"Excited, bunny," he told her. "The word is excited."

She let out a sigh and he realized that she actually felt a little limp and shaky in his arms, so he tightened his grip on her. "Sorry," he said, actually meaning it. He didn't like leaving her unsatisfied.

"Let's go to my place," she said, eyes widening hopefully. "It's only a five-minute walk."

Damn, he hated disappointing her, more every second, yet . . . "I wish I could. But I have an important conference call in about half an hour."

She blinked. "Well then, I'm not sure what you're doing fooling around with me in the ocean, because you'd better get going."

He couldn't help laughing. "I don't have to be in the office—my cell phone is in a backpack under your beach umbrella. And I figured I'd have time to fool around with you *here*, but I doubt I'd have time to fool around with you *there*." He pointed to her building. "Since we'd have to gather up our stuff and walk and wait for the elevator. I don't want to rush that way with you, you know?"

She sighed in understanding—but then he decided they should both turn it to their advantage. "Look at it this way," he told her, gazing into eyes made greener by the sun's reflection on the emerald waters. "By the time we get to have sex later, we'll both be so ready that we'll want to go all night."

He saw her swallow visibly at the promise before she said, "Later? As in when?"

"Go out to dinner with me. Over in the village. There's a place called Sharky's, right on the bay—totally casual, lots of fun." Then he remembered she was here on business. "And *please* don't tell me you have to work tonight."

She bit her lip before a slow smile crept onto her face. "No, I don't have to work."

His chest filled with warmth. "Then it's a date."

After leaving the water, they spent more time together on the beach in between what turned out to be a *series* of business calls—none, unfortunately, relating to solving his problems, but more about day-to-day operations—and Brandon found he enjoyed her company even when sex wasn't on the table. Of course, he supposed it really *was*—just with more of a buildup than last night—but he liked just hanging out in the sun with her. He *really* liked putting on her sunscreen and he wasn't shy about touching every inch of her he could that way, even if it aggravated his hard-on. He loved how slick her skin looked in the afternoon sun. He liked watching her get a little tipsy and even sleepy as they sipped on umbrella drinks. When she drifted off, her mouth half open, he found himself simply studying her, thinking she appeared just as erotic to him—in a different way—than ever before. Because she looked just as gorgeous, but also vulnerable. Real. She was beautiful without being . . . too polished, too plastic, too perfect.

When finally she revived and had tied a sexy little skirty

thing around her hips and they prepared to part ways, he pulled her close, unable to help asking, "Did you get over your excitement in the water?"

She looked like she was weighing her answer, finally saying, "I'm doing okay."

"Liar," he said, grinning.

A cute expression took over her face. "Fine. It's all I can think about. Did I fall asleep for a while? Because I think I even dreamed about it."

He let out a low groan. "What did you dream exactly?"

"Pretty much what almost happened. I was riding you in the water."

His dick stiffened all over again, at the vision, and at knowing he'd even inspired her sun-soaked dreams. "Damn, bunny, that's hot." He ran his fingertips lightly, playfully, over the bare curves of her waist.

"You want hot, buddy—you should've been there."

He let out a low laugh and said, "Tease."

"Only until tonight," she promised.

"Don't come without me," he said.

"Huh?" She looked up at him through puzzled eyes.

Clearly the alcohol and sun had dulled her usually sharp mind. So he pulled back just slightly and cast his gaze right at the crux of her thighs. *"Don't come without me,"* he said again.

This time she smiled, and he saw a glimmer of lust return to her gaze. "Oh. Okay."

He felt a grin sneak onto his face when he decided she wasn't taking this seriously enough. "I mean it. I want to make it happen. Promise me you'll wait."

She nodded, still looking sleepy and playful. "I promise," she said.

And I promise to make it well worth waiting for, he thought as he watched her walk away, her ass sashaying across the sand in a way that kept his eyes glued there until she was out of sight. He had some very naughty plans for his hot little beach bunny.

I watched for White Bikini Babe today. I'm not sure why. Maybe I wanted to thank her. Or maybe I wanted to see if I felt less intimidated by her now. If she passed by me on the beach, though, I missed her. I was too busy . . . <u>being</u> her. Being my own version of her and enjoying every strange, exhilarating minute of it.

Hard to believe it was just over twenty-four hours ago that I began this hedonistic little game. Perhaps even <u>harder</u> to believe that it isn't over yet, and that has it feeling a bit like . . . erotic Monopoly, a place where you just go round and round the board, passing Go over and again. Only instead of amassing property and money, I'm amassing . . . a collection of erotic experiences.

But I'm getting ahead of myself. Two erotic experiences—last night on the beach and today in the ocean—do not really a collection make. Yet I already feel myself rounding that third corner and racing past Park Place and Boardwalk, heading for Go once more—later tonight. And the amazing thing about erotic Monopoly is, it doesn't matter if I pass Go just one more time or a hundred. No matter what happens, I've already won.

Now it's only a question of how many times I'll win again.

Chapter 5

Wendy felt wired—with sexual need. Erotic images raced through her head. Erotic images that had really happened—the way she'd pinned Brandon to the sand last night, straddling him; the way she'd arched for him on hands and knees as she'd sucked on his finger; the sight of his hand between her legs beneath the clear ocean water a few hours ago.

And it would continue. Tonight.

When he'd suggested the restaurant, Sharky's, in the village, she'd almost mentioned that the outing would be perfect for her work since she needed to check out as many of the resort's hot spots as possible—but she'd quickly bit her tongue, deciding to keep work talk out of this. They had so far—so why spoil the fantasy with anything like reality?

Now she found herself shedding her bikini, staring again into the wide bathroom mirror at an entirely new set of tan lines than those she'd had yesterday. The old ones were still visible, but the new ones were more prominent due to more time in the sun today. Studying the sexier outline they made on her body, the way the tan dipped lower past her belly button and arced higher onto the curves of her breasts, she couldn't help thinking she looked erotic and . . . beautiful. She bit her lip, remembering Brandon's hands on these same curves. Like earlier today, it almost didn't seem real, as if those hours, last night and today, were just oh-so-vivid fantasies. She wondered where they would have sex tonight. And she hoped it would be someplace where he could see her body, really *see* it—the tan lines, the curves, *all* of her.

So her cunt already felt heavy, ready, as she stepped under the cool spray of the shower. And when she let her mind drift back further in the day, to Brandon's piratelike friend, Pete, her pussy actually quivered. God—where had *that* come from?

But she knew. It had come from the thoughts that had assailed her just before Brandon had shown up. She'd been thinking about fucking Pete, too.

He wasn't her normal kind of guy with his long, messy hair and beach bum look, but something had sizzled in the air between them—definite chemistry—and she'd found him undeniably hot in that rugged, pirate sort of way.

As she moved the bar of scented soap over her skin, feeling as if she washed away the coconut sunscreen to reveal the fresh tan underneath, she couldn't decide which man she wanted to focus her thoughts on at the moment. Perfect, handsome beach stud Brandon or rough, swarthy pirate Pete. It surprised her, in fact, that they were even friends—they seemed so different. But Pete had mentioned the friendship going back to college, so maybe it was just an unlikely pairing that had endured over time.

She'd promised Brandon she wouldn't climax without him, of course, but as she showered, her own touches felt too good, igniting still more longing. Despite her worries about being in public, her whole body had hummed with pleasure when Brandon had caressed her in the water, and she still suffered the frustration.

That was the point of waiting, she knew, the reason he didn't want her to come without him. And yet as she ran wet palms over her breasts and downward across her stomach, one hand eased between her legs.

She bit her lip, still amazed at how smooth her pussy felt, hairless. And equally amazed at how simply "free to be" she felt right now, like some untamed, exotic, pleasure-seeking creature. She felt free to touch herself as the water sluiced over her skin, heightening every sensation. And she felt free to think thoughts she never had before—ever. Thoughts of two men at the same time. Thoughts of one to the right of her and one to the left. Thoughts of two sets of male hands exploring her body. Thoughts of two men kissing her, her mouth, her neck, her breasts. Thoughts of two hard cocks, one in each of her fists. Then more thoughts of those cocks, taking turns fucking her, filling her up.

She braced herself against the shower's tile wall as she came, startled by the ferocity of the orgasm that pumped through her, the pulsations almost overwhelming to the degree that she had to sit down on the edge of the tub enclosure for a moment, her legs too weak to feel steady.

"Oh my God," she heard herself breathe as she came back to herself. Not because of the orgasm, but because of the thoughts that had made it so powerful. Had she really just fantasized about being with two guys at once? Her brain pulsed just as hard as her nether regions at the realization. This wasn't like her. She wanted to be wild, she wanted to live these dirty fantasies, but she'd never crossed that line in her mind before. She'd never even *thought about* crossing it. Anytime she'd ever heard of such a thing, it had struck her as unnatural and perverse, the height of sleaziness. Yet here, now, the notion suddenly struck her as more of a forbidden pleasure than a perversion.

Not that she would—or even *could*—ever do that.

It was one thing to fuck a guy's brains out on the beach after she'd just met him.

And to discover she could enjoy—*appreciate, adore, cherish, devour*—a bold sexual encounter that came without romantic emotions or attachment or a future.

It was even bearable to have entertained—very briefly—the idea of being with another girl when she'd found herself wondering if the pretty salesclerk at the Beach Bazaar was flirting with her.

But to do what she'd just fantasized about doing was . . . *unthinkable*.

Except for the fact that she'd thought it.

And the sky hadn't fallen, the world hadn't ended, life was going to go on.

Which made it, like everything else she'd experienced in the past twenty-four hours, shockingly . . . freeing. Just to think about. Just to play with in her mind. Just a little.

As she stepped from the shower, reaching for a plush towel, she caught a glimpse of herself in the mirror and realized that a naughty little smile played about her lips.

It was true. You really couldn't go back into the box.

She wore a simple summer dress of cotton with thin shoulder straps and a small flowery print. She'd gotten it last year for her annual beach sojourn with her sister and nieces, and feared it was more pretty than sexy, but she hadn't counted on needing more than one sexy dress when she'd gone shopping yesterday.

Thankfully, it was close-fitting and the bodice low cut, giving her some cleavage, or she would have felt positively frumpy in it after her more recently worn apparel.

When she went downstairs to meet Brandon at seven sharp, her chest practically sizzled at the sight of him. She knew he was hot, but when she was away from him, it seemed her memory didn't accurately capture the *zing* he sent through her when they were face-to-face. From those blue, blue eyes to the dark stubble on his chin to everything down below, he was easily the most attractive man she'd ever known. And despite the fact that his rather immense cock had been a little difficult to take at first, now the very knowledge of what lay hidden in his pants made her pussy swell, just thinking about it.

When he flashed an appreciative smile, she could tell—thankfully—that her appearance hadn't instantly doused her sexy image. Still, as she climbed into the golf cart next to him, she couldn't help saying, "Hope the dress isn't too Mary Sunshine."

He cocked a grin in her direction. "I think you'd look hot in anything. And besides," he added, turning his gaze to the cart path that ran through the resort, "all I ask from a dress is that I can get under it with ease, and this one qualifies." With that, he smoothly slid his right hand up over her knee and higher under the cotton skirt.

The unexpected touch shot straight to the apex of her thighs. "God," she breathed.

"What?" he asked.

She turned to look at him as the cart puttered along, and spoke low. "You make me wet."

"Jesus," he muttered, flinching. "Are you trying to make me wreck this thing?"

"It's your own fault," she pointed out with a soft laugh, "for instituting touching this early."

He shrugged, a small grin tugging at the corners of his mouth. "You're right. Remind me not to touch you for the next few hours so we can have a civilized evening out like normal people before I fuck your brains out again."

She nearly shivered at the promise, and cast him a look. "Talk like that isn't helping the situation. My panties are going to be soaked by the time we reach the restaurant."

He shot her a suggestive glance before looking back to the path. "Guess you'll just have to take them off."

Her whole body tingled as she lowered her chin, delivering a coquettish expression. "You are a naughty, naughty man."

"That's *your* fault, bunny."

Walking into the village tonight felt entirely different than it had the previous evening. Last night she'd been openly on the prowl, seeking sex with a stranger, needing something new and dangerous. Tonight she looked more like everyone else in the resort, dressed like the young wives and mothers out with their families, and she was on the arm of a handsome man. Tonight felt . . . safer, yet even more exciting. Because tonight there was no fear, no anxiety over the unknown, just a mouthwatering anticipation for what was to come.

When they approached the outdoor hostess station at Sharky's, the pretty young girl working there looked awestruck by Brandon, then—despite the long list of names in front of her—told him she'd get him the next available table. Wendy blinked in surprise, watching as Brandon waved off the offer. "No need to keep all the people who got here first waiting longer than they already have. Just add us to the list and we'll come back in half an hour. Although," he added with a wink, "a table by the water would be nice."

"Of course, sir," the girl said.

As Brandon took Wendy's hand and led her away, she asked, "Um, what was that about?"

He gave his head a short shake. "I come here a lot and they know me, that's all."

She raised her eyebrows in question. There were plenty of places where *she* went often, without getting treatment like *that*.

"I'm an excellent tipper," he added with a laugh.

"Apparently," she murmured, still stunned.

But her mind quickly moved onto other things, like the fact that Brandon was *holding her hand* as if they were some sort of romantic couple. And that—despite herself—she liked it. In fact, she just liked being out with him. She enjoyed perusing some of the gift and specialty shops with him—although she was thankful that her orgasm in the shower had helped her remember she was here to work, which meant checking the place out, and this was a good opportunity for that. And she liked when they stumbled upon a band playing pop hits in a parklike square in the center of the village and settled on a bench to watch little kids dancing to the music. He held her hand the whole time and something about it made her feel . . . full inside. Not in a sexual way, just in a . . . human connection way.

She bit her lip, pondering her emotions. *This is just sex, just sex, just sex.*

And she was sure, despite a moment of curiosity, that it was just sex to Brandon, too. A nice evening out between lovers didn't make it any more than that. After all, she'd had nice evenings out with *tons* of people in her life, from her mother to casual friends, and a nice evening was simply . . . a nice evening. No more, no less.

Sharky's was exactly what Brandon had promised—a casual outdoor eatery on a large covered deck edging the bay. A band of guys in their forties played standards like "Brown-Eyed Girl" and "Suzy Q," and while some people ate, others had fun on the small dance floor, and still more strolled through the restaurant to reach the narrow pier that led out over the water to a marina. It was the type of place decorated with fishing net and starfish and various shark-themed items, as well as a few pairs of women's panties, which were pinned up on an out-of-the-way rafter, high enough to avoid turning the restaurant into an un-family-friendly place.

Their table indeed sat next to the wooden railing by the water, inviting a pleasant breeze beneath the large awning. They both ordered seafood and drank rum-laden hurricanes, and when Brandon asked her how her work was going, she still decided to keep it vague, answering simply, "Fine."

"Good meetings today?"

"Productive," she answered shortly.

"Do you work for the mafia?" he asked, smiling.

She gave him a *very-funny* grin in return. "I just prefer not to mix work with pleasure."

He nodded. "Not a bad rule to live by. I'm pretty much the same way myself."

"Then I won't ask you about your work, either. So . . . tell me how you met Pete. He said he'd known you since college, but you two seem . . . very different."

Brandon leaned his head back in a light laugh. "We met

when we were in college—but we didn't go to the same school. We both worked summers here, though, right on the beach, setting up and taking down all those chairs and umbrellas."

She raised her eyebrows. "That sounds tedious." But at the same time, she was thinking: *Now I know where you both got all those muscles.*

"It was hard work—but a great summer playground, too."

"It's a pretty good playground *now*," she added.

He nodded. "Of course, Emerald Shores wasn't here back then—this stretch of the coast was a lot less developed and most of the hotels and small resorts were a few miles farther west, and that's where we worked. As for us being different—yeah, we're not exactly twins. But we both have strong work ethics, entrepreneurial attitudes, and . . . good taste in women." He lowered his chin conspiratorially. "I thought he was gonna steal you away this afternoon."

She simply propped her chin on her fist and cast a catlike smile. "Well, let's just say it's a good thing you showed up when you did."

The band played through dinner, and when the first notes of "Heard It Through the Grapevine" filtered through the air, Brandon held out his hand and said, "Let's dance."

She couldn't help being surprised. "Really? Because you don't seem like the dancing type." They'd slow danced last night, of course, but this was different.

He shrugged. "I'm a little drunk. And I always liked this song when I was a kid."

She wasn't usually the dancing type, either, but his honesty made him too cute to resist. Especially when he started to sing to her on the dance floor, replacing the "honey, honey" part with "bunny, bunny." They didn't really dance so much as move to-gether, his hands at her hips and her arms looping around his neck. And it should have been a playful, silly, easy thing . . . except that there was really nowhere to look but into his eyes, which were as warm as they were sexy. Exploring their depths made her wonder about him. What kind of work *did* he do? *Was* he an en-trepreneur, as he'd implied? Was he insanely rich? An overpriced golf-cart rental was one thing, but getting special treatment when you walk into a restaurant was another. What was his family like, his childhood? How had his voice sounded before he'd left behind that Alabama accent? She knew he loved the beach, but what else did he love? His mother? Puppies? James Bond movies?

Stop this. You aren't supposed to want to know *him, or even know stuff* about *him. He's your stranger in the night, your physical-pleasure-only fuck. And you need to keep it that way.* Good God, the *last* thing she needed was to go home attached to her hot beach lover.

After tonight, you'll probably never see him again. Yes, he'd wanted more after last night, and it turned out she had as well, but one more night of sex with him would be enough to quell any curiosities, and certainly enough to prove to herself that she was more than capable of getting hot guys, having hot sex, liv-ing the dream. *If* she could quit all this looking-into-his-eyes-and-wanting-to-know-him-better crap.

So when the song ended, she was glad to hear the band say they were taking a break. Which meant no more dancing. Which was good.

"Walk out on the pier?" Brandon asked, taking her hand.

Okay, walking out on the pier she could do. It was dark out there, and maybe it would give her the chance to remember what she was here for: sex. Sex, sex, sex.

And in fact, as they strolled out into the dark sea air, occasionally passing another couple or family but mostly finding themselves alone, that was exactly what she found herself thinking about—his body, and hers, and what they'd started today out in the ocean but hadn't finished.

So when they reached an intersection where the pier split off, one branch stretching to the marina across the water and the other leading out to a point overlooking the bay, she had no objections whatsoever when Brandon led her down the more private route, not stopping until they reached the end of the pier.

Leaning against the railing, she drank in the moment. Sounds and lights from the restaurant in the distance behind them. A sense of quiet, lavish luxury from the yachts docked at the marina. And before her, a wide-open bay that felt like . . . possibility.

Brandon wrapped warmly around her from behind, just as he had in the water this afternoon, already hard against her ass. Mmm, yes, nothing like an erect penis to get a girl back in a dirty mood. She couldn't resist rubbing against him a little—he felt too good not to.

As he used his hands to caress her body, he leaned near her ear and whispered. "You didn't come without me, did you?"

She considered lying. It wouldn't have mattered; it would have just been part of the game. But something compelled her to honesty. Odd, but even as she pretended to be someone she wasn't with him, when it came to sex she'd been brutally open with him so far, and something in her wanted to continue that. She peeked over her shoulder, feeling a bit sheepish about the answer, though. "Um . . . yes."

He didn't appear overly surprised or wildly disappointed. He simply said, "When?"

She bit her lip. "In the shower."

His head tilt was half chiding, half playful. "Damn, you didn't last long."

She found herself turning in his arms to face him, lifting her palms to his chest. "The water just felt so good and . . ." She stopped. She liked being sexually honest with him, but how far did she want to go?

"Tell me," he said, his voice deepening. "Tell me more."

Something in the request made her flow with fresh moisture. Maybe it was the invitation to totally let herself go, to hold *nothing* back, nothing at all. She reminded herself of what she kept telling *him*. *You're a bad girl, you're a bad girl. Be that. For him. Completely.* "The water felt good," she said, peering up at him, "and I was all soapy and soft. My pussy was throbbing and . . ."

"Shit," he murmured, his eyes gone glassy in the moonlight, clearly aroused. "What did you think about? Your body?"

"No." She shook her head, remembering. "More."

"Tell me."

Tell him. She swallowed back her hesitation and said, "You, mostly. Vague thoughts. You watching me. Then you fucking me. And your friend Pete." *Oh God, did I just say that part?* Her first reaction to her own words was mortification, but her second was . . . more of that new sense of freedom. She was putting it all out there, being a carefree sexual being, right? Since when *had* she started holding back with him? And why? She wasn't going to do it any longer—at all.

"Jesus fucking Christ, really?" Brandon asked.

She sucked in her breath. "Should I not have told you? Is that a turnoff?"

"Uh, no. Just the opposite. It's hot as hell. What was happening in your fantasy? Both of us fucking you?"

She let out a sigh of relief. Because she wanted to do this now, wanted to tell him—all of it, no matter how wanton it was. "Something like that—both of you naked with me in the shower, sort of . . . taking turns with me. It was all vague, though. I had all those drinks at the beach, remember?"

At this, Brandon let out a hardy laugh, but then lowered his voice again to say, "Damn, bunny."

His very tone echoed through her chest, making her breasts achy. "Do you believe me now?" she asked. "That I'm a bad girl?"

He arched one eyebrow. "Getting there."

"Well, see if *this* gets you there," she said. "I want to suck your cock so bad right now I can taste it."

He let out a low moan and she loved it—loved that she'd told him her shower fantasy, loved how much he turned her on, loved the amazing boldness he inspired in her. And she suddenly did want to suck him, right here, right now, because his erection pressed even more rigidly against her than before, stretching up between them like a granite pillar in his pants— and because if their pleasant dinner had dulled her sense of being a wholly sexual entity and nothing else, the last few minutes had restored it, taking her back to the animalistic place where she'd been last night, wanting to dive headlong into sin and pleasure.

Brandon angled his mouth across hers in an almost punishing kiss, and even as it caught her off guard, she liked the rough feel of it and met it with equal pressure. "Do it," he said against her lips.

"Mmm, I will," she purred into his mouth between kisses, "as soon as we're alone someplace."

He pulled back just enough to cast another chiding smile. "We're alone right now."

She couldn't help laughing a bit in response. "Just like we were alone in the water today? Famous last words."

Looking over his shoulder while keeping her pinned to the railing, he said, "No one's anywhere near us—they're all on the main walkway between Sharky's and the marina."

She simply looked at him. Because she'd never in her life given a guy a blow job anyplace more daring than a car, and even then, she'd been certain they were *very* alone.

Clearly sensing her indecision, Brandon braced his hands at her hips and smoothly switched their positions until he was the one with his back against the railing. "I promise if anyone even *starts* in this direction, I'll stop you before they have a chance to see." All amusement had left his gaze now—it had gone hot, fiery . . . and oh-so-seductive. Then his voice dropped an octave. "Now suck me. Suck my cock."

Heat infused her body at the command. In fact, it made her crave him, crave having him in her mouth. The truth was, she'd never been that into giving blow jobs before, but something about this hot game she'd created was pushing her into still new places. There for a little while, she'd felt like things were getting too soft between them, too much like a date, romance, and she'd found herself regretting the flowery sundress that made her look too much like she *usually* did. But now things were all the way hot again, and she felt driven toward total incineration.

So she dropped to her knees—another thing she'd never done with a guy—and ran splayed hands up his thighs, focusing on the bulge in his khakis and listening to the hot sigh he emitted above. She began to work at his belt, zipper, pleased when, although still hidden behind dark silk boxers, the full column of his erection pushed free from the open pants.

She ran the flat of her palm over the silken length, listening to Brandon's low groan. And she wanted to please him so badly, wanted to excite him more than she'd ever wanted to excite a man before. Yes, this dress had been a mistake. All hesitation on her part—of any kind—had been a mistake. She wanted to be wild for him in every way, wanted to prove to him, and herself, that she was just as naughty as she claimed.

Reaching inside the silk, she wrapped her fist around hot steel and released his jutting cock from his underwear. Oh God, the very sight of it—so close up—made her chest contract, her heart beat faster. It looked even bigger from this angle, small veins lining the hard length, the rounded head dotted with moisture. Big, powerful. She could still feel the way it had pumped into her last night, the memory turning her breath shallow.

Instinctually, she squeezed and caressed, aware of music and laughter in the distance yet feeling as if the darkness cocooned them. "So hard," she whispered into the sea breeze, then licked him, dragging her tongue from the bottom all the way to the top of the shaft. She looked up at him as she reached the tip, swirling her tongue to lick away the pre-come gathered there. She felt it in her pussy, and his low growl heightened the sensation.

His fingertips caressed her cheeks, raking back through her hair as he gazed down at her. "Do it, baby," he prodded. "Go down on me."

Never in her life would Wendy have imagined that being in such a submissive position could bring her so much pleasure. Never in her life had she enjoyed obeying a man's commands. But the woman she had become in this game made all that different.

Opening wide and flattening her tongue against her bottom lip, she lowered her mouth over the sizable head of his cock, and sank down. The sensation of taking him inside her that way barreled through her like hot liquid, racing down her throat, through her chest, making her gush with still more dampness in her panties. Above her, a ragged moan escaped him as his fingers threaded through her hair. "God, baby, yeah," he said.

Then she simply closed her eyes and fucked him with her mouth. Up and down, again, again, and deeper, a little deeper with each descent, making his length wet so that her lips slid more easily. Below, she grasped the root of his cock and fondled his balls, but mostly, she just felt the way he filled her mouth and let delivering such pleasure bring *her* more pleasure than this particular act ever had.

She tipped back her head as far as possible, yearning for him to watch her, wanting to look obscene and hungry for him. She drank in his moans like a sweet, fueling elixir that pushed her further into passionate oblivion. When he began to thrust slightly, she wanted more—so she looked up at his face and hoped he saw that in her eyes.

With every passing second, she grew more intoxicated on pleasuring him, continuing to feel amazed by his size and even more amazed that she could swallow so much of it. Everything took on a sense of eroticism—the air around her was sweet with it, the sound of laughter and music in the distance sang with it, even the way the hard wooden planks beneath her bit into her knees somehow felt erotic.

"God, baby, good," he breathed above her. "You suck me so fucking good, honey."

She even liked that he held her head in place now, that she couldn't back off of his erection if she wanted to, that he was virtually in control of her now. And the very awareness of *liking* that filled her chest with a strange, heady pleasure . . . a certain self-knowledge . . . self-acceptance . . . and full-on lust that she'd never felt before.

Above her, his breath grew heavy and when he plunged harder, deeper, between her lips, she welcomed it, amazed by the intensity. Every nerve ending in her body responded as she closed her eyes again and joyfully surrendered to letting Brandon fuck her mouth. "Jesus God," he muttered above. "So damn good . . . so soft, wet . . . yeah, oh yeah."

She was lost in it, drunk on it—when Brandon whispered, "Shit," planted his hands on her shoulders, and pulled her abruptly to her feet. "Somebody's coming."

Dizziness assailed her, but she turned her head to see two young couples making their way up the pier. They were talking, joking around, and seemed not to notice Brandon and Wendy. She leaned into him to keep her balance, comforted from the jarring situation when he wrapped an arm around her and pulled her close.

As she got hold of herself, she glanced down to see his magnificent cock still arcing up between them, and couldn't help whispering, "How was *that?*"

His voice came low, breathless. "I was about to come in your mouth."

"I would have loved that," she said without hesitation, even though she'd never let that happen with any guy before and had never particularly wanted to.

"I wanted to stop," he told her, "didn't want to get you messy out here, but damn, bunny, you suck me good."

Her chest tingled, and she'd never felt quite so flattered in her life. She didn't think any guy had ever complimented her on that before. But then again, she'd never gotten so into the act before, either.

"Let's go somewhere," she suggested. The two couples had stopped to look out on the water about halfway down their branch of the pier and would probably leave soon, but she was tired of being interrupted. "Someplace private. Someplace where we can take our time and won't have to stop."

Heat laced his smile. "My place?"

"Race you to the golf cart."

They started to take off, hand in hand, when Wendy pulled up short, stopping them.

"What?" he said.

She looked down at his open pants. "Might want to zip up there, buddy."

"Jesus," he murmured, then reached down to stuff himself back inside his zipper, a task that looked fairly challenging given his size. Once he had his pants back together, he took her hand back in his to say, "What a dangerous little bunny. You make it so I can't even think straight."

"The sooner you get me to your place, the sooner neither one of us will have to worry about that anymore. Now let's go. I want to do things with you that . . ." But she faltered then, letting her voice trail off.

He flashed a sexy, inquisitive smile. "That what?"

Stop being shy. No hesitation. "Things that I've never done before."

Normally, Brandon thought the golf cart was the best way to travel Emerald Shores, but at the moment, the damn thing wouldn't go fast enough. Good God, Wendy was enough to drive a man wild. It was bad enough he'd gotten all worked up with her in the water today—and hadn't gotten to come. Now he'd nearly exploded in her mouth only to have that stopped, too. He was starting to think she had a point about not fooling around anyplace they could be caught, and that was what had him racing—as much as a golf cart could race—to his penthouse condo right now. His cock throbbed like crazy in his pants.

Next to him, her cheeks were prettily flushed and her eyes glimmered with a lusty anticipation that made him that much more eager. Was she a good girl or a bad one? It was a conundrum he hadn't yet solved. Normally, he didn't sit around dividing chicks into categories—but she'd started the wheels turning in his head on this particular topic.

The dress said good, but the blow job definitely said bad. Whereas last night's dress had said bad, but something in her eyes had leaned closer to good. Today on the beach had been the same—she'd worn a bad girl's bikini, but damn, she'd somehow looked so innocent asleep in the sun.

And he liked the good girl part of her just fine, but at this moment, he was *way* into the bad. Or at least the *wanting* to be bad. Maybe something about a girl wanting to be bad was even hotter than the true bad girl. A girl who *wanted* to be bad had to let go of herself, had to let loose her inhibitions, had to reach deep down inside to find a new, dirty part of herself and release it.

When they reached his building, he led her quickly inside and onto an elevator. Alone there, he couldn't help pulling her into his arms and making out with her as the elevator rose. Shit, if it was possible, the tongue kisses they exchanged made him even harder. "I want you so damn bad," he murmured in her ear, caressing the side of her breast.

"I can't wait to let you have me," she purred back.

Oh yeah, he liked the bad.

As they stepped into his penthouse, though, the mood changed, slowed down. Hell. He supposed he should have expected it when her eyes went wide. "Wow, nice place," she said, taking it all in.

Maybe he should have warned her. But how do you say, *Prepare yourself—I happen to be pretty fucking rich and I live in a showplace*? Just one of many reasons he seldom brought women back here—but with her, he hadn't thought twice about it.

"Thanks," he said.

She turned to give him a teasing smile. "Do *you* work for the mafia?"

A short laugh escaped him. "I thought we were leaving work out of this."

"We were, but *this*"—she motioned around her at the lavish furnishings in the open layout condo—"this bears some explanation, don't you think? How does a guy go from putting out beach umbrellas in the summer to living *here*?"

He tilted his head, quirked a grin. "Let's just say I've . . . made fortunate choices."

She lowered her chin derisively at his vagueness. "Yes, I'm sure the mafia pays well."

He chuckled again, then moved on. "If you really want to see the *best* part of this place, come here." With that, he headed toward the doors that led onto the balcony.

During the day, you could look up and down the beach through the row of picture windows lining the seaward side of the penthouse, but at night, they only admitted darkness and to really see anything, you had to go outside. When Wendy stepped through the door, he placed an instinctive hand on her ass, following her out.

"Holy crap," she murmured as they approached the railing. "This is amazing. And . . . mmm, the breeze feels great."

Brandon smiled at her bluntness and closed his arms around her from behind. He leaned in to her, letting the salty sea air soak into him, as well. "Believe it or not," he said near her ear, "as much as I like this place, *this* is the main reason I live here. This view."

"I bet in the daytime you can see forever."

He nodded, cheek to cheek with her, his hands splayed, one across her hip, the other caressing her breast. "It always makes me feel . . . somehow both big and small at once. Like there's this huge, beautiful world out there, too big to ever really be fully explored or fully controlled. But at the same time"—he couldn't help laughing at himself a little—"I always have that 'I'm king of the world' feeling when I look out on it."

She laughed softly, as well—but her laughter faded when his palms skimmed down onto her thighs. She drew in her breath, and he kissed her neck, his cock pressing into the valley of her ass, rigid and more than ready. He'd never fucked anyone out here before—and as he slid his hands upward on her soft skin, under her dress, it dawned on him that it was high time he had.

His touch glided higher, slowly higher, on smooth as silk legs—until he found the *real* silk at the juncture where they met. When he stroked his fingers through her slit, her pretty gasp heightened his need even further. Her head dropped back, inviting more little kisses across her neck, shoulders.

Upon easing his fingers inside the lacy edge of her panties, a small jolt shook him—just from the mere connection with her female flesh. His fingers sank into her moisture, forcing a ragged sigh from his throat. "Smooth and wet," he murmured deeply in her ear.

"I told you—you make me soak my panties."

He smiled, even though she couldn't see it, his chest swelling with a masculine arrogance he couldn't push down. "Then we should definitely take them off," he said, slipping his thumbs through the bands at her hips to send them dropping to her ankles.

After emitting a little gasp, she looked over her shoulder at him in the darkness, and *now* he let her see his wicked smile. She bit her lip, looking lusty, weak, like a woman who needed to be fucked. And he was more than happy to oblige.

It took only one hand to undo his zipper and extract his aching cock. With the other, he raised her dress in the back, watched the way she arched her ass slightly in invitation—even as she turned her eyes back toward the ocean.

Gripping her bare hips with both hands, he nudged the tip of his erection at her damp opening. A hot little moan echoed from her, urging him onward—so he slid deep, slow, tight, until he was fully sheathed in her warmth.

"Oh *God*," she breathed.

Like last night, he feared he might be too big for her. He knew the whole world thought big dicks were great, but he'd been around enough to know that for some women, his was hard to take. "Is it okay, bunny?" he whispered.

She let out a heaving, thready breath, but then finally said, "Uh-huh."

"Are you sure? I don't want to hurt you."

"It's . . . so big."

"Do you want me to take it out? Would it be better lying down?" He knew for a fact that it *would* be easier for her lying down.

Yet she said, "No. I want you . . . to fuck me hard."

Oh. Okay. So his naughty little beach bunny was adjusting to the size of his cock. *Thank God.* Withdrawing from her body right now would have been nothing less than torture.

"Tell me again," he said. Because he needed to be sure *she* was sure. And because he wanted to hear her say it a second time.

"Fuck me hard, Brandon. Please."

That was all the prodding he needed to tighten his grip on her hips and begin thrusting, thrusting, into her tight warmth. Jesus God, it was good, filling *him* as much as he was filling *her*. With each stroke, she cried out, arching her ass farther, curling her fingers around the balcony railing like she was holding on for dear life.

And he went faster, rougher, soon pummeling her sweet flesh, driving into her with all his strength, fucking her hard, hard, hard, just like she wanted, just like he wanted, too—until the orgasm he'd been needing all day broke over him like a sweet downpour after a long drought. Of course, he hadn't exactly been in a sexual drought, but as he exploded, shooting his come deep inside her, it felt that good, that powerful.

When the climax waned, he slumped over her, wrapping around her tight and muttering, "God, baby. God, you drained me."

In front of him, she panted her own exhaustion, then glanced over her shoulder, looking tired but still perfectly naughty. "That was *so* good."

He found himself returning her weary grin. "And we're just getting started."

After which he summoned his strength, hoisted her into his arms, and carried her inside.

*T*here are moments with him when I forget. Who I am pretending to be here, who I am with him. There are moments when I am . . . me. There are moments when I yearn to know him better than I do, better than I should want to. Better than you know a guy you're just having meaningless sex with. That part surprises me. I mean, when I first saw him, I just never thought ahead to that as a possibility. He was too beautiful, with too much potential for arrogance and superiority.

But then, I never expected one night to turn into two.

Luckily, though, when things get hot between us, I forget that. Mostly.

Mostly, it turns into what I wanted from him from the very first glance—hot, wild, make-me-scream, make-me-crazy sex. Then that's all I can think of, all that matters. Passing Go. And staying outside the box.

Chapter 6

Wendy wrapped her arms around his neck, her panties looped over one wrist, and kissed him as he carried her inside and across the room. She remained vaguely aware that he hadn't bothered shutting the door and that the sea breeze followed them in as sheer white curtains blew around them, making the world feel dreamlike for a moment.

But then, in ways, *all* of this felt dreamlike—still.

The sex.

The man.

The woman she became with him.

He laid her on a king-size bed that faced the windows and said, "Take your dress off. I want you naked."

He stood, looking down on her as she followed the command, aware of the wetness on her inner thighs, and for the first time in her life not minding the messiness of it. He kept his eyes on her, all the while unbuttoning his shirt, dropping his pants, shedding his underwear, until he was naked, too. Beautifully so.

He was a vision of rippling muscles, perfect male flesh that she hadn't seen enough of last night on the beach. She found herself wanting to touch his hard, masculine body, run her fingertips over the ridges and valleys of his skin. And—oh God—his cock was growing again, that quickly, as large already as most men she'd known with a full-on erection.

The backdrop to his perfection was a wall of windows that made the ocean and sky part of his home. Pale yellow walls and ceiling shone warm and golden in the dim lighting but probably imitated the sun during daylight hours. The sprawling studio-style condo possessed only one small wall erected to separate the bed from the living area and lavish state-of-the-art kitchen, the space as open as the beach itself. And so he fit here in this setting—as well as he did on the ocean shore—and she couldn't have imagined a more perfect place for Brandon to live.

"Lie down," he told her, waiting as she reclined. For a guy who seemed genial and easygoing most of the time, he had the ability to take firm charge of things during sex. She didn't usually like bossy men, but when Brandon got bossy about sex, she instinctively trusted him to know what would make them both feel good.

When he straddled her hips, his majestic phallus expanding to still greater lengths, she thought he would fuck her again, and she tried to spread her legs beneath him. But when he reached behind him with both hands to push them closed, then gave a small, precise head shake, she realized that wasn't what he wanted.

Next, he bent to drag his tongue from the bottom of one of her breasts to the top, passing over the turgid nipple on the way. The moment he drew back, a burst of air lifted the curtains across the room and wafted coolly over the wet pink peak to make her tingle in delight. A low moan escaped her, and she saw the satisfaction wash over his face.

Then he bent again, to the other breast, but this time he

swirled his tongue around the beaded tip, then sucked it into his mouth, hard, deep. She cried out, surprised by the severity of the action—how it hurt a little but she felt it echoing through her *everywhere*.

He continued to suckle her and she found herself running her hands through his hair, over his shoulders—until her breath came heavy, as if she'd just run a long distance, until her pussy pulsed with hot need. "More," she heard herself beg.

More what? She didn't even know.

But he responded by releasing her breast from his mouth, sitting upright on her again, and easing his body up hers until his thighs stretched across her torso just beneath her tits. His cock was completely erect again and looked impossibly huge from her vantage point as it arced magnificently upward from her chest.

That was when he took the rock-hard shaft in his hand and began to feed it to her.

"Unh . . ." she heard herself moan, opening her mouth, accepting what he gave her with all willingness. He was direct without being forceful, leaning toward her, sliding several inches of his length between her lips, making her taste herself there, the remnants of their sex on the balcony still present.

She remembered last night on the beach, wanting to look obscene for him, and earlier on the pier, as well. She knew she looked that way now, and in better lighting this time. She met his gaze, hoping he could read her eyes. *I want this. I want this experience. I want your cock. I want to know what it is to taste all of life, to live to the fullest, to know every emotion, every sort of sex, every dirty bit of it. When I'm ninety and people think I'm a sweet, docile little old lady, I will look back on this moment and smile a secret smile and know I missed nothing.*

Of course, there was no way he could read all of that, but maybe it was enough just to feel it herself, just to bask in the knowledge that she'd taken control of her sexuality, that at least in this facet of her life, she would never have regrets now, never have what-ifs or doubts or curiosity over naughty fantasies. Because she was *doing* this, *living* this, and it was the most thrilling thing she'd ever done.

He fucked her mouth, slow and deep, and sometimes she looked at him, and other times she closed her eyes and simply felt the nearly overwhelming wonder of it. He never went *too* deep, made her take *too* much—he seemed to instinctively know what she could handle.

When he finally pulled out, her mouth felt stretched, well used and a little sore—and if a woman had to have a sore mouth, this was the best possible reason she could think of.

She had no idea what would happen next, what pleasure he would lead her to—but she simply waited, trusting him, feeling swept along, as if she were traveling in a strange land and he was her guide.

Their next stop on the journey was . . . her breasts again. But this time it had nothing to do with his mouth—he lay his still damp hard-on between them and used his hands to lift them, to press the soft flesh up around his hardness, and then he began to slide.

"Oh . . . oh God," she heard herself say. Because it seemed—just like fucking her mouth—as if this were something that should pleasure *him*, not her. Yet this, too, filled her with such delight and satisfaction that she could barely contain it. The very sensation of having his hardest part against one—or two—of her softest. The slick slide. The raw visual as she watched the rounded head of his shaft jut between her breasts. The moisture, which grew as his pre-come gathered and then became spread across her inner curves, helping him to fuck her there even more wetly.

Without planning it, she covered her hands with his, wanting to push her breasts even harder around his stiff cock. He let go, let her take over, as he braced his hands on the teak headboard and thrust in earnest, same as if it were her pussy, emitting low groans at each hot drive.

He wasn't holding back—she could feel it. He was fucking her tits hard, hard, and he was going to come this way soon, and her body forgot to be selfish at all—she knew only the intense need to pleasure him. Hadn't it been that way all night? Sucking his cock on the pier, and then he'd fucked her on the balcony without making her come. And maybe she *should* be starting to feel selfish, but she simply wasn't. Somehow she knew he'd make it right in the end. At the moment, she was still basking in the simple yet profound pleasure of *experiencing* this, experiencing things with him she'd never even thought about before—letting her body respond favorably, and her mind, too.

"Ah, God," he groaned, then used his hand to withdraw his length from the tunnel her breasts had created. "I'm gonna come," he growled. "Keep pushing your tits together."

So she did, watching as he aimed his dick downward, toward them, and she wasn't surprised when the bursts of white semen arced geyserlike across her breasts, but she flinched anyway—from the sensation—and lay amazed at how erotically beautiful she thought the evidence of his orgasm looked decorating the part of her body that had taken him there. Three, no, four hot shots of it, Brandon moaning his release—and then he replaced her hands with his, firmly massaging, rubbing it into her skin just like the sunscreen earlier today.

He held his index finger to her mouth and said, "Taste me."

As soon as she did, she instantly wanted more, so she reached for his nearby cock instead, pulling it into her mouth and sucking him dry. She tasted only a little more of him—sweet, odd, salty—but the sensation left her even more aroused than she'd already been.

"You are *amazing*, bunny," he told her, the first hint of a smile she'd seen in a while beginning to make its way onto his handsome face.

"Lie down with me," she said.

Now that he'd come, he'd stopped being so "in charge" and did as she asked, leaning over to kiss her sweetly.

And that was when it hit her. *No condom.* Out on the balcony. They hadn't used a condom. "No condom," she said suddenly without preamble.

He looked just as surprised as she suddenly felt, his gaze going wide. His eyes fell shut with regret. "Damn it. I'm sorry, bunny. I don't know what I was thinking."

"That you had to get inside me before you erupted?"

He sighed. "Something like that. But I'm usually a lot more careful."

"Well, that's reassuring." She meant it wholeheartedly. God only knew how many women he'd been with, but she was betting on a high number.

"What about you?" he asked. "Are you usually careful?"

I usually don't have much sex. At least not lately. But when she had . . . "Yeah, I am."

Next to her, he sighed in relief. "Then maybe this isn't a disaster of epic proportions."

"I guess not," she agreed. "As long as"—she connected her gaze to his on the pillow next to her—"you're *sure* you've been careful."

"Scout's honor," he said, lifting two fingers and making her laugh at the very idea that he'd ever been a Boy Scout.

"Because I'm guessing I'm not the only bunny you've played beach blanket bingo with."

A confirming even if slightly sheepish smile graced his face. "But you're the only one who's kept me battling a raging hard-on all damn day."

Good to know. Not that it mattered. "Your own fault," she pointed out. "You were the one who wanted to fool around where we couldn't really fool around. And you were the one who chose not to sensibly take care of it in the shower like I did."

He raised his eyebrows pointedly. "Are you trying to make me hard *again*, bunny? Reminding me of the whole shower thing and your dirty little fantasy. *Damn.*"

"Sorry," she said, not feeling very sorry. "But yeah, I actually wouldn't mind it. I mean, uh . . ."

This time he gave her a full-blown smile. "Don't worry, I'm well aware that I owe you an orgasm or two. You've been very generous and I intend to return the favor."

"Good," she said. "How?"

He laughed, then made a *tsk*ing noise. "Patience, patience, my naughty beach bunny."

"Easy for *you* to say, after coming twice."

He shrugged. "True. But you'll just have to trust me." And with that, he sat up and got out of bed.

"Where are you going?"

"Bathroom," he said. "I'll be right back. Don't go anywhere."

As if. He couldn't have *paid* her to leave his bed at the moment. Not just because she was so turned on, but because there was something about him—something about them *together*. She'd wanted to see if she could be sexy enough to catch a guy like him. But now it was about much more than that. She'd known sex with a hot guy who truly aroused her on sight would be great, but sex with Brandon surpassed all she had imagined. Sex with Brandon was continuing to broaden her horizons, take her speeding around that Monopoly board again and again until she was almost dizzy. And she wanted to get dizzier still.

As she lay on her back, looking around the expansive space, she found herself wondering once more—just how much money did Brandon *have*? It didn't matter, for various reasons, but seeing his home confirmed that he had to be überwealthy. Beachfront property was expensive *enough*—but a penthouse condo in a gorgeous building nestled by the beach in a swank resort? She couldn't even begin to estimate the price tag—although given her duties this week, she could probably nose around and find out if she wanted to.

She couldn't help thinking he was charmed. Just like White Bikini Babe. People like them simply just didn't know what it was like to be average, to lead an average life. Not that she held it against him. But the realization made it seem all the more surreal to suddenly be a part of his world. Even if it *was* only temporary.

"Do you have any idea how gorgeous you are?"

Her eyes had fallen shut, but at this she opened them and smiled. His words reminded her—she really *had* pulled it off, hadn't she? Even without the bikini or the sexy dress, he thought she was hot. It remained beyond amazing to find out a guy like him found her "worthy." Lying naked among his rumpled white sheets—high-end Egyptian cotton if she wasn't mistaken—with her arms flung sensually up over her head, she'd never felt more beautiful.

"Yes," she heard herself say. Not out of arrogance, but simply because she believed it now. If he thought she was gorgeous, it must be so.

"Good," he said, lowering himself back to the bed. "A woman as beautiful as you should know it."

No way would she ever tell him that a few days ago she *hadn't*, that it was only because of him that she'd come to understand it. She wanted him to keep thinking of her the way she thought of White Bikini Babe—he wanted her to think she'd always been this *confident*, this *exciting*.

He'd situated himself farther down the bed than where she lay, and he slid one hand behind her calf, the other beneath her bare foot, lifting it to his mouth for a kiss. The ministration skittered up her thigh, straight to her cunt, reminding her that he'd also paid a bit of attention to her feet last night when they reached the beach, too.

"Mmm," she purred, then enjoyed watching—and feeling— as he began to kiss his way up the inside of her leg.

Soft kisses traveled up her calf and to the side of her knee—and since he now sat between her legs, they'd naturally parted. As he lowered another kiss to her sensitive skin, his gaze dropped to her slit. "I love that you shave your pussy," he murmured.

She bit her lip, very aware of his eyes on her there, and her voice came out sounding airy, dreamy—from pleasure, she supposed. "Not a fan of pubic hair, huh?"

He chuckled gently. "I have nothing against it, but I like being able to see every bit of your pretty cunt."

His words left her a little breathless. Not to mention wet. And very glad she'd experimented with shaving.

As he kissed his way closer to her pussy, it tingled, heavy, hungry. And maybe it should have made her feel . . . dehumanized or something that he kept his eyes so focused on it, but it didn't. Instead, it made her . . . a porn star. The porn star she could never be. And didn't really *want* to be—but it was just one more way of being desired, of becoming a wholly sexual creature for a night. Or two, as the case was.

His first kiss on her most tender flesh landed to the left of her slit, on the pale skin she'd bared. He kept his eyes open as he placed a kiss on the other side, too, not looking up at her face, but directly at her cunt. She instinctively found herself parting her legs even wider, as wide as she could. *Look at me.* She wanted him to think she was as beautiful there as he did everywhere else, since it was a part of her, after all. An *important* part, now that she thought about it.

He explored her with his fingers, as well, gentle touches at first, running a fingertip along the rim of her pussy, then using two fingers to tease and stroke the pink lips within. He gently pinched and rubbed her clit, making her whimper as he touched his tongue to her below.

Soon he pushed two fingers inside her moist passageway, using his other hand to hold her open as he delivered short, soft licks to her swollen clit—and through all of it, he studied his work, kept his eyes on her cunt as if he were a scientist conducting an important experiment or an archaeologist exploring a newly discovered artifact. She'd never been touched or licked so meticulously.

"Lie back and close your eyes, bunny," he said. She'd propped herself on her elbows to watch him . . . watching her.

She hesitated. Then remembered that with Brandon, her temporary dream lover, she held nothing back. Because there were no real consequences to honesty. "Maybe I like to watch."

He lifted a grin to her eyes. "Then we have that in common. But I need you to relax."

She raised her eyebrows. "You sound like a doctor about to perform some unpleasant medical procedure."

He let out a laugh. "Don't worry, baby—I never want to hurt you. Only pleasure you. Now be a good girl and lie back and relax for me."

True enough, the man knew how to bring her pleasure. He knew how to bring pleasure through means she'd never imagined could *be* so pleasurable. So she lay back and closed her eyes.

She felt his fingers sliding in her moisture, thrusting all the way in. She felt his licks and kisses at her clit, which made her squirm and sigh and begin to undulate rhythmically, meeting both types of delicious pressure. And then she felt . . . God, something big and hard, pressing where his fingers had just been, opening her wider. "Oh . . ." she moaned. She'd have thought it was his cock, but she could still feel his breath on the flesh between her legs, so that was impossible.

As it began to enter her, she opened her eyes and propped up again. "What *is* that?" She strained to see what he held in his hand. Was it a . . . ?

"A cucumber," he replied as if it were a totally normal answer.

She blinked. She'd totally missed him carrying that back to the bed with him. "Why do you have a cucumber?"

He raised his gaze from her cunt to her face. "Because I like to slice them up and put them in salads. Why else?" Then he smiled. "Right now, I want to put it inside you."

Dear God. She sucked in her breath, taken aback. "Why?"

He let out one of his sexy little Brandon laughs. "Well, I'm guessing you don't have a vibrator on you at the moment—and I want to watch something go inside you. Something bigger than my fingers. I want to watch your pussy take it, open for it, and close around it."

Holy crap. His words literally stole her breath. Even as they somehow made her pussy do exactly what he wanted—open for it. She let out a light groan as he pushed the cucumber deeper. "God." To her befuddlement, it felt . . . good.

Still on her elbows, she couldn't help watching again, this time more in amazement than anything else. She'd heard the occasional joke about cucumbers and had once attended a bachelorette party where one of the games had been to see who could put a condom on a cucumber the fastest—but she'd never actually thought about putting one *inside* her, for God's sake. And yet, between her legs, Brandon thrust it firmly, driving it deeper and making her moan again, and it filled her just as satisfyingly as any penis.

"Ah, bunny, your pussy looks so fucking hot like this."

A frisson of excitement swirled through her stomach, even as she heard herself saying, "Still, it seems sort of . . ."

"What?" he asked, his gaze still planted squarely between her thighs, where her vagina swallowed a vegetable.

"Odd," she said.

Only then did he raise his eyes back to hers. "The word you're looking for is kinky. And I warned you last night—I *am* sometimes."

Kinky. Kinky *was* better than odd. Kinky was . . . kind of hot. And as that idea echoed through her, her pussy took the cucumber even deeper.

His low groan said he'd noticed, and he took the opportunity to begin moving it in and out of her moisture. Her breath grew heavy as the sensation assailed her. Again, it was the same as a cock. The same, she supposed, as a vibrator, but she'd never owned one, used one, because she'd always figured that if she needed to pleasure herself, her hand would do, and it usually did. So she remained amazed that this felt so freaking good.

"Fuck it, bunny," he instructed her.

He wanted her to move against it, wanted to watch her pussy in action. She obeyed. She tried simply to feel, to forget, but that part was harder. "I can't believe I'm deriving pleasure from a cucumber," she said on a heavy breath.

Her lover laughed. "You're not deriving pleasure from a cucumber," he informed her. "You're deriving pleasure from *me*. But even if you *were* deriving pleasure from a cucumber, so what?" When she glanced down at him, he was flashing a wicked smile. "And by the way, a real bad girl wouldn't blink at deriving pleasure from a cucumber."

She smirked playfully, even as he continued moving the cucumber in and out. "Smart-ass."

"Just calling it like I see it. And if the halo fits . . ."

She gasped. "Oh, *please*. You might not think I'm a bad girl, but you *cannot* think I'm an angel, given the things we've done together the last two nights."

"Fair enough." He offered a shrug, still working the vegetable-turned-sex-toy.

"I'm going to convince you yet that I'm the baddest girl you've ever met."

He grinned—and shoved the cucumber deeper in her cunt. "If the *cucumber* fits," he said, meeting her gaze and letting his amusement fade, "then fuck it for me."

And so she did. But this time she *really* did it—she stopped thinking, she let her eyes close as the pleasure grew more invasive, more overwhelming; she let herself be a kinky bad girl for him. She loved feeling his eyes on her there even if she wasn't looking anymore, and she let it make her still hotter, still wetter—until she could hear her own wetness as the cucumber thrust inside her, again, again.

He gave her still more pleasure, *unbelievable* pleasure, when he bent to lick her clit, hard. It felt much different, much more powerful with something inside her below—it was *double* the pleasure, two entirely different kinds that couldn't be delivered by one man the normal way. A man could fuck you and a man could lick you, but he couldn't do both at the same time—only now *this* man was doing that, and the pleasure was wild and pervasive as she lifted herself against his mouth, as she fucked what he held in his hand with intense total abandon.

She cried out and soaked it all in. She clutched at the bedsheets, balling them in her fists. She reached over her head, pressing her palms to the headboard for leverage. And when Brandon sucked her clit deep into his mouth, she exploded, the climax roaring through her like a freight train. "God, yes! Yes! Yes!" she screamed as the pulsations rolled through her.

Oh Lord. She'd just fucked a cucumber. That was the reality of getting kinky that hit when the orgasm was over. But when Brandon eased the cucumber out, lowered a gentle kiss just above her slit, and whispered, "Damn, bunny, that was so fucking hot," it made everything okay.

She lay quiet for a moment, recovering, then peered down to ask the weird question that had just entered her mind. "So, are you still going to eat this particular cucumber?"

He grinned up at her, eyes twinkling. "Sure," he said. "It'll be just like eating you in a whole different way."

She lifted her hand to cover her mouth—hiding her smile at how nasty her hot lover could be. And if she was smiling, that must mean she could be pretty nasty, too. *I really* am *a bad girl now, inside and out.*

He watched her sleeping among tousled sheets. Her nipples remained erect and beautiful, even in slumber. He liked her body. No, more than that. He'd seen plenty of naked women in his day, but he was more fascinated just watching her sleep than he could ever recall being with anyone before. Something about her was so . . . natural, genuine. Most women he'd been with had either seemed to put on airs of some sort or they were all beauty, no brains. So maybe he was fascinated by more than just her naked body. But at the moment, that was the part that held his attention.

She lay on her back, her tits drooping toward either side, but he didn't mind. Again, something in how natural that looked also became beautiful. She had a small scar just below one of them—he wondered what from. Her belly button made a small oval pool just above a small pooch of tummy that, like everything else, made her all the more lovely and real. She was a real woman, nothing fake or sculpted about her.

But was she a bad girl? He still voted no. Like he'd told her, the cucumber wouldn't have freaked out a bad girl so much. On the other hand, within moments of meeting her, he'd understood that she was open to casual sex with him. Why *was* that? Was she lonely? A beauty like her with a great personality—nah, couldn't be. Was she on the rebound from a bad breakup? Maybe she was what he'd originally thought—just a woman who liked sex as much as he did and wanted to indulge in it.

But since then he'd seen too many moments when she seemed surprised. About fooling around where someone could see, about cucumbers. On one hand, she'd seemed completely experienced and ready to party, but on the other, he sometimes got the idea he was taking her places she hadn't been before.

Ah, hell. Maybe he shouldn't ask himself those kinds of questions. Normally, he didn't care why a woman wanted to fuck him—so long as she wanted to fuck him. Like every other woman, Wendy would be gone from his life soon enough and nothing would matter but the fact that they'd brought each other some pleasure. Okay, some fucking *intense* pleasure. Still, in the long run, his curiosity about her wasn't important—in fact, it was wasted thought.

Just then, she shifted, rolling over on her stomach, one knee bent out beside her. And, like every other view of her, the curve of her back, the roundness of her ass, struck him as beautiful. Yes, she'd be gone from his life soon—but already, he found himself wanting to remember her. More than the others. He wished he could take a picture of her like this to help preserve the moment—but then he laughed inside. His sexy bunny would have a fit if he even suggested that. Again proving that she wasn't really a bad girl.

He'd come twice already, but watching her, he hardened again. She was just too pretty sleeping to . . . let her keep sleeping.

So he found himself easing up behind her on the bed, running his hand slowly from her shoulder down over the curve of her waist and onto her sweet bottom. It brought to mind a memory, the vision of how she'd looked last night on her hands and knees on that lounge chair as he'd moved in to fuck her from behind. Hell, maybe she *was* a bad girl, after all. What the hell *was* the exact definition of a bad girl anyway? He'd thought he knew, but she was changing his perceptions. His naughty beach bunny didn't fit neatly into any one slot.

Rubbing his hand in a circle on her bottom made her stir slightly, then look over her shoulder with a smile. "Did I sleep long?"

He shook his head. "A few minutes."

"Mmm. Good. I don't want to miss anything."

That made him grin. "Don't worry, bunny. Anything I do to you worth feeling would definitely wake you up."

She licked her lips, then murmured, still sleepy-sounding, "That feels good."

His hand on her ass, she meant. "I can make it feel better," he promised, then used both hands to begin massaging, kneading her rear.

"Mmm," she nearly purred, and the sound went straight to his dick, turning it still more rigid.

As he continued kneading Wendy's hot, round ass, which she arched slightly for him now, he studied her there, the same as he'd studied her pussy, wanting to visually drink her up, every bit of her. Then he remembered. His promise to her last night. His really *dirty* promise. With his eyes on her lovely rear, he suddenly wanted to keep it—right now.

So as he massaged her soft flesh, he splayed his fingers wider, and he let both his thumbs begin to stretch inward—toward her anus.

Almost immediately, he heard her reaction—a soft, pleasured sigh. He smiled inwardly, his chest expanding with lust. He loved that she liked ass play.

Kneading her more deeply still, he let his thumbs dig into her flesh as well, knowing it would stimulate her where he wanted it to. His reward was another hot sigh—and slow, labored breathing. *Yes, baby, that's so good.*

When one thumb brushed over her asshole—which puckered slightly for him now—she let out a quick little gasp, then shivered slightly. He couldn't resist bending down to give her ass a tiny nibble, so pleased that she was as sensitive there as in other key places. She let out a sexy hiss in response.

Raking his middle finger beneath her, upward, though her pussy, he found it delightfully moist—which was exactly what he'd been after, a little lubricant. Then he began rubbing the same fingertip in a small circle directly at the hot little fissure of her rear.

Her breath came harder then, pretty and excited—her eyes were closed, her lips parted in passion.

"Feel good, bunny?" he asked softly.

"Yes." The reply came on a quick breath. "Oh, yes."

"Good," he whispered, then pushed the tip of his finger inside.

A small, low cry escaped her, hardening his cock still more, and he began to drive his finger inward, in the rhythm of sex, again, again, pushing it deeper with each small thrust. She hugged her pillow tight now, releasing rough, jagged breaths, and he knew he had to take this further, use more than just his finger on her. The raw lust coursing through him demanded it.

So as he finger-fucked her and listened to her hot, naughty whimpers of pleasure, he leaned over to the bedside table and used his free hand to open the drawer, glad he kept a little tub of Vaseline next to the bed.

When he drew his finger out, she flinched and said, "You're done?" He adored how innocent and disappointed she sounded.

"Not even close, bunny," he assured her. Then he uncapped the Vaseline and dipped two fingers inside.

Swirling the petroleum jelly on her anus, he promptly re-entered her, with both heavily lubricated fingers. She cried out, clearly stunned, but just as quickly settled back into the soft moans of pleasure. He pushed his fingers in all the way, but instead of thrusting, this time he began to move them in a counterclockwise circle inside her, as much as was possible, to begin opening the tight passageway wider.

"Relax for me, baby," he told her, his voice low, when she began to let out jagged little cries of joy, her body jerking a bit. "Relax and enjoy."

Her voice sounded shaky. "I think I could come . . . just from this."

Behind her, he smiled. "Don't. Not yet anyway."

"Why?"

"More to come," he said simply.

Wendy felt crazed with the strange pleasure echoing through her. Just like last night on the beach, she was astonished that anal penetration could deliver so much pleasure. And such a *different* and *intense* pleasure, too. It seemed to curl and twist through her body like a plume of smoke. But it was harder, more solid than smoke. It was like a wiry rope wrapping around her, around her torso, across her shoulders and neck, even her arms. She felt the strange sensation *everywhere*.

And then, suddenly, his fingers were gone, and she wondered what was happening, and she found out when something much larger began to nudge at the opening. "What are you . . . ?" she asked, jerking to look over her shoulder—but the angle didn't allow her to see what he was using.

"Cucumber," he said.

She yanked her gaze to his face. "Are you serious?"

He looked taken aback, like she'd just accused him of something. "Yeah—why?"

She swallowed, suddenly nervous. "It's . . . big."

He smiled—soft, sexy, indulgent. "Actually, it's not nearly as big as *me*."

"But it's a lot bigger than your fingers."

He laughed softly. "That's the idea." Then shook his head lightly. "You don't want me to?"

It was the first time tonight that he'd asked her, given her a free choice. And she felt like she was letting him down. And maybe missing out on something. She hesitated.

He lowered his chin lightly. "It'll go easier than you think, baby—I promise."

"Okay," she said. That easily. Dear God, was she crazy?

"Just relax," he told her, "and lift your ass for me, just a little—okay?"

She lay back down on her stomach, arms wrapped around the pillow beneath her, and remembered—this was pleasure, not pain. So far it had *definitely* been pleasure. *Unimaginable, unfathomable* pleasure. She closed her eyes and, when the pressure came, bit her lip. And wanted it. Wanted it so bad. Same as when she wanted a cock in her pussy, yearned to take it inside. Only this was a different part of her body—and she suddenly wanted Brandon to fill it.

A low moan rose all the way from her belly when he pushed the cucumber in. Her first thought—he was right; it had gone easier than she'd imagined. Her second—*Oh God, I'm really doing this. Really being fucked in the ass.* And by a freaking cucumber, no less, but she tried to blot that part out.

She felt so full back there. In a good way. Invaded. In a good way.

Then he began to move it gently in and out.

Oh Lord. She cried out, crazed by the sensation. If she'd thought she'd felt his fingers everywhere . . . God, she felt this *in her hands, in her feet, in her face, her very lips.* She heard herself panting, and also heard Brandon's voice. "That's so good, baby. You're taking it so good for me. Please tell me it feels good."

"Yes," she managed on a whimper, but talking was hard now—even thinking was difficult. This was all about having something done to you, something so overwhelming that it consumed you.

"Ah, bunny, that's so damn hot. I wish you could see how amazing you look."

"Obscene?" she found the strength to suggest.

"Yes," he said, quite seriously. "And beautiful."

That turned her on even more somehow, and she found herself licking her upper lip and raising her ass higher for him.

He moved the cucumber in and out, again, again, and from his hot breaths she thought he sounded as aroused as she was.

And then the cucumber was gone, and she couldn't decide if she was happy or sad, but she felt very odd and strange and empty—until pressure returned, hard pressure, and Brandon's hand was on her hip and the warmth of his legs mingled with hers, and as he pushed inward, she realized *he* was fucking her ass now—*him, his cock. His freaking enormous cock.*

"*Oh God, oh God, oh God,*" she heard herself cry as he eased slowly, slowly inside her.

"Jesus fucking Christ," he cursed under his breath behind her, clearly as impassioned as she. "Tell me you're okay, baby," he whispered near her ear then. "Tell me it's good."

The truth was, she couldn't tell yet. She simply felt consumed by the very fullness. "I'm not sure. So big. Isn't this impossible?" The question had just come to mind and she'd blurted it out.

When he answered, she heard more than saw his small lust-filled grin. "Lubrication makes a lot of things possible."

"Clearly," she managed.

His arms closed snug around her now, circling her stomach, one palm curved around the outer side of her breast. His breath warmed her ear.

And she realized . . . "It doesn't hurt." She let out a sigh of relief with the words. "It still feels impossible to me, but it doesn't hurt."

"Mmm, bunny, that's so good," he growled in her ear, then kissed her cheek.

Then he began to move. In her ass.

Slow at first—small, slow drives of his cock. And she thought she'd die of that strange, powerful pleasure that made her forget everything but sensation.

She heard herself begin to whimper and moan, felt her lips trembling. Like before, she felt the thrusts everywhere, as if his cock stretched all through her, touching every region of her body, every inch of her skin.

And when his breath grew just as heavy as hers, when he began to thrust deeper, harder, her brain ceased to process anything but *feeling*. An overwhelming heat expanded within her, and she began to sweat profusely, everywhere at once, the pleasure pouring from her body in the form of perspiration.

He remained wrapped tight around her, and the plunges of his cock made them move as one—sobs echoed from her as he emitted hard, heavy groans through clenched teeth. This was amazing. This was impossible. This was the most profound pleasure she'd ever known. It had captured her. It controlled her. She was out of her mind with the overwhelming joy of it. And she knew she couldn't really come from this—or at least she didn't think she could—so when she *did*, when a raging orgasm ripped through her with no warning, she could only conclude that her clit had brushed hard enough against the sheets beneath her to make it happen.

Not that she cared why it happened. This was no time for analysis. It was a time to scream, to moan, to whimper, and to tremble in her lover's arms. It was time to take an entirely new kind of joy when he rasped, "God, yeah," then moaned and growled through his own climax, holding on to her tight through the last thrust.

When he pulled out, her body—her anus—felt strange, unpleasantly open. But within a few seconds, it seemed to contract back to normal. It still felt unusual, but no longer as stretched. She sensed Brandon rolling to his back behind her, but she was too weak to move at all.

"You okay?" His voice came as weak as she felt.

She could still barely speak. "Mmm-hmm."

They lay quiet for few moments, until he said. "Sorry, bunny, but I'm not eating the cucumber after this."

A hard laugh lurched from her throat, and he laughed, too, and she finally rolled to face him.

Their eyes met.

"You never did that before." Anal sex, he clearly meant. He looked all-knowing and pleased.

"I hate that it's so obvious."

"I love that you're so willing."

"Me, too." She granted him a smile, filled with erotic joy to know she'd done something that felt so *forbidden*. She'd never felt more wild.

A moment later, regaining her strength, she rose slightly and leaned over to give Brandon a long, slow, lingering tongue kiss. Then she located tissues, tidied herself, and bent over the edge of the bed to scoop up her panties.

After she put them on and reached for the dress she'd dropped in a heap on the floor, as well, Brandon said, "You don't have to rush off. It's late."

She gave him a small smile, suddenly feeling more empowered and in control of herself than ever. "Precisely why I have to rush off. I have an early meeting."

He sighed, looking hot and cozy still nestled into soft pillows, a sheet pulled to his waist. "Actually, I do, too, now that you mention it."

"I was beginning to think you live a life of leisure," she said, raising her eyebrows.

He smirked playfully. "No, but I can usually set my own schedule, take time off when I want."

"Lucky me."

"No," he said, shaking his head against the white pillowcase, "lucky *me*. Which reminds me, how's your afternoon look?"

She bit her lip, tried to hide her smile. This would go on. Another day. Another night? "Free," she said.

"Good. I'll take you parasailing."

"Another thing I've never done," she admitted.

"Another thing I'll enjoy showing you. Although," he added with a wink, "probably not as much as I enjoyed *this*."

Who am I?

Am I the woman I was when I came here? The woman who wears sensible panties and sensible shoes and dates average men (if I date them at all)?

Or am I really the bad girl now, the bad girl I become when I'm with _him_? Do I give guys blow jobs in public places and beg to be fucked and delight in turning myself into a stranger's personal porn star?

Which woman is real? Both? Neither? I've lost the ability to tell.

When you pretend to be something, can you really _become_ it? Just from the very act of pretending? Is it that easy, that fast?

And when I go home, who will I be then?

Chapter 7

When Wendy headed out the next morning, she felt as if she could tackle the world. The sun was shining, the call of seagulls echoed nearby, and it was a beautiful day in paradise. She donned a summer suit the color of orange sherbet that only added to her good cheer.

Like yesterday, she found herself noticing details and effortlessly connecting more with the people she encountered. When she had breakfast at a small deli near her building, she complimented the earrings worn by the young girl behind the counter, who seemed so sincerely touched that Wendy realized the rich patrons of Emerald Shores probably seldom took the time for such niceties. And when she re-entered the building that housed the resort's corporate offices, she greeted the receptionist in the vast first-floor lobby with a smile. "Those flowering shrubs I keep seeing everywhere are gorgeous!" she said. "The ones with the bright pink flowers. What are they?"

"Bougainvillea," the woman said with a smile. "It blooms all year here as long as it doesn't get too cold. I believe you're meeting with Mr. Worth and Mr. Penny this morning?"

Wendy nodded. And whereas a few days ago she would have been somewhat nervous about meeting the top dogs at such an immense, upscale resort, today she felt totally comfortable, totally confident. Amazing what some adventurous sex could do for a girl!

A few minutes later, she was greeted by a well-put-together woman in her fifties, who said, "I'm Mr. Worth's assistant, Joanna. Welcome to Emerald Shores." They made pleasant small talk as Joanna took her up on the elevator, explaining that the CEOs shared the top floor of the structure.

It wasn't as tall as Brandon's building, nor was it directly on the ocean, but her memory of his penthouse condo urged her to say, "Great view, I bet."

Joanna smiled. "It's pretty breathtaking, I'll have to admit. Very relaxing when the job gets stressful. The whole side of the floor that faces the ocean is glass, so the water is always just a glance away."

"Wow, that sounds incredible."

"Mr. Worth insisted upon it when the building was being designed. He created Emerald Shores from nothing as a very young man."

"Wow," Wendy said again. This time because she hadn't imagined one sole person being behind the resort—she'd envisioned it being the brainchild of a whole conglomerate of developers. "I'll enjoy meeting him," she added. *As long as he doesn't tell me someone saw me having sex on the beach—the activity, not the drink—and that I'm going to lose my job because of it.*

The moment they stepped off the elevator, she caught a glimpse of the gulf waters out the window wall to her right. "That's my desk," Joanna said, pointing to one of two near the window. The other desk was unoccupied at the moment, but Wendy presumed it belonged to Mr. Penny's assistant.

"Color me jealous," she replied. "I love my job, but my

desk looks out on another skyscraper across the street from mine."

Joanna cast a conciliatory smile, then said, "Right this way. Mr. Worth and Mr. Penny are waiting for you in Mr. Worth's office." Then she opened the double doors before them to show Wendy inside.

Her first observation was that Mr. Worth had one hell of an office. Bigger than her apartment back home, actually. It held a grand, expansive desk, tons of dark wood bookcases, a bar, an enormous aquarium filled with brightly colored fish, and a large glass conference table by the window wall.

The second, when she spotted two men at the table, was that Mr. Worth was . . . *Brandon?*

Or maybe he was Mr. Penny—but either way, one of the two men standing up to greet her was definitely the man who'd fucked just about every orifice on her body last night! How the hell could this be?

Her mouth dropped open, and when their eyes met, she tried to keep hers from going wide—given that there was another guy in the room, and that he didn't need to know about the orifice fucking, or any fucking at all, for that matter.

She could see from the look on Brandon's face that he was just as shocked, but like her, trying not to let it show.

How was this even *possible?* He was one of the Emerald Shores CEOs? She couldn't remember either man's first name, but she knew neither had been Brandon.

He stepped up to her in a crisp charcoal-colored suit and shook her hand. "I'm Brandon Worth," he said with a professional smile, even though the way he looked at her was much more personal. "*James* Brandon Worth," he clarified.

And then she remembered seeing the name on various papers: James B. Worth, CEO.

"And this is my business partner, Charles Penny."

Numbly, she shook Mr. Penny's hand as well, still trying to recover from her disbelief. The man was a husky but well-dressed guy about Brandon's age—probably mid-thirties, like herself.

Not that she gave a crap about Mr. Penny. She was still trying to get over Mr. Worth. *She'd been having sex with the chief executive officer of Emerald Shores!*

"And you're," Brandon began uncertainly, "Gwendolyn Carnes."

She tried to smile as she met his gaze once more. "Most people call me Wendy," she explained, and Brandon leaned back his head to say, "Ah."

Oh boy. This was insane. Just freaking insane.

It was at that moment when they both noticed Mr. Penny looking at them oddly.

"Turns out that Miss Carnes and I are already acquainted," Brandon explained. "We met a couple of days ago—over in the village."

"Call me Wendy," she was quick to say. *Or bunny.*

When Joanna came in bearing coffee and a plate of croissants, it gave Wendy a chance to wrap her head around the situation. A little anyway.

No wonder he'd seemed so rich. He *was* rich. *Mega*rich. And he'd conceived this entire place himself?

But she had to quit thinking about that.

Come on now—put on your game face. Sex aside, and shock aside, this is an important meeting. Walter is counting on you. You have to be professional. And tough. You have to do Walter proud. You're talking about gambling millions of dollars of Walter's money on this place. Focus!

Of course, it was easier said than done. When she looked across the table at Brandon, besides seeing a handsome young CEO, she also saw her lover, the man with the magnificent cock. And mouth. And hands. And he wasn't bad with a cucumber, either, even if that still embarrassed her a little. As Charles Penny spoke to her about their grand future plans for Emerald Shores, the warmth of a blush began to climb her cheeks, and she prayed he didn't notice. Because she was thinking about cucumbers, not resort expansion. *Stop this. Pay attention.*

Finally, after both Brandon and his associate made sweeping speeches about the grandeur of the resort, how ten years into its existence it was still a cutting-edge vacation destination, and how Walter's investment could help take Emerald Shores into the future and make them all a lot of money, Brandon smiled and said, "Wendy, we'd love to hear what you think of our little slice of paradise here on the Gulf Coast, and where you stand in terms of advising Walter."

Stay focused. Don't look at him. She planted her eyes on her notes instead. And when she did need to lift her gaze in order to appear conversational and professional, she either looked at Mr. Penny or looked slightly past Brandon's face to the pale ocean horizon beyond the glass behind him.

"It probably goes without saying that I've been very impressed with the resort. You've created a tropical paradise that meets the needs of every traveler. Emerald Shores provides a unique, upscale experience that can be whatever a vacationer wants, whether it's casual or posh."

They both looked pleased—even if she only caught Brandon's expression in her peripheral vision—and she wondered if the next part would surprise them.

"However," she went on, "perfection lies in the details, so once I realized what a gem Emerald Shores truly is, I naturally found myself seeking out flaws. And I believe that for this resort to reach its full potential, some small but pertinent changes will need to be considered."

She lifted a glance, just to gauge their reaction. Both looked content enough, and Charles Penny said, "Mr. Carlisle explained his usual way of doing business, so we were aware you'd likely bring such items to us. We'll be most curious to hear what they are." Then the two men exchanged looks that told her they took so much pride in the resort they couldn't believe she'd found room for improvement.

Well, sorry, but get ready, boys. From there, Wendy read off a long list of changes she felt would benefit Emerald Shores.

She knew that every time she paused, they thought she'd finished, yet she would then continue on. She finally concluded with, "The snack and drink bars should open earlier—it gets hot on the beach and people need to stay hydrated long before eleven a.m. during the summer months, so you're missing out on revenue there *and* irritating patrons. Not all the beach umbrellas and cabanas should be reserved in advance—I saw several couples and families who arrived and on their first day were surprised and angry that they had no access to an umbrella as they had not brought their own. The golf carts are a great concept, but let's knock down the price—you'd rent a lot more of them, and that would reduce the traffic on the shuttle system, which also needs to be reworked and better organized. Service seems sporadic and slightly undependable as it is. All outdoor pools need speakers, music piped in to them—a little calypso music adds to that tropical paradise feeling and reminds people they're on a lavish vacation in a special place. And the pools need better refreshments, too."

When she stopped talking, they stayed quiet for a moment, until finally Brandon said, "With all due respect, Wendy, isn't all of this rather . . . small potatoes?"

Now she met his gaze. For some reason, the challenge made it easier. Or maybe she'd just finally gotten used to the idea of whom she'd been fucking. Either way, she put on a professional but pointed smile and replied, "I see them more like pickles, Brandon."

He looked perplexed, and next to him, Charles Penny looked completely dumbfounded. "Pickles?" Brandon asked.

"On its own, each seems small. But put them all together and you've got . . . a great big cucumber. If you take my meaning."

She saw him struggle to hide his smile. "I do. Little things add up to bigger ones. But with all those . . . flaws, as you called them, I do hope to hear that you've found just as many things at Emerald Shores to your liking."

This time, she didn't hesitate to let a full smile stretch across her face. "Don't worry. Overall, I've found my visit *very* pleasurable." And her panties went damp even as the words left her.

"Well," Mr. Penny interjected—drawing her eyes back to him, "we'll certainly take everything you've suggested under advisement. We'll need to talk, of course, and get back to you on it, asking you to bear in mind that we're focused on *new* projects for at least the remainder of this year. In the meantime, though, I hope we can count on your support with Mr. Carlisle."

"I'm afraid that before I can make any recommendation to

Mr. Carlisle, we'll need a firm commitment on what changes you're willing to institute and by when. Your expansion plans sound great, but what's already here can't be neglected. I've prepared a full list of the items I mentioned," she said, sliding it across the table.

At this, Mr. Penny nodded solemnly, clearly a bit perturbed that she was actually making a *demand*, and Brandon simply continued looking stunned—*by* her demands, or still simply by her presence, she couldn't tell.

"I'll be here for three more days and I have a lot yet to see. I'll call with any additions to my list, and in the meantime, it's been a pleasure to meet with you both."

Both men returned the sentiment, and as she rose to her feet, Brandon rushed to make his way around the table. "Let me show you out."

He accompanied her to the double doors just around the corner and out of sight from the table, then leaned near her ear with a wicked grin. "Do you have any idea how hard I am right now?"

"Let me check," she returned, then pressed the flat of her palm to the front of his pants—to find a column of pure steel that made her pussy flutter.

"Mmm," she purred. Then said, "See you for parasailing, Mr. Worth."

Brandon stood on the beach, watching one of Pete's boats glide across the water near the horizon, a billowy yellow parachute floating in the sky behind it. Then he turned his eyes toward the boardwalk in the distance behind him, waiting for Wendy to arrive.

He still couldn't believe it. Just couldn't fucking believe it. Of all the women in all of Emerald Shores . . . what were the chances?

Not that it mattered. He was pretty sure they were both very capable of separating business and pleasure. He'd just never fucked anyone before who held his livelihood in her hands.

The good part, though, was that maybe she didn't *know* she held his livelihood. She probably didn't realize Walter was one of their last shots for getting an injection of new revenue. There were always other investors to approach, of course, but the clock was ticking—the resort had some big bills to pay at the end of the second quarter, which was coming way too fast.

He'd continued not letting himself think about that and letting his beach bunny be a nice distraction from big worries. Hopefully she'd *still* be a nice distraction, as long as he could forget she held the reins to his future.

And maybe that distraction was why he'd asked her to spend the night last night—another thing he was still trying to understand. He'd attempted to shroud the invitation in consideration, in not wanting to make her go home late—but the truth was that he'd *wanted* her to spend the night with him. He'd wanted to sleep with her—actually *sleep*. He'd wanted to wake up with her this morning. Shit. Just because he'd fucked her in the ass? No—because it definitely *wasn't* his first time for that. And if he was honest with himself, it wasn't really about the nice distraction she'd been providing, either.

The fact was, he'd felt . . . some sort of connection with her. More than just the sex part. He'd felt her trust, her openness; he'd felt her holding nothing back from him.

"Hey."

He looked up at the perky sound of her voice. "Hey." Then he smiled, shook his head at their shared shock in his office a few hours ago, and they both simply laughed.

After which he couldn't resist giving her a long once-over—damn, she wore that bikini well, every curve ripe and begging to be touched. "Bunny, I'd never have dreamed you were hiding *this* body under that pretty suit you wore this morning."

She simply raised her eyebrows in reply. "And I'd never have dreamed you were hiding *that* job under this easygoing-guy veneer."

"Well, life is just full of surprises, isn't it?" he said with a wink. Then he added, "You're cool with this, right? I mean, this doesn't change anything between us, finding out what *I* do and what *you* do?" *And that you're basically holding my balls in a vise right now even if you don't know it.*

"I'm cool with it if you are. I've never had occasion to . . . you know, combine work and pleasure, but I see no reason that *that* has to affect *this*."

"Agreed," he said, but instead of shaking hands like this morning, he sealed it with a kiss.

A few minutes later, the *Sky Pirate II* came pulling up to shore, dropping off a group of pretty college girls in scant bikinis, all of whom appeared to have enjoyed flirting with Pete—and likewise, Brandon felt sure. Although his buddy had a whole staff who worked for him, he often drove one of the boats himself, simply because he enjoyed it.

Long ago, when the idea for Emerald Shores had first been forming in Brandon's head, he'd approached Pete about being a partner in the venture, but Pete had turned him down, having his eye on the parasailing business and knowing it was more of a sure thing. Both guys had turned out happy, he thought with some satisfaction, watching his friend jump over the side of the large speedboat painted with his logo, then start wading to shore to meet them.

Just like yesterday, Pete kissed Wendy's hand in greeting and Brandon simply shook his head and chuckled. But then he remembered her fantasy, the one about being with both of them—and his dick got a little hard as the three of them started toward the *Sky Pirate II*.

"This guy showing you a good time, I hope?" Pete asked her as they sloshed through the waves.

She cast Brandon a sideways glance that stiffened him further. "*Very* good," she said.

Pete flashed a cocky grin. " 'Cause if he doesn't, you just come find *me*, honey, and *I'll* take care of you."

"I'll definitely remember that," she said, openly flirting back with him right in front of Brandon, then casting Brandon a teasing smile.

Ten minutes later, Pete had driven them out into deeper waters and outfitted them with life jackets, explaining to Wendy how the double lift worked, allowing both her and Brandon to be taken up together in a joint harness. They sat side by side, rigged up and ready to go, and when the boat picked up speed again, the parachute would catch the wind and lift them into the air.

"Nervous?" Brandon asked as Pete departed the lift platform at the rear of the vessel.

She just looked at him. "After last night, and this morning, this is nothin'."

And he believed her. Something was changing in her. He'd thought she seemed confident enough when they'd first met, but this was different—it ran deeper. More than before, she seemed ready for anything.

Seconds later, the boat took off, speeding forward over the blue-green water until Pete reached over from his driver's seat to hoist the parachute and lift Brandon and Wendy skyward. She gave a little gasp at the initial ascent, but then simply held on to her harness and started enjoying the view.

Once they were all the way up, Brandon took the opportunity to point out different parts of the resort, and landmarks farther away as well, up and down the beach.

"My God, it's so peaceful up here," she said. "That wasn't how I'd envisioned it. You get such a different look at things." Then she slowly drew her gaze away from the far-reaching scenery and turned to him with a sly smile.

"What?" he said.

"It just hit me all over again. You're Mr. Emerald Shores. Since you didn't know who *I* was, why didn't you mention it?"

"I wasn't trying to be deceptive. I just *never* mention it when I meet a woman."

She leaned back her head as if in understanding. "Gold digger precaution?"

He shrugged. "Not exactly. It just . . . gets in the way of getting down and dirty. And then, there's always the worry of blackmail."

She lowered her chin doubtfully. "Afraid I'm going to tell the local papers you molested me with a cucumber?"

He tried to smile but suspected the gesture didn't quite make it to his eyes.

Which she misunderstood, going more serious on him. "Don't worry—I would never do that."

"I know you wouldn't. But once, a few years ago, a woman *did* tell the local media some things we did, and it came off pretty scandalous and had some of my investors upset. So, since then, I just keep it under wraps."

He saw the understanding in her eyes—and was a little surprised he'd just told her about that. He hadn't intended to. "Oh," she said softly. "Sorry that happened. I'm a pretty big believer that what someone does in the bedroom—or on the beach, or the pier—is their own business, so you don't have to worry about anyone finding out."

"Thanks for that. The woman I mentioned . . . well, she was a bad reminder that not everyone is as nice as you."

Next to him in the sky, she rolled her eyes and got indignant. "You *still* think I'm *nice*? I let you fuck my ass with a damn cucumber and you think I'm *nice*?"

He couldn't help laughing—at the whole situation. "Sorry to break it to you, but *yeah*. You're *nice*. Live with it, bunny."

"You know," she said, "after we had sex on the beach, I had this insane fear that someone from the Emerald Shores offices could have seen us and that I might lose my job. And it turns out I was fucking the freaking *CEO*!"

"Hey, CEOs need sex, too."

"Clearly a lot of it," she said, and they laughed some more.

That was when he caught her giving him another one of those inquisitive looks. "What?" he asked.

"I guess I'm just . . . amazed by you. How on earth did you go from beach-umbrella boy to being the man who runs *this*?" She motioned toward the shore, all the beautiful colored stucco buildings that had created a skyline where one hadn't been before. And it made him feel good, *really* good—but he always tried to be humble about it because he understood that success was often about the luck of the draw. So he shrugged and said, "I just had an idea—for an incredible place. A place that could be a vacation destination or a home, but where you never had to leave if you didn't want to. A Disney World for beach lovers. So after college, I put a business plan together, used money I'd saved to hire an engineer and architect to draw up my ideas, and I started pitching it to developers and investors. And it has . . . surpassed my wildest dreams."

"Where does Charles Penny come in?"

"College friend—who had an aptitude for business. I'm more the creative guy—he's the guy who makes sure we run things right. I actually approached Pete with the idea way back when, but he already had his eye on a . . . simpler sort of beach life. Not that I'm downplaying his success any—he's done very well with this business. We both wanted to live here and work here—be beach bums in our own way for the rest of our lives. And it's worked out pretty well."

"Seems that way," she said, casting a sincere smile. "Did you tell him? Mr. Penny? About how you knew me?"

Brandon shook his head. "We've never had that kind of friendship—it's mostly about business for us."

"Ah."

"Kiss me," he said without planning it, and he wasn't even really sure why—but like other times with her, it had just hit him once more how damn much he simply enjoyed her company.

One kiss turned into two—hot, lingering tongue kisses that left him hungry for more. When their mouths parted, her eyes were glassy with passion, too. "I never made out with a guy up in the sky before," she told him, looking around again at where they were.

"Not a member of the mile-high club then?"

"Well, that wasn't really the form of sky I meant, but no, if you must know."

"A shame we don't have occasion to get on a plane together," he said, then wanted to kick himself—it sounded like he was suggesting they travel together or something. Which sounded like a thing you didn't really do outside of a relationship. Shit, what was going on with him?

But she didn't seem to hear it that way. Instead, she'd heard it exactly as he'd wanted her to. "Don't worry," she told him. "I've still got a few days before I leave and I suspect there's still plenty of new stuff we can do together here. New to me, anyway."

"I like the way you think, bunny. Want to come back over to my place for dinner tonight? I'll cook."

"Sure," she said warmly. "But, uh . . . don't make anything with cucumbers please."

Wendy had found the tranquil ride across the sky elating. But then, she'd found *everything* rather elating today. One night with Brandon had made her feel . . . worthy, like a worthy sexual being. But two, it seemed, had made her feel simply . . . ready for more. One had knocked down the walls of her sexual box, but two had made her feel like some kind of female warrior ready to go out and conquer all the untamed new land she'd discovered outside.

When she'd put on her bikini after lunch, she'd experienced what she could only describe as . . . a sense of newness. Yesterday, even if her first night with Brandon had made her braver, she'd still felt a bit nervous donning the bikini, almost as if she were masquerading as . . . well, as a woman who wore that kind of bikini. Today, though, she *was* a woman who wore that kind of bikini.

Was it because of the things she'd done with Brandon—the feminine freedom she'd found with him? Or because she'd taken charge in her big meeting this morning? Or was it—somehow—the irony that she was fucking the CEO of Emerald Shores? She didn't know, but she simply loved the way she looked in it and no longer wondered if she could pull if off. Today she *owned* that bikini, owned the way she *looked* and *felt* in that bikini—it had become a natural, sensual extension of her body, like something she was born to wear.

So by the time they landed gently back on the boat and Pete killed the engine to come back and help them unharness, and he asked, "How'd you like it?" she didn't hold back. Everything about the day so far had her bubbling with a self-aware confidence that grew by the hour.

"It was *amazing*. I loved it! I felt like . . . a bird or something up there."

"Sexiest bird I've ever seen then," Pete said easily without looking at her as he unsnapped something near her hip. And when his darkly tanned arm brushed her leg, a frisson of heat skittered upward, straight to the juncture of her thighs. She glanced down at his dark hair, the sides again falling from his low ponytail, and felt his warm breath on her arm—and couldn't help being reminded of her shower fantasy.

After which her pussy began to pulse.

Because just yesterday that had seemed . . . impossible.

And today it somehow seemed . . . well, not quite as crazy a thought.

"So what are you two up to for the rest of the day?" Pete asked, finally rising upright to glance at both of them.

Brandon answered. "We'll probably hang out on the beach awhile. Then later we're having dinner at my place."

Pete drew back as if in warning, then looked to Wendy. "Letting him cook? That's dangerous territory, honey."

She looked at Brandon. "You sounded so confident, I assumed you were secretly a master chef or something."

He laughed in his cute way. "I get by okay, but the truth is—although you wouldn't know it to look at him, Pete here is pretty damn good with a grill."

She shifted her eyes to the man in question. "Is that so?"

The swarthy beach pirate only shrugged. "It's a gift."

"Why don't you join us?" she said. No hesitation. She'd blurted it out as soon as the idea had hit her.

To which Brandon flashed a look of surprise, while Pete simply smiled in what she suspected was a long-standing silent game of one-upsmanship.

"Unless you mind," she directed toward her lover.

He only laughed. "Hell, why not? We can at least be assured of a good meal that way."

A little while later, after they'd exited the boat and Pete was busy loading the next parasailers, Brandon took her hand and smiled into her eyes. "So . . . what was that about?"

She didn't have to ask what he was referring to. The invitation. To make their private dinner less private.

The fact was, she'd been asking herself that very same question ever since the conversation. Given the things they'd done together last night, and how gloriously *changed* the evening had left her, it did seem an odd thing to do.

She shrugged, trying to play it off as nothing, then put on a teasing smile. " Maybe I just like having two gorgeous men flirting with me at once."

As they started—hand in hand—up the busy shoreline, sprinkled with people throwing Frisbees and kids with plastic shovels and pails, his expression turned knowing and sly. "I think you want to have two gorgeous men do more than *flirt* with you, bunny."

She pulled up short, jerking both of them to a halt, her feet sinking into the wet sand. "What do you mean?"

His sly look edged into a wicked grin. "You want to explore your hot little shower fantasy. You want both of us to fuck you."

Something in her stomach curled inward at his words. "No," she said automatically, shaking her head insistently as they walked on, weaving around two attractive girls in skimpy bikinis who sat in beach chairs at the water's edge, letting the surf wash up around their legs. But she felt herself blush—and hoped it wouldn't appear to be anything more than an effect of the sun.

When she glanced up at him again, his eyebrows arched—he clearly doubted her protest. And true, she *had* fantasized about being with both of them at once. And also true, she'd now invited Pete on what had, prior to that, been a "date" that would surely end in more kinky sex. But even if she'd had that flash of thought—that the idea of a ménage à trois with Pete didn't seem as crazy as it had the first time it had come to mind—that was still a far cry from actually doing it.

"Look," she said, "inviting him to dinner was an impulse

move. But there's a big difference between fantasizing about something and really living it. So if that's what you think I'm after here, sorry to disappoint you, but you're wrong."

To her surprise, the expression on his face didn't change a bit. "Whatever you say, bunny," he replied, but he obviously didn't believe a word of it.

Which raised the question in her mind: Did *she*? Believe herself?

Did she really just want the easy fun of having two sexy guys' attention this evening? Or did she secretly—so secretly that she couldn't even admit it to herself—really want the harder, rougher fun of having two sexy guys' attention on her in a much more daring way?

No, she told herself—again, still. That *wasn't* what she wanted. Because to fuck a hot stranger—Brandon—was one thing. It was a little slutty maybe, but it wasn't *shocking*. Women slept with strangers on vacation all the time. But a woman who fucked two guys at once? That was a woman who she didn't even *know*, had never *met*. A woman whose needs and desires and view of the world she couldn't understand. Until now, the very idea of such an act was practically foreign to her—it was something that happened in a porn move, not in real life.

Two guys at once. Two guys at once. The words kept echoing through her brain as they continued their walk up the beach, and her heart beat harder, and she began to sweat but didn't think it was from the sun any more than her blush was. Could she? Would she? No. No, of course not.

But later, when she and Brandon were playing in the water, he was rubbing up against her from behind, and she turned in his arms to find him flashing his hottest, lustiest look, and he said, "I can't quit thinking about the moment you walked into my office this morning. The moment I realized Walter Carlisle's assistant was the woman I've been fucking like crazy, and how hard it turned me in a heartbeat. It's got me hard as a rock again right now, bunny."

And just like everything with Brandon, it turned her nipples hard and made her pussy surge with excitement, and it reminded her—she *wanted* to be his porn star. She loved *thrilling* him. She loved thrilling *herself*.

And then new questions rose in her mind.

How far will you go, Wendy?

Who are you now?

WHO ARE YOU NOW?

I am beginning to feel like I'm in a carnival fun house. Nothing seems real. And yet I barrel haphazardly forward. I catch glimpses of myself in mirrors that make me look different than I did before . . . recognizable in ways, yet also distorted into something new. The floors are slanted, the walls are tilted, and so I go whichever way they seem to carry me, propelled in a new direction at every turn. It's like a Picasso painting come to life—and suddenly it's *my* life.

In the corner of the painting rests an hourglass, or maybe one of Salvador Dali's crazy melting clocks. Maybe I would slow down if not for that proverbial ticking clock, that speeding hourglass. But it's almost as if I can hear the sand sifting through, quicker and quicker.

I have only so much time here before my carriage turns back into a pumpkin, and maybe that's why I am letting myself be carried so easily on this journey. He is a fantasy come to life, *I* am a fantasy come to life. Don't I have to live as much of that fantasy as I can, *while* I can?

I began this game in pursuit of pleasure, power, control. Don't I need to grab as much of those things as possible before the sand empties and the game comes to an end?

Chapter 8

She began this third night of her wild, crazy affair with Brandon by slipping on sexy underwear and a flirty, low-cut sheath dress that stopped midway down her thighs. She finished the outfit with more new shoes—she'd bought them today while out shopping for the dress—strappy platform heels that might have resembled stripper shoes if they hadn't been a springy shade of pale yellow that complemented the dress.

How convenient that shopping at Emerald Shores this week actually qualified as work. She'd considered going back to the Beach Bazaar—to look for a dress, to see if her pretty Asian friend was there—but had decided that shopping could only count as work if she went to new places she hadn't checked out before. So she'd found the dress at an upscale shop in Bayside Village called the Sand Dollar, and she'd picked up the shoes in the retail area where she'd shopped the first day at a cute boutique called She Sells Shoes by the Seashore.

Now she looked in the mirror, applying makeup and running her fingers through her hair, no longer really seeing herself. Or not the self she used to see anyway. Was she crazy or did something about her truly look different now—something in her expression, in her eyes? Probably no one else would be able to see it if she asked them, but *she* could see it. A new confi-

..., a new sense of her own feminine power
...ut through her skin.

...stion that hung over the night—because of
...ng it earlier—she refused to think about it. Every
...me to mind, she forced it aside. Perhaps because she
...t want to say yes to it, but she found she didn't exactly want
...o say no, either.

Inherently, she didn't want to be that kind of woman—the
kind who could fuck two men at once with little consideration
or worry, men she didn't know or care about. When she thought
about that sort of woman, the image wasn't a good one—this
woman wasn't someone she wanted to know or whom she particularly respected. And since she *wasn't* normally that sort of
woman, how might she feel afterward? Would she have trouble
looking herself in the mirror? Would she harbor regrets and feel
sleazy every time she remembered it?

Still, the vague images in her fantasy continued to float
pleasingly through her mind, and even as she walked along the
winding path toward Brandon's place, a warm breeze kissing
her skin as it rustled through palm fronds overhead, the cloudy
visions made her breasts feel heavy and her pussy tingle.

Part of her wanted to forge ahead with her "no hesitation"
plan, throw caution to the wind, tell herself that what happened
at Emerald Shores stayed at Emerald Shores. But that silly saying
about Vegas was just that: silly. You still had to live with yourself afterward. And among the many things she'd learned from
being with Brandon, one of them was that fantasizing about
something and actually doing it were *very* different. When fantasy became reality, it was *real, there, in your face*, and more in-

tense than she could have imagined. You couldn't shut your
and decide it was over.

So as she reached Brandon's building and hit the butto.
that would prompt him to buzz her in, she concluded that her
explanation on the beach was completely true. She'd invited
Pete to dinner for *fun*. Simple, easy, flirty *fun*. She liked the idea
that Brandon's equally hot friend was attracted to her; she liked
watching the playful banter between them; she liked knowing
she *could* have them both if she *wanted* to have them both. But
that was all.

When Brandon greeted her at the door, he gave her a tingle-
inducing once-over, then said, "Damn, bunny—you look amazing," easing her into a warm embrace that moistened her panties
further. His hands closed gently over her ass, squeezing slightly,
as his dick—already half hard—nudged her in front.

"Mmm, and you *feel* amazing," she assured him, still a little
astonished that she could sound so silky and seductive without
even trying—it was simply more sexuality spilling from her beneath his influence.

That quickly, though, she found herself glancing past his
broad shoulders, vaguely curious if Pete was here yet.

Apparently, she wasn't being very sly about it since Brandon
informed her with a teasing grin, "Your other boyfriend's on the
balcony."

She rolled her eyes, but still her pussy fluttered. "Stop it—
he's not my other boyfriend." *And does that make you my* main
boyfriend? But she kept that question inside.

"Whatever you say," he told her again, like on the beach.
Then he added, "Hope you like pork chops—that's what the grill

We have kind of an arrangement—he'll

1 to, but he gets to choose the food."

ough," she said, glad the topic had edged

.ready.

.ie watched Brandon puttering around the kitchen,

, pots on the stove and then getting her a drink, she real-

.d that, for her peace of mind, she had to turn it *back* in that direction—briefly. "You didn't say anything to him, did you?" she asked. "About your suspicions—about *me*?"

A small, *still*-suspicious grin formed on his face. "No. Why? Should I have?"

It almost galled her that Brandon persisted in thinking she had ulterior motives here, so she was going to set him straight, once and for all. "Because I'm serious," she told him and for good measure closed her hand around his wrist, hard, looking intently into his eyes. "I *really, truly* don't plan on pursuing anything like you suggested earlier. And I keep getting the idea that you don't believe me."

His smile softened on her, his eyes going kinder, along with his voice. He covered her hand with his free one and said, "I believe you, bunny." Only then, just as she was starting to feel relieved, his expression changed once more, leaning back toward sexy, knowing. "But things don't always go the way you plan in life. Sometimes . . . desire wins out over intent."

Despite the fact that Brandon's words had made her a little nervous, dinner turned out easy, fun—exactly as she'd hoped. There was easy talk peppered with bits of flirtation that contin-ued to make her feel sexy and attractive. Wine flowed, and the meal—seasoned chops accompanied by garlic mashed potatoes and a green bean soufflé Brandon had whipped up from a family recipe—was delicious. She discovered that even as much as she enjoyed the obvious contrasts between the two men—the smart, handsome CEO versus the swarthy "sky pirate"—she also sincerely liked Pete and could see enough similarities to understand why they had a long-standing friendship.

Pete, she learned, had a father in the air force, which had resulted in him living a transient childhood. Their last stop, just before Pete graduated from high school, was at nearby Eglin Air Force Base, and Pete had determined "to put down some roots and never leave again. And to let my hair grow as long as I damn well pleased." He'd grinned, adding, "So far, it's worked out for me."

"How did your dad feel about that? Your hair, I mean?" she asked with a smile. She'd gathered that the elder Mr. Faber had been a fairly strict father, in keeping with his military background.

"He's cool with it," Pete assured her. "All in all, he's a good guy and just wanted to make sure he instilled some values in me. Once he figured out I had some ambition and didn't want to be a *total* beach bum, he pretty much let me do my own thing."

"So what about *you*?" Brandon asked, shifting his eyes to Wendy. He sat between her and Pete at the round table on the balcony. To the west, the sun set rapidly, leaving the sky over the ocean streaked with pinks and purples so vibrant that the scene began to feel a bit otherworldly despite the "normalness" of the evening.

"What *about* me?" she inquired.

"Well, you know how *I* ended up here and how Pete ended up here. Now that I know what you do for a living—how did you get into this line of work?" Even cool Pirate Pete had looked adequately stunned when they'd shared with him earlier the coincidence they'd discovered this morning when she'd strolled into Brandon's office.

"No big, fabulous story," she explained. "I was working in an investment advisory firm in Chicago—I'd gotten my Series 6 and 7 licenses, which enabled me to buy, sell, and advise on securities—but I didn't enjoy the corporate environment much, or the pressure of the job. Walter Carlisle was a company client, and when he came in one day to discuss his portfolio, he mentioned he was interviewing for a new assistant. I'd talked with him before and liked his easygoing style—I could tell he was a wealthy man who knew his business, but he didn't act superior or shove his success down anyone's throat. I sent him a résumé and the rest is history."

"And you're happy in this job?" Pete asked.

She nodded, draining her second glass of merlot. "The setting is a lot more laid-back, but the work is still interesting and challenging. And I learn a lot just from watching Walter."

Brandon grinned, arching one eyebrow. "A mogul in the making."

She thought about rolling her eyes and protesting the statement—normally she would have; normally she didn't see herself ever taking on that type of role. But maybe more than just her senses of sexuality and femininity were changing here. Walter had enough confidence in her to trust her evaluation of Emerald Shores and to let her make demands of the CEOs. Who knew where that could lead someday? So she simply smiled and said a light, airy "Could be."

Then she smiled inwardly again at the whole unlikely turn of events—how had she ended up in a hot, kinky affair with one of the CEOs? Despite the typical conversation taking place, that knowledge hung over the meal—at least for her. And she enjoyed the aura of masculinity around her, discovering she liked being the only girl at the table with more than one guy, especially guys who dripped as much testosterone as these two.

As Brandon poured the last of their second bottle of wine into her glass, she commented on the stunning sunset. "If being a mogul will get me a view like this, that provides some serious motivation."

"Yep, bud," Pete said to Brandon, "I gotta admit, there are rare moments when I regret not going in with you when I had the chance. Look at this—penthouse with a view, the hottest chick on the beach, and she's smart, too. You've got it all, man." He concluded with a wink toward Wendy that made her pussy tingle as she cast a coquettish smile back in his direction.

But Brandon replied with a laugh and said, "What are you talking about, dude?" Then turned to Wendy. "You should see this guy's house."

Wendy raised her eyebrows, trying not to let her surprise show. She knew Pete had done well for himself, but she hadn't pictured him living anyplace fabulous. "Oh?" she directed toward him.

He shrugged. "I've got a nice little place up the street in Destin."

Brandon added dryly, "A nice little mini-mansion with a pool and a hot tub and one of the priciest addresses in the area."

"Wow," Wendy said. "Color me impressed."

Again, though, Pete just shrugged. "You guys should drop by. I'm having Stacy over for dinner tomorrow night if you want to join us."

Wendy smiled and asked, "Who's Stacy? Your girlfriend?" Until this moment, she'd been thoroughly convinced that if Brandon hadn't found her on the beach yesterday, she'd have ended up in bed with Pete—but maybe not.

Although Pete was quick to deny it. "Just a girl I've known a long time. But we decided to try the dating thing, so we're starting with dinner at my place."

Wendy was back to raising her eyebrows again. "So you're inviting us along on a first date?"

He shook his head and laughed. "Don't worry—with Stacy, things are totally casual. No big deal."

"Are you sure? Because maybe she sees things differently."

Now Brandon chimed in. "Nah, Stacy's the most easygoing chick around. And it's not like they've never . . ." He trailed off and Wendy prodded him.

"Never?"

"Well, they kind of epitomize the phrase 'friends with benefits.' "

"Ah." Wendy leaned her head back in understanding, cognizant of the fact that Pete didn't look even remotely embarrassed. And she found herself envisioning—just for a fraction of a second—Pete pounding into some sexy girl, grunting, moaning, hot and sweaty. But then she forced the vision away. Because her pussy was already wet *enough*, and because she had her *own* guy to get hot and sweaty with and he was certainly nothing to sneeze at. "Well, if you're sure it won't be weird and she won't mind."

Pete was already shaking his head again. "Nothing weird, and she'll be glad to meet you. She's a more-the-merrier kind of girl—loves a party."

"Speaking of a party, we need more wine," Brandon announced.

Wendy sensed him getting ready to push to his feet, so she reached over to cover his hand with hers. "I'll get it. I need to tinkle anyway."

And as she got to her feet—thinking, *Did I just say the word tinkle?*—she felt the effects of the wine swirling through her and decided she'd probably had enough. Now she hoped she didn't ruin her sexy image by falling off her quasi–stripper shoes.

"Be right back," she heard herself say, glancing at the two men, then scurrying through the door.

She rushed to the bathroom, careful to keep her balance, thinking that peeing would help. Standing up had suddenly made her feel *sooo* drunk—and more than just drunk, really. While she'd been very pleasantly aware of her body and the dual masculine presences on the balcony all through the meal, standing up had somehow . . . escalated it. As she walked, her breasts had felt heavier—her pussy, too. The lace of her panties rubbed slightly against her crotch, and the underwire in her new bra seemed to frame her tits in a pleasingly tight way. So maybe by the time she went to the bathroom and uncorked a fresh bottle of merlot, she'd feel more . . . in control of her responses.

Only that didn't happen.

Moments later she found herself standing at the kitchen counter, carefully working a corkscrew, and every subtle move she made heightened her awareness of herself. The gauzy fabric of her dress seemed to caress her skin like a sea breeze, and her breasts heaved lightly with each turn of the corkscrew.

She suddenly wished Pete would leave—so she could have her way with Brandon. She remembered pushing him down in the sand that first night and she wanted to take that kind of control *again*. She suddenly didn't want to wait; she wanted pleasure *now*. She wanted his big dick *now*. She wanted his hands and mouth on her *now*.

Although maybe, it hit her just then, it wasn't particularly control she wanted at the moment—she rather liked when *Brandon* took control. The issue for her at the moment was actually timing—the *now* part of the equation. Given her body's sudden readiness, she'd turned instantly impatient.

Only at the same time, she *didn't* want Pete to leave. Because he was so brawny and sexy. She could scarcely recall ever meeting a man who made a mere T-shirt and jeans look so good. And she'd noticed a tattoo on his arm—the sleeves of tonight's T-shirt must be shorter than other ones she'd seen him in—and she wondered now what the design was. And she kind of wanted to touch it for some reason. She'd never known a guy with tattoos before.

Finally she popped the cork, and it was time to go back out on the balcony. The cold, wet bottle felt good in her hand as she walked to the door, her cunt still overly sensitive, her skin practically humming with lust. *You'll feel better after you sit down.* After all, she'd felt fine—much more normal—before she'd stood up. *You've just had a little too much wine.* In fact, she probably shouldn't drink any more. *This will be fine. You'll sit with them a little longer, talk a little more, and then Pete will go home. And maybe you'll be sorry to see him go in a way, but then you can fuck Brandon like a wild animal if that's what you feel like doing. You can expend all your lust for both men on him—and he'll love it, and you'll both come like crazy, over and over again.*

"So what have you been doing," Pete asked as she moved

through the open door, "to check out the whole resort in just a few days?"

"Well, hitting the beach, of course. Trying some of the restaurants. And *shopping*," she added playfully, letting her eyes go girlishly wide.

"Women and stores—a dangerous combination," he said as she stepped up between the two guys to begin filling his wineglass. "Any purchases?"

"Um . . . these shoes," she said, then stepped back and struck a pose to show them off.

"Holy God," Pete said, glancing down in admiration. "Those are fucking sexy."

"And believe it or not," she added, teasing, "I don't make my living twirling around a pole."

"You could."

She lifted her gaze for a glance into Pete's eyes and knew her panties were officially soaked now.

But she had to regroup. So she started pouring wine into Brandon's near-empty glass and went on. "Now that I think about it, I've bought everything I'm wearing at the moment since getting here—right down to my boy-short panties."

Oh God. Had she just done that? Brought up her panties?

She tried not to act embarrassed—and maybe it didn't even matter, given the friends-with-benefits discussion.

"Boy-short panties?" Pete scrunched his brow. "What are *those*? They sound . . ."

"Ugly, I know," she replied on a giggle. "But they're *really* sexy." *Oh yikes—shut up about your undies already.*

On the other side of her, Brandon was shaking his head and

looking perplexed as well. "I don't know what they are, either. Have I, uh, seen you in them before?"

She didn't even bother blushing by this point—instead the warmth that ascended her body was about something else, about discussing their sex in front of Pete, even if only in a very mild way. Did it plant a picture in *his* head, just like the mention of Pete's sex life had planted one in *hers*? Was Pete imagining Brandon plunging his cock into her right now? Was he hearing her whimpers and moans in his imagination? "Uh, no," she replied, short, simple.

"Then . . . what are they?"

She'd been just about to go back to her chair and take a seat, but now, instead, she set the wine bottle on the table and used her hands to try to "draw" the slight V-shape of the wide panties across her hips. "They're the same basic width all the way around—but they mold to the body in a very hot way."

"Why don't you just show us?" Brandon suggested.

Her eyes shifted to his and she knew, felt—it was almost as if he was daring her. Or telling her . . . that her desire was stronger than her intent.

Was it?

Part of her wanted to say no, to show him she was truly serious about not fooling around with them both—because she *had* been, *totally*.

But another part of her still yearned to be wild for him, to be his personal porn star. That same part of her felt the tick of the clock she'd written about in her journal earlier—the sifting sand, racing away, reminding her she might never feel this hedonistic again, or have such sensual, sexual opportunities laid before her. And that same part of her had also thought the panties looked amazingly sexy in the mirror when she'd put them on earlier, and she simply suffered . . . the urge to show them off.

She'd never felt so brazen and free as when she stepped back slightly, bit her lower lip, then used both hands to gather the flirty skirt of her dress in her hands—slowly, so slowly, teasing, stretching it out. Her inner thighs tingled, and her cunt felt heavy with anticipation as she lifted the dress higher, higher, until the front was raised to her waist and her pink lace panties were on display—her pussy maybe, too, through the delicate fabric.

As Brandon and Pete both looked at her there, their eyes going glassy with lust while they studied her unabashedly, her face went warm—her whole body, in fact.

"Jesus," Pete muttered beneath his breath.

Brandon lifted his gaze to hers to say, "So pretty, baby," in a low voice that turned her inside out.

She simply drew in her breath, ribbons of pleasure running down her thighs. She liked this too much, being on display for them.

"And from the back?" Brandon asked in that same smoldering voice that told her how aroused he was. Neither his look nor his tone held any dare now, no private *I told you so*—just pure, deep, sensual longing.

Pulling in her breath again, Wendy slowly turned around, looked out over the ocean, arched her ass the same as if she were offering herself up to be fucked, and reached with both hands to lift the dress in back.

She knew what the panties looked like from that view, too. They hugged every contour of her flesh and revealed the lower curves of her rear, at the same time visually slimming her hips and covering a few imperfections—all making her feel sexy as sin itself.

"Ah, God, bunny," Brandon rasped.

When Pete didn't issue a response, she surprised herself—a common occurrence this week—by peeking over her shoulder, lowering her chin, and saying in her sultriest voice, "Do *you* like them, Pete?"

His eyes shot upward from her ass to her face—he appeared lost in lust, his very expression tightening her nipples into even stiffer peaks than they already were. "Nice ass, honey. I'm hard as a rock just looking at you."

Mmm. Her pussy wept. And her stomach pinched with un-adulterated desire.

And it all got worse—or better, depending upon how she looked at it—when Brandon said, "Why don't you take your dress off, baby?"

Something in her throat constricted. Never in her life had a "point of no return" seemed so glaringly obvious to her. *Do it and this will happen. A ménage à trois. Do this and you are a changed woman forever.*

But hadn't this game been *about* change? Excitement? The very hottest sex? White Bikini Babe wouldn't hesitate in this situation. So neither did Wendy.

Reaching behind her to slowly lower her zipper, she looped her thumbs through the shoulder straps and let the dress fall in a bunch to the balcony floor. Then she turned to face him.

On top she wore a pale yellow demi-cut bra with pink straps, dots of pink flowers embroidered across the cups, and a pink bow between her breasts. The underwire lifted them nicely, putting the upper curves on display—she knew from the mirror in her room that they looked big and round and plump.

"You take my breath away, bunny," Brandon whispered in the waning twilight.

"Good," she whispered back.

Then he said, "Come here," and reached for her.

He molded his hands to her hips, then placed a kiss just below her navel, above the V in the panties, making her wetter still. "Turn around," he growled then, and she rotated carefully on her sexy heels until his hands splayed over both sides of her ass, his fingertips digging in for a massage that stretched all through her as she automatically arched and lowered one hand on the table for balance.

Which left her rather bent over, facing Pete. Their eyes met—she'd not quite realized exactly how big and blue his were—but he wasted no time letting his gaze drop to her breasts. And, oh God, she liked it there—it was like a touch, making them feel large and swollen and in need of attention. Her whole body hummed with desire now—which, indeed, had quickly, crazily, gotten *far* bigger than her intent.

As Brandon continued to knead her ass, his thumbs stretching pleasingly toward her anus to stimulate it as well, she found herself arching deeper, higher, hissing in her breath at the pleasure—the pleasure of this whole situation—and in effect thrusting her breasts closer to Pete, who seemed completely entranced.

"He . . ." she murmured breathlessly to Pete about Brandon in explanation, "seems to . . . have a thing . . . for my ass."

Pete didn't lift his eyes from her chest as he replied, "And I think I . . . have a thing . . . for your luscious tits."

"Oh . . ." The words moved through her like liquid, making her cunt spasm, and she leaned her head back with a lustful sigh, pointedly offering her breasts to him.

Pete's palm rose to the side of her tit, making her moan, and with that touch, everything changed.

She became that kind of woman she'd never understood before.

She lost the ability to analyze her moves—or even think clearly.

She felt her sense of judgment and decision leaving her and she let it go willingly now. She didn't need it here—it would only get in the way.

All that happened from this point forward would be about following instincts and soaking up pleasure—*dark, forbidden,* and utterly *intoxicating* pleasure.

*A*t moments I feel guilty. Not guilty about the sex, but about Walter. What would he think if he knew what I'd been doing down here besides analyzing the resort? Would he be disappointed? Shocked? Horrified? I can't help thinking it would be all of the above.

But then I remind myself that he told me to have a good time and not to work too hard. I'm not sure he meant it as literally as I've taken it, but I guess what it comes down to is . . . I've never done anything like this in my life. Not just the sex part—but I've never shirked a duty, I've never behaved unprofessionally, I've never played on the job.

This is my . . . renaissance. My rebirth. My revival.

Such a thing could have come in many ways. It could have been through a job, through art, through working less, or more, through new friends, or hobbies, through anything that made me feel new inside. But my personal renaissance just happened to come through sex.

And sexual or otherwise, doesn't everyone deserve a renaissance at least once in their life?

So instead of feeling guilty, I've decided to instead silently <u>thank</u> Walter, and this journal seems like the best—and only, really—place to do it. So thank you, Walter, for helping me find new parts of myself that I never could have predicted lay hidden inside me. Thank you, thank you, thank you.

Chapter 9

When Pete's thumb stroked across her nipple, she gasped and found herself writhing within both men's grasps. Behind her, Brandon still caressed her ass, his touches scintillating—she'd never realized quite how sensitive her bottom was before meeting him. As Pete took her breasts full in his hands, squeezing, massaging, she thrust her fingers back through his thick dark pirate hair and kissed him, hard, loving the way his tongue instantly invaded her mouth and the rough scratch of stubble on her skin.

Behind her, her bra loosened, and she realized Brandon had undone the hooks, so she shrugged free of it, letting it drop to the balcony floor as well, baring her tits for Pete. He let out a low groan, stopping their kisses to look at them, then resumed his full, vigorous caresses, flesh to flesh.

Having two men's hands on her was the most heady, wonderful thing Wendy had ever experienced. Touches came from all directions, covered more area—pleasure seemed to surround her. And she wanted still more of it. *Much* more.

Brandon seemed to read her mind as he said, "Stand up, baby," putting his hands on her hips to help her do so. When she did, pausing the hot action, taking a moment to *feel* what it was to stand between two hot guys in nothing but a pair of panties and fuck-me heels, it was almost unreal. She felt beautifully on display. And so ready for more that she could taste it.

Brandon stood behind her, his tremendous hard-on nestled at the valley of her ass as he reached around, dipping his fingers into the front of her panties, stroking through her wetness to make her moan. Pete stood in front, holding her tits, bending to lick and suckle them.

She heard noises leaving her—whimpers, sobs. Her whole body felt electrified. She parted her thighs and moved against Brandon's touch in front, his cock in back, as she watched Pete suck her elongated nipples, letting the draw of his mouth reach deep down inside her. Her legs grew weak, but still she needed more somehow—so she reached down to start working at Pete's belt.

Mmm, God, he *did* feel hard behind it, and suddenly there was no shyness—she couldn't wait to get to his sturdy erection.

His breath came heavy at her breast as she worked the belt and zipper, then finally reached boldly into his blue jeans to pull out his cock. She couldn't yet see it, given their positions, but it felt thick and delightfully rigid in her fist as she began to squeeze and pump it. "Aw, God," he growled warm against her tit.

Then he rose up, grabbed on to the hair at the nape of her neck, flashed a look of raw hunger, and gave her the roughest kiss any man ever had. It burst through her like sparks from a flame, burning out only once they'd drifted deep into her body.

Now she had to get to Brandon's cock, too—that was what her instincts told her, that she wanted both guys' dicks, right now, in front of her, to do with whatever she pleased. She turned toward Brandon and began working at *his* pants as well. He helped her, delivering passionate tongue kisses as they fumbled through the process, until finally his majestic shaft popped free from his khakis.

She closed both hands around it—oh God, *so big*, so big that it never ceased to amaze her. And it instantly felt more familiar than Pete's, easier to hold on to in a sense—but in a larger way, that didn't matter. All that mattered was having two of them. All to herself.

Turning toward the balcony railing and the ocean beyond, she took Pete's cock in one hand and Brandon's in the other—and, oh, the power that vibrated through her body! One hard penis felt commanding *enough*, but two . . . Well, the mere sensation of holding them, working them in her fists, was nearly overwhelming.

The power drove her onward.

So she followed her next instinct and stooped down between them, still gripping both guys' long appendages tight. Facing Brandon's, finding herself closely eye to cock, she lowered her mouth over it, taking it inside.

Above her, her lover let out a gut-deep groan that spurred her ministrations, and behind her Pete murmured, "God, yeah."

Oh Lord, it was amazing. Simply to take him in her mouth while another man watched, while she held that other man intimately in her hand. She moved up and down on Brandon's raging erection, working vigorously, wanting to be wild for him, for them both, and for herself, too.

A few moments later, she released the cock from her mouth, pleased by how wet it looked in the dim light echoing from inside, and turned to the other waiting shaft. *Mmm, yes.* Not quite as massive as Brandon's, Pete's cock still stood pleasantly full and long, slightly curved, and was completely inviting, given her current state of mind. *No hesitation.* So she pressed the flat of her tongue to its tip, licking away the pre-come, then went down on him.

He let out a deep, masculine sob that filled her with satisfaction. And though this could have felt strange—like too much too soon with him—instead it only felt fabulous and freeing and perfect.

She was their perfect sex toy. Or they were hers. She wasn't sure, but both ideas appealed and kept her enthusiastically sucking, sucking, taking him in as deep as she could, pleased by everything around her. Her nakedness. The two majestic cocks on either side of her. The hot men attached to those cocks—their eyes on her, their low sounds of pleasure. Pure hedonistic revelry was hers.

She took turns, moving back and forth between Brandon and Pete until her mouth felt so wantonly, joyously stretched that she couldn't go on any longer.

When she slowly rose to her heels between the two men, she felt brazenly beautiful, looking back and forth between them and hoping they could somehow see, or sense, how swollen and well used her lips felt.

"Shall we take this inside?" Brandon asked softly. But she heard the *real* question. *Do you want to keep going?*

No hesitation. "Yes. Please. I want you both," she said. And she took both guys' hands and led them in through the wide open door.

She led them straight to Brandon's big bed, and when they reached it, he drew her into an embrace and spoke low. "Tell me what you want, baby." Again, more unspoken questions. *Are you sure? Exactly how far do you want to go?*

He still, somehow, thought she was a good girl, but she'd never felt less "good" in her life—all traces of that person, at this moment anyway, had vanished.

She looked him in the eye. Wanted to make him *see*. Wanted to make him see her like he never had before. "I want everything," she promised him, her voice gentle but sure. "I want you both to fuck my brains out. I want to come and come and come. I want it all."

Brandon's eyes went glassy with a familiar lust that drove hers even higher. "Then you'll *have* it all."

And after that, he didn't ask anything else.

After that, it was only the hot, wanton sex she craved.

Brandon began kissing her, hard, rough, just as Pete had, making her mouth feel utterly well used after all the oral sex she'd given them. He massaged her breasts, pinching the hardened nipples between his fingertips and making her moan in response to a sensation that hovered somewhere between pleasure and pain. "Damn, your tits are phenomenal," he growled before taking one into his mouth—again hard, deep. There was nothing soft about this sex, and she didn't want there to be.

Behind her, Pete moved in, caressing her hips and ass, kissing her neck—which she bent for him—then reaching down inside the back of her panties to stroke his fingers through her hungry pussy. "God, you're juicy," he breathed, and she could both hear and feel how drenched she was and loved the idea of her moisture being on his hand.

"You both make me so wet," she managed, breathless with passion. "Need you both naked. Need you to fuck me."

That was all the guys required to hurriedly shed their clothes before moving back in to touch her, rub against her, press their hard cocks in her softest places. She ran her hands over bare male asses, broad shoulders, muscular chests. She saw Pete's tattoo—predictably, the flag of a pirate ship, complete with skull and crossbones. She continued working the men's incredible shafts in her hands. And she felt as if she were being swallowed, wrapped up in a big velvet blanket where every inch of her skin was pleasured by touch after touch after touch—only there was no blanket; there were only men.

When they moved onto the bed, the two men kneeling on either side of her legs, she bent to start removing her shoes, but Brandon reached down, covering her hand to stop her. "Oh no you don't," he said. "Those stay on."

Lying nestled on soft sheets, switching her glance back and forth between the guys, she motioned down to her panties. "What about these?" she asked, playing the coquette. "Do these stay on?"

"Those are so hot," Pete said, "I almost wish they could."

"But they'll have to go," Brandon added, then reached for the clingy lace that hugged her hips. "Lift your ass, bunny," he said, so she did, allowing him to slowly peel them down and off over her sexy heels.

She immediately felt Pete's eyes on her crotch, which she'd shaved again today to keep it perfectly smooth, and having a new pair of male eyes on her sent a fresh thrill ricocheting through her like a pinball.

She looked up at him. "Do you want to see how wet and pink I am?" No hesitation.

From the look on Pete's face, she thought maybe he'd come just from that. "God—show me, honey."

She spread her legs wide, happy to reveal the folds of her

inner flesh. Her body's instincts urged it, urged her to spread as wide as possible, so hungry was she now to take something inside.

"Fuck," he whispered, and then she felt Brandon's gaze there, too.

The next thing she knew, Brandon was swirling two finger-tips over her clit in hot little circles that reminded her he knew exactly how a woman needed to be touched, and Pete, who still sat up facing her cunt, easily slid two of *his* fingers up inside her wet, open passage. *Unh, yes.*

Her sighs of pleasure filled the air and much of that pleasure came from the visual aspects of the moment as well as the physical, looking up to find two incredible men hovering over her, concentrating together on her needy cunt.

"*Mmm*, pretty pussy," Pete growled, and she pumped against his fingers harder as her own hands rose mindlessly to knead and caress her breasts. "I want to fuck you with my tongue before I fuck you with my dick," he said then.

She didn't protest.

And Pete wasted no time making good on the promise—as Brandon drew his hand away, Pete situated himself between Wendy's legs and stroked his tongue upward through her feminine folds. She gasped—just that one lick felt like having her whole body illuminated from the inside out, the pleasure from it vibrating through her.

Then he did exactly what he'd said he would—he fucked her with his tongue. He pushed it up inside her, and even though a guy's tongue was short compared to his fingers or cock, it still felt hot, especially when he thrust it in and out. She panted in rhythm to his movements as Brandon kissed her breasts, her shoulders, her lips. Brandon thrust *his* tongue, too, into her mouth, and she met it with her own, lost in being the center of attention in a way she never had before.

As Pete resumed licking upward through her wetness, connecting with her clit each time, she continued to make out with Brandon and found herself tugging needfully on his cock. Without even quite realizing what she wanted, she pulled it upward, upward, until Brandon whispered to her, his eyes heavy-lidded, "Back in your mouth?"

"Uh-huh," she sighed, then waited impatiently until he rose to his knees beside her head and held his dick down, feeding it to her. She took the large head in and felt him slide deeper, deeper, where she wanted him. Oh God, he filled her mouth so incredibly full, and like other times before, she loved the idea of how she must look to him right now, so beautifully obscene.

She moaned around his immense shaft as the heat from Pete's ministrations spread through her, taking her closer and closer to climax. She fucked his face as he worked tenaciously at her clit, and she soaked in the pleasure, deeper, deeper, until finally the much-needed orgasm broke over her like a tidal wave.

As the ecstasy slammed through her, she pumped against Pete and screamed against Brandon's cock, thrashing about until finally the waves lessened and then receded completely—and she lay still on the bed.

It was in those few seconds after coming that sanity returned to her—the ability to think, to reason, to do something more than just *feel.*

Look at where you are. With two men. In the middle of an official ménage à trois.

It reminded her of that moment on the beach her first night

with Brandon—after she'd come, she'd waited for some sort of guilt or regret to assail her. But it hadn't happened. And it didn't happen now, either.

Instead, what struck her was more like . . . a sense of glorious celebration. She smiled at them both. She told them her orgasm had been powerful and amazing. She said she wanted more of them—so much more. "Fuck me," she begged. "Please fuck me."

"Don't worry, baby," Brandon said. "You're gonna get all the cock you can handle."

Should that have scared her? Turned her off in some way? It did neither, filling her with nothing but desperate anticipation.

"Get on your hands and knees," Brandon told her, and she hurried into the position that she relished because it made her feel so naughty.

"Are you going to spank me again?" she asked hopefully over her shoulder.

He arched one brow and clearly tried to hide a devilish grin. "Only if you're a very bad girl."

"Getting badder all the time," she assured him, not hiding a lascivious smile.

"So I see. And I like it."

A second later, his hands closed warm over her hips and his cock plunged into her. She cried out at the impact—oh *God*, he was big—but she was so wet that he'd gone in surprisingly easy. As always, the sensation of being so completely filled radiated through her body and made her let out a hiss of pleasure.

When he began to pound into her, hard, just like she wanted, each stroke vibrated through her and made her cry out. Pete knelt next to them on the bed, reaching under her to caress her swaying breasts and play with her ever-sensitive nipples, and she didn't hesitate to say, "Pete, bring that gorgeous cock here. Put it in my mouth." Completely bold. Completely sure. Queen of sex.

Pete sighed his lust at the demand and wasted no time getting to his feet. Her hands were planted near the edge of the bed, so he stood in front of her and took his dick in hand, inserting it between her lips the same as Brandon had a little while ago.

She could only describe the resulting sensation as euphoria. Pure, raw, ecstatic pleasure roared through her at having two big cocks in her body at the same time. When she'd made the request of Pete, she'd not even realized it would produce that effect—be the first time she'd taken both of their large, hard shafts into her at once—but the second Pete's erection had entered her mouth, she'd been overwhelmed by how utterly full she was, unnaturally so, obscenely so.

Brandon fucked her cunt while Pete fucked her mouth, and she sobbed with joy and got lost in the naughty pleasure. She didn't know how long they fucked that way—two minutes, five, ten?—but as they proceeded, Brandon indeed began to bring his hand down, slapping her ass, grunting with each strike, adding yet one more blessed and naughty sensation to the mix.

Like before, she couldn't think, stopped trying. Simply absorbed. Simply felt.

When finally she couldn't maintain the position any longer, she pulled her head back, releasing Pete's cock from her mouth, smiled up at him, and told him she wanted *him* in her pussy now. In response, he groaned, brushed his thumb across her swollen lower lip, and gave her a look that said *he* thought she was the queen of sex, too.

As Pete rummaged in his jeans for a condom, Wendy rested atop the rumpled sheets, her body feeling well used but still hungry. Brandon lay facing her, running his fingers through her hair, over her breasts, telling her she was hot and beautiful.

I am not me anymore, she thought in that moment. *I simply am not me.* In ways, sure. But she would never be the same. And she didn't *want* to be.

Once sheathed, Pete lay down behind her and ran his palm up her outer thigh. The pace had slowed now, and though she'd wanted it hard and fast earlier, this change was welcome since she was growing tired.

"Are you ready for me, honey?" he whispered, his voice deep, sexy.

"God, yes," she breathed, adding, "Do it like this, from behind. So I can make out with Brandon while you fuck me." Again, all confidence. No fear. Taking what she wanted. Telling her men how it was going to go.

Despite having just had Brandon's enormous shaft inside her, when Pete entered, she still let out a low groan—from that always incredible sensation of being impaled on a guy's hard cock. Mmm, God, it was delicious.

As Pete began to move in her, as she began to meet his thrusts, she looked into Brandon's eyes—*no hesitation*—and let him see all the lust and pleasure there. Could there be any moment more intimate between a man and woman than to gaze at each other while another man fucked her? She didn't think so, and she found herself savoring such a strange and unique human connection—but at the very same time, she reminded herself that he was not a man to get attached to. No matter how sexually giving he was. No matter how caring or respectful. No matter how . . . plain fun he was to be with in every way.

Besides the fact that he was her . . . her conquest, her own personal "freedom ride," he was now also a business associate, weird as that was. And after this was over, she didn't expect to have any direct contact with him through work—but if Walter invested in Emerald Shores, Brandon would indeed be at least a distant presence in her life, and she didn't want to be hung up on him from afar. If she saw his name on a piece of paper or on the computer, she wanted to flush with the warmth of remembering this moment, this week, and all the pleasure he'd opened her to—she didn't want to feel sad or lonely or anything else that came with getting attached to a guy she shouldn't have.

"Feel good?" Brandon asked her then.

Her stomach curled with the weird pleasure of it. "*Very.* Do you believe I'm a bad girl *now*?"

"Mmm-hmm," he told her, sounding wholly convinced— finally, then gently twirled one erect nipple between his fingertips as he leaned in to kiss her.

His long, deep tongue kisses echoed through her as strongly as the drives of Pete's shaft. At the front of her pussy, Brandon's cock, still erect and damp, rested at her slit, nuzzled at the indentation there—and as she moved against Pete, it also rubbed her clit against Brandon's hardness.

"Ohhh . . ." she heard herself sigh against his mouth and instinctively hooked her leg around his hip to press against him more insistently even as Pete kept thrusting, connecting with what she suspected was her G-spot.

Brandon continued kissing her as he massaged her breasts and found her rhythm below, beginning to move in time with her and Pete. They rolled together like tumultuous ocean waves, writhing, meeting, creating perfect friction on all sides, and soon moans from all three of them filled the air.

She wished she could see them from above, all tangled together. With one hand, she rubbed Brandon's chest; with the other she reached behind her, to Pete's firm ass, pulling him more deeply inside her. *Perfect pleasure*. Those words wafted through her head. She'd found that, and she was wallowing in it, literally.

She and Brandon kept kissing, but she occasionally turned her head to kiss Pete, as well. In between, he dropped kisses on her bare shoulders, her upper arm. Her pussy felt more swollen and stimulated than ever in her life, by one cock *inside* her and another *outside*.

When Pete's arm circled her, his hand cupping her breast, she looked down to see the back of his hand now also bumping up against Brandon's chest. And when Brandon's mouth left her lips to head south, to suck the tit Pete held, she wondered if his mouth touched Pete's hand. She wondered if, below, their legs mingled. She had the urge to see that: her two men touching.

And she was pretty sure that if she suggested such a thing, her two big, masculine guys would probably have heart attacks, so she wasn't going to ruin the moment, but as the three of them moved together in sexual union, she enjoyed the idea, the notion that their legs *were* touching, that on some level they were gleaning pleasure from each other as much as from her.

Wendy was the first to climax. Adding visions of her guys touching each other to the glorious pleasure already echoing through her body pushed her over the edge. As the pulsations rocketed through her, she moaned her ecstasy, clinging to Brandon with one arm around his neck, using the other hand to grab on to Pete's hip and make him fuck her still deeper as she exploded. The orgasm went on and on, longer than usual, and she soaked up every drawn-out second of it.

Pete went next, just on the heels of Wendy, groaning, "Fuck, *now*," between clenched teeth, then driving *hard, hard, hard* into her, and she welcomed it, loving that she'd made him come.

Before Peter had even completely finished, Brandon moaned, "Ahhh—me, too," and she hadn't quite expected that, hadn't quite known if what they were doing could take him there, but it did, and he shot his wet white come upward, spraying both their stomachs with a shocking warmth that made her gasp.

As Pete pulled out of her, she rolled to her back between them and both guys began to rub Brandon's juices into her, producing the most erotic sight Wendy had ever beheld. Brandon focused on massaging it into the flesh of her cunt while Pete rubbed it into her breasts using both hands, as if it were lotion.

And then they slept, and Wendy had never experienced sweeter slumber.

God, she was fucking amazing. The truth was, he hadn't thought she'd do it. Or that even if she did it, that she'd be . . . well, a lot more timid, and that she'd leave it to him to take the lead.

It wasn't the first occasion on which Brandon had shared a woman with Pete. Or even the second or third. They'd known each other a long time and were fortunate enough to live in a place and an age when more women were agreeable to such liaisons.

But it was the first time that sharing a woman with Pete had made Brandon come so hard, or had him blathering to her about how beautiful she was. He hadn't been lying—she'd pretty much convinced him she could be a perfect bad girl now. Yet at the same time, he knew how much more there was to her: brains, ambition, humor.

Maybe . . . maybe he was starting to care for this woman. Or maybe he'd just let himself spend a lot more time with her than he usually did with any one particular girl and that alone accounted for his feelings. But then, he'd kind of felt this way from the start with her, hadn't he? After that first night on the beach, he'd wanted more of her and been worried he wouldn't get it.

He watched her sleeping, her lips softly parted, her nipples still slightly erect even now. Pete lay on the other side of her, just as naked, sprawled so that one sun-darkened arm fell across her not quite as tan stomach.

Sharing her had been about more than the hot kinkiness of it. Sharing her had been . . . like urging a baby bird out of its nest. Maybe that was a silly—and far too placid—analogy, but it was what came to mind. He was teaching her to be naughty—and not just for him, but also for her. He thought she was like a but-terfly spreading her wings for the first time—but then wanted to slap himself. Since when was he so sappy? Especially about a girl? Or sex, for crying out loud.

And still, as he studied the way his buddy's arm rested across her body, it felt different than ever before. He felt a strange con-nection to her that he couldn't explain to himself. Sharing her with Pete had been like . . . like a communion of sorts. It was clear to him that she was in a period of sexual experimenta-tion, and he simply found himself wanting to help her experi-ence everything she could. The weird part, though, was that he wanted it in such a soul-deep way. He wanted to *give* her things. He wanted to make her life fuller than it had been when she'd met him.

Just then, her eyes fluttered open.

"Hey, bunny," he whispered.

She smiled.

"Good?" he asked, feeling the need to check on her, to make sure everything was still fine.

She shook her head, but smiled cutely, replying, "*Bad.* Remember?"

He grinned back. "Bad bunny," he scolded.

As she shifted slightly, Pete stirred and opened his eyes. Then he seemed to remember where he was and what they'd just done. "Damn," he said, "that was fun."

Watching Wendy's eyes, Brandon saw how much that pleased his naughty little beach bunny—and it made him a little hard all over again, that quick.

Biting her lip and looking pretty as sin, she reached out to grab both guys' wrists, to pull their hands together, atop her cunt. She still lay on her back, her large breasts falling heavy toward her sides, so naturally beautiful that, like last night, Brandon wanted to somehow capture the way she looked right now, put it in a bottle or a drawer, save it for some later point in time when she was no longer with him. In her he saw some perfect culmination of purity and sin that blurred all the lines and made his feelings for her a little less scary than they probably should have been.

"I want you both to touch me, together, at the same time."

So bold now, his bunny. Well, she'd been pretty bold from the start, but the kinkier they'd gotten together, the more shy she'd acted at moments. Until tonight—until she'd taken them both on and started bossing them around. It made him smile inside. And stiffened his dick further.

He knew she liked the way he rubbed her clit—it was an easy enough thing to tell and something he happened to be skilled at—so like earlier, he automatically gravitated there, while Pete eased his fingers deeper, underneath, between her legs. She spread instinctively, then issued another command. "I want to take turns sucking your cocks while you touch me," she said. "So I want you both to turn around, put your heads down there"—she pointed toward her crotch—"and look at my pussy while you play with it."

Jesus God—she was a continual surprise to him. She really *was* getting badder all the time.

And he wasn't about to argue with a woman who so clearly knew what she wanted, and apparently neither was Pete, so they both resituated as she'd directed, as Pete grinned and said, "You can suck my cock all you want, honey."

The strange thing, Brandon discovered, was being face-to-face with Pete while they pleasured her. The geography of their three ways didn't usually go like that, bring them up close and personal with *each other*.

But soon enough they both seemed focused totally on her beautifully exposed cunt, the flesh already engorged again, even after her orgasm. Her pink inner lips parted to reveal her opening, and her clit was noticeably swollen, too. He could smell her arousal along with the general scent of sex on all of them.

"Damn, look at this pretty little pussy," Pete said, and Brandon watched his buddy thrust two big fingers inside her. Her juices seeped out around them and made him want to sink his dick there. When Pete began moving his fingers in and out, they made noise in her wetness.

Above, Wendy's breath grew ragged, heavy, and her voice came out raspy. "Kiss me there, Brandon. Kiss me there while Pete touches me."

He just looked at her, his own breath hitching. Even more so when she added, "And, Pete, use your other hand to hold me open for him, so he can lick me better."

He and Pete both hesitated. But Wendy was propped on her elbows now, watching, waiting, and even if this close contact with Pete felt a little weird, he supposed neither of them wanted to mess up the hot, perfect harmony of the night.

So as Pete reached, using two fingers to part the top of her pussy, Brandon leaned in to lick her, careful not to let his tongue touch Pete's fingers—although it was hard to avoid brushing them slightly with his chin—or Pete's other hand with his nose. But when that happened, neither of them even flinched, so he decided it was no big deal—it was what the lady wanted, and they both seemed committed to giving it to her.

His hot beach bunny continued to watch, even as she reached out both hands to stroke their dicks. She seemed riveted by the sight of them working at her pussy, which made him lick her harder, made him bear down with his tongue, taste her deeper, flick it across the nub of her clit with vigor, regardless of whether that meant he touched Pete's fingers that way. Below, Pete's other hand played with the lower part of her cunt, teasing it, stretching it, fucking it with his fingers. Catching such close-up glimpses of that got Brandon even hotter, and as he grew more aroused by eating her while Pete touched her, he quit caring so much if his mouth, or any part of him, touched his friend.

Hell, he'd known the guy nearly twenty years—what was the big fucking deal?

Finally, Wendy kept her promise and drew his cock into her mouth. *Ah, fuck yes.* So warm, wet. Brandon lifted his gaze from her cunt to her face to watch her suck him.

He scarcely even understood how girls got his particular phallus into their mouths given the circumference, but with Wendy, he was even more amazed than usual, and her reckless enthusiasm for cock sucking tonight tightened his chest. Badder and badder. Bad bunny.

He moaned against her clit as she took him in deeper, her free hand still pumping away at Pete. Shit, she was hot. Fucking *astounding.* Pleasure expanded through his chest—as well as his cock—and he went down on her more roughly still, sucking her clit into her mouth almost forcefully. She let out a cry around his shaft and rocked against his mouth, against Pete's hands.

But then she released him from her lips and turned her head the other way, taking Pete into those moist depths. "Ah—ah, yeah," Pete groaned near Brandon's ear, again reminding him of their close proximity. He again watched Pete's dark fingers below him, thrusting in and out of her opening, glistening wetly each time he withdrew them.

When Brandon felt her soft tits close around his erection, he looked back up to see that she'd managed to get his dick there while she continued to suck Pete. She moaned in pure elation, and he wasn't sure he'd ever seen such a hot, dirty sight. His bad bunny loved having two cocks to play with, no doubt about it. He licked her harder as he began fucking her tits, his dick still damp from her ministrations and making his plunges into that pillowing valley smoother—slick and warm.

They all moved that way for a long while, all moaning and groaning, but Wendy more than either guy. Wendy, Brandon realized, was nearly out of her head with pleasure. She sometimes extracted his cock from between her breasts and ran the length across one of her beautifully beaded nipples, or she would release Pete's dick from her mouth, trading it for Brandon's while rubbing Pete's over the pink tip. She sucked on one while she caressed her tits with the other.

Like earlier, they all writhed together in heated unison, like a finely tuned sex machine, all of them pumping and grinding, delivering pleasure, and taking it, too.

Wendy's excitement grew, increasing Brandon's, as well, until she no longer sucked *either* guy's cock, but instead ran them both roughly over and between her voluminous tits.

She was going to come soon, he knew. And he watched, half entranced, half *horrified*, as he realized that his cock was rubbing more than just her tits now—it was rubbing against Pete's cock, too. She was making it happen, drawing them together over the flesh of her breasts, pressing the heads of both shafts together, and simultaneously licking them.

Jesus God. Part of him wanted to stop. He couldn't be doing this. He wasn't gay or bi—he'd never wanted another guy in his life.

But he *didn't* stop. She was so wild and dirty, and so close to exploding in his mouth.

So he sucked her clit, and he soaked up the pleasure she delivered, and at first he tried to forget part of that pleasure was coming from Pete's cock, but then he just quit thinking so hard, and just *felt* the pleasure, building, growing, starting to consume him.

He glanced at Pete, but found his eyes closed and was glad. That meant he could enjoy this without Pete knowing.

Shit, he was *enjoying* it. How the fuck was that possible?

Still, he licked his bad bunny's swollen nub, harder, harder, driving her onward, until finally she screamed and pumped more intensely at his face and Pete's fingers, and her orgasm hit so hard that it nearly rocked through *his* body, too. He nibbled her clit as she came, took it between his teeth, made her pull against him that way when she bucked.

"Oh God, oh God, oh God . . ." she moaned, her release moving through him like hot liquid. Soon she was purring, "So good, so good," coming down from the high, and making him think maybe they would stop now. Stop moving in this particular way, change positions, *something*.

Only they didn't. All three of them kept heaving and thrusting at one another and Brandon realized it didn't really matter what he thrust *against* in that moment—as long as it was flesh, it brought pleasure.

Pete's dick was hard against his—and God help him, that excited him. He was used to the softness of a woman, not the rockhardness of a guy. He kept moving, fucking her tits, sometimes her hand, at the same time still meeting with the other stiff shaft in the bed. His stomach contracted.

When Pete finally opened his eyes and glanced upward to where their cocks mingled, Brandon caught the stunned look in his eyes. Then heard Wendy's voice—who'd clearly seen as well. "Please don't make me stop," she pleaded. "They look so beautiful together, it's *so* hot, *so* fucking hot."

And neither guy stopped moving.

They didn't say a work or look at each other, but they didn't stop moving, thrusting, sliding.

Fuck, it felt good. *Too* good. Her tits were like a pillow beneath the two dicks now, and Wendy rubbed them directly together, cock on cock, hard flesh against hard flesh.

He couldn't believe he was doing this, letting this happen.

But he tried not to think about it. He tried to think of pleasing her—tried to ignore the fact that it pleasured him, too.

He was going to come soon. From this—rubbing his cock against Pete's.

No, from all of it, from everything.

Yeah, that was better. Think of it that way and it didn't interfere with his mounting excitement as much.

And part of him—the *I'm-not-gay* part—didn't want Pete to hear his reaction, but he couldn't stop his hard breathing, and when he knew he was about to erupt, he couldn't hold in a whispered, "Fuck. Now. God."

Then came the mighty rush of hot come, spewing all over Wendy's tits and stomach, and he heard his own moans and had to let them out because what difference did it really make now?

And still, it satisfied him, on more than one level, when Pete's orgasm followed, that he was muttering, "Shit, shit, here I go," and when he felt Pete's hot semen splatter across *his* cock, *his* stomach.

Now, finally, the three of them went still.

He opened his eyes to glance upward at his messy bunny. Unlike other times, he didn't rub it in, but he couldn't help thinking it was beautiful, his and Pete's come mixing together—for her. And it was even more beautiful when *she* reached down to massage it thoroughly into her breasts, biting her lip, watching herself do it. God, he wanted to wrap around her right now.

But he had weirder things to deal with. So he said to Pete, over her thighs, "Let's not ever talk about this."

Pete met his eyes only briefly to say, "Agreed." Then he got up and started getting dressed.

It gave Brandon the opportunity to ease up beside Wendy in the bed, but he remained freaked out, thinking: *For no other woman would I have allowed that to happen.* And he didn't plan to let it ever happen again, but he was still shocked and unable to deny that . . . it had felt *good.*

Apparently he wasn't the only one bringing people out of their shells here—apparently there were things she could draw from him, too, things he'd never even imagined.

Wendy lay in bed with Brandon. Pete was gone, and she was amazed—at herself. Her breasts still gleamed with her lovers' come. *Both* of her lovers. Good God, what had happened to her?

But she knew the answer. Pleasure had happened to her. And confidence. And freedom. And she had the man who lay next to her to thank for all of it.

Of course, who knew? Maybe if she hadn't found Brandon, she would have found some other guy in the village that night, some other guy who was hot and smart and sweet and sexually generous. Or maybe she would have hooked up with Pete on the beach the next day and she'd have had just as good and bold an experience. But then, Pete had approached her because she'd looked familiar, because he'd seen her with Brandon the previous night. If not for that, Pete probably would have been one more hot guy in trunks to walk past her that day and set her blood humming—with no result.

When she thought of what Brandon had done tonight—not just sharing her with Pete, not just encouraging her in that direction, but what he'd done *with* Pete, sort of, for her—it blew her mind.

She'd never been particularly aroused by the idea of guys together before, but suddenly, having two magnificent hard cocks at her disposal, she'd realized it excited the hell out of her when they touched each other. Her chest contracted now just thinking about it.

Yet then a rather icky, morbid thought hit her, and she turned to Brandon in bed. "You really wanted all that, right?"

He blinked, then met her gaze. "Huh?"

"None of what happened tonight was because . . . well, because of business? Because you want my endorsement with Walter?"

He pursed his lips, then propped on one elbow to peer down at her. "*Of course* I want your endorsement with Walter, but I thought we agreed not to bring our business into our pleasure. And let's get something straight here, bunny. When it comes to sex, I do what I want—nothing more, nothing less."

"So, uh . . . what you did with Pete, that was really . . . for me. And for you. Not for the resort in any way."

He blinked again, and this time looked a little caught off guard. "Do we have to talk about that?"

"Just answer me."

He sighed. "It wasn't about the resort, okay? Believe me, the resort was the last thing on my mind."

"Okay," she said, relaxing.

He lay back down, staring up at the ceiling fan turning above the bed. "On the other hand, I don't plan to do it again and I'm kinda freaked out that it happened at all, so I'd rather not discuss it."

Next to him, she couldn't help smiling, teasing him. "I thought you were a little kinky."

"Emphasis on the *little*, bunny. There's a big difference between being kinky and being into other guys."

She couldn't believe how troubled he sounded about it—given all the new things *she'd* done over the past couple days. "Come on, relax—it's not that big a deal," she told him. "Look at it this way. At least I didn't try to put a cucumber up your ass."

At this, he let out a loud laugh, then met her gaze, still smiling.

"Thank you, though," she added, "for, you know, not stopping."

"I couldn't bring myself to spoil your fun."

She lowered her chin, bit her lip. "Well, not all men would have cared so much about . . . my fun."

"What can I say?" he told her. "I'm just an all-around good guy."

She giggled softly, but then her humor faded, because he really was amazingly generous that way. So she followed one more instinct tonight by leaning over to kiss him on the cheek.

Their eyes met and she felt something moving between them—something good, sweet, and she knew in that brief moment that their souls had connected.

But it's only temporary. That can happen in life. You can have profound connections with people without having a lasting relationship come from it.

Did White Bikini Babe ever share that kind of connection with a lover? Wendy sighed, doubting it. But she still refused to let herself care too much for Brandon. For all the reasons she'd had when this started—it wouldn't seem so much like a grand success if she ended up falling for her hot stud—and for the newer reasons, too. It plain wasn't healthy to be hung up on a business associate. Especially when there would be millions of dollars concerned.

"I should go," she said, starting to sit up, look for her panties. The rest of her clothes, she remembered, were out on the balcony.

But Brandon closed his hand around her wrist. "Stay. It's late. No reason for you to walk back in the dark tonight. And I happen to know you don't have any meetings scheduled in the morning." He concluded with a wink.

"I still have work to do, though."

"What's on your agenda?"

"Well, given that there're golf, tennis, basketball, shuffleboard, mini golf, and bike rentals on the property, and that I haven't yet checked out *any* of those, I was planning on doing that."

"Do you golf?"

"A little. Not well. But I know when to use a wood and when to use an iron."

"Great. We'll go golfing in the morning. I'll show you our best course. It was voted one of the top twenty in the country last year."

Despite herself, the idea appealed. Even though she knew it would be wise to put some distance between them tomorrow. She already knew she'd be seeing him tomorrow night, of course—on his way out the door, Pete had reminded them about dinner at his place. And she couldn't even really think that far ahead right now, to what it would be like to face Pete after tonight, and to meet the girl he was dating, knowing what she'd done with him less than twenty-four hours earlier—but the one thing she knew was that it wouldn't be smart to keep spending more and more time with Brandon.

"The problem with that," she said, "is that if I'm with *you*, I won't get to see how the average patron is treated. Just like at Sharky's."

He shrugged, but didn't look worried. "True. But how about this? You golf with me in the morning, then you can investigate incognito for the rest of the day."

She sighed. "Fine." But it wasn't really. Because apparently that meant she was spending the night with him. Risking attachment. Then spending the morning with him. Risking more attachment. *Your job, from this point forward, is to make sure this stays just about sex. Sex, sex, sex. Nothing more. Nothing emotional.*

So her plan was . . . to keep fucking his brains out.

And when she looked at it that way, it didn't sound too difficult.

I have had two men inside me at once.

I have craved two cocks.

I have felt them erupt on me like hot volcanoes, and I have rubbed their mingled come into my skin.

I never knew. How much I could want such things. How dirty I could be.

Does "the forbidden" exist only in our individual minds? I fucked two men last night and the world didn't end, I still woke up and ate breakfast this morning; my life is going to go on.

Is it that simple? If you decide it's not forbidden anymore, does that make it so?

Chapter 10

The next morning, Wendy and Brandon showered—together—where she braced her hands on the tile wall and he pushed his cock into her from behind, and she remembered to keep it all about sex, even bathing.

They stopped by her condo on the way out so she could change into shorts and gym shoes, then they had breakfast at a delightful in-resort eatery called the Cracked Egg.

Over breakfast, they talked a bit more about Brandon's early years—in the small southern Alabama town where he'd been born and raised. It sounded quaint and picturesque, and having been a city girl all her life, Wendy found herself almost envying his small-town upbringing.

"Why'd you leave?" she asked.

"I told you before—the beach is in my blood. Always was, as long as I can remember."

Which made sense to her—something about the beach simply suited him. He belonged here.

"My family's still there, though," he added, "so I get home for holidays, and my mom's birthday."

"Brothers and sisters?" she asked, taking a sip of coffee.

"One of each, and I'm the youngest."

"And the most successful, I'm betting."

He grinned. "Yeah, everybody at home makes a big deal out of what I do, but I've found that success in life is pretty much in the eye of the beholder. My brother runs a feed store and has five kids, and he couldn't be happier. My sister's dream was always to teach high school English—and that's what she does, so she's very satisfied."

When Wendy had first met Brandon—or even yesterday, finding him in that huge office, looking so crisp and handsome in his suit—she'd never have suspected humility to be part of his makeup. Yet on this particular topic, it shone through, and she found it unduly appealing.

They talked a bit about her then, too—she'd grown up in a bustling Chicago suburb with her parents and older sister. "Where I lived a completely average middle-class life. Girl Scouts, piano lessons, that sort of thing."

He lifted his gaze from his coffee cup to her eyes. "There's nothing average *about* you, bunny."

Given that she'd always *felt* very average—happy but indeed *average*—the sentiment touched her. And it also made her a little wet in her panties, given that she knew at least part of it had to do with the passionate sex they'd shared.

When they walked into the pro shop at the golf course overlooking the bay, they held hands. And when the older man behind the counter smiled at them, even before realizing it was Brandon Worth who'd come to play a round of golf, it made Wendy realize—the two of them were getting too cozy here, just as she'd feared. They looked like a romantic couple.

You have to make this about sex again. Just about sex.

"We'll play the front nine," Brandon told her, motioning to a huge diagram of the course mounted on the wall in a thick wooden frame. "It gets hot early this time of year, so every golfer here starts out at the crack of dawn. We'll be behind them all, so we can take our time and not feel rushed."

"Sounds good," she said absently, wondering, *How exactly do I make golf about sex?*

Just then, her eyes fell on a rack of women's golf clothing, most specifically on a little white skirt that would generally be deemed way too short—*unless* it was for golf or tennis. She wasn't sure why that made it okay, but she knew it did. And the shorts she wore were perfectly stylish, but they didn't feel *sexy*. The flirty white skirt *would*.

So she found one in her size, along with a pink pullover designed to hug the body—the perfect sexy little golf outfit—and spotting a dressing room in one corner, she called over to Brandon at the counter, "I'm going to try these on."

He only chuckled. "You're a shopaholic, aren't you?"

Not usually. But starting to be. She'd never liked clothes so much before she'd started wearing ones that looked hot on her.

The ensemble fit like a glove, and in her opinion, made her look like one hot golfer. She tore off the tags to take to the man behind the counter, but left the clothes *on*.

And just before opening the door to go back out, she followed yet one more instinct—she reached up under the skirt and took her panties off, shoving them in her purse.

Risky? Definitely. But she wanted to make sure Brandon thought way more about fucking today than about anything like romance.

When Brandon saw her, he gave her an appreciative once-over, then spoke low enough for the older guy not to hear. "How the hell am I supposed to concentrate on golf now?"

You're not. Mission accomplished. Or the start of it anyway.

She golfed even worse than usual. Because wearing a tiny little white skirt with nothing on underneath, it turned out, was pretty damn arousing. By the time they were on the fourth hole, she was tingling and swollen between her legs. Brandon had no clue, though—he seemed focused on the game, and was busy giving her pointers and thinking she cared about her score.

It also turned out that Brandon had been right about a couple of things. It was hot out, even in the morning, which she knew from being on the beach early in the day—but *here*, there wasn't even a sea breeze to cool them. And the golf course was pretty much deserted except for them. She hadn't quite imagined there would be *no one* else playing, but when she mentioned it to Brandon, he said, "Most people who golf here are serious about it, and they know what the weather is like. It's different in early spring and fall, but this time of year, it's a ghost town on the courses after nine thirty."

Well, all the more easy for me to get your mind on sex, if I don't have to worry about anyone seeing anything. When she'd taken off her panties, it had been with an eye toward discreetly flashing him at some point, or maybe just taking his hand and sliding it between her legs while they were in the cart. But now she could be more aggressive. And the more she played with being aggressive, the more she liked it.

So it was on hole seven, which was beautifully verdant and pristine—*and* remote, the green itself circled by a thick growth of trees—that she decided it might be a good place to make her move.

Before deciding exactly what that move *was*, though, she reached in the cooler they'd brought along, grabbing out a bottle of water. Sweltering, she held the cold bottle to her neck, and then to her chest, where her top opened in a V. She sighed as the icy bit of wetness refreshed her a little.

"Knock that off, bunny," Brandon said with a chiding grin from a few feet away. "You look too good wet. You're gonna give me a hard-on."

She glanced at him expectantly. "Is that a problem?"

"Right now?" He looked amused. "Yeah. I'm golfing."

She tilted her head. "So you'd rather golf than fuck?"

"I take my golf game pretty seriously." His expression was playful, but he clearly meant it, too. She'd been able to tell since the first hole that this was something he didn't do halfway. Now that she thought about it, Brandon didn't do much of *anything* halfway, and she decided that must be the secret to his success.

Still, she couldn't help taking this as a direct challenge. So when they approached their balls—both on the green, but a good distance from the hole—she slowly bent over at the waist to adjust hers just slightly, her ass pointed in Brandon's direction. She knew the move would surely put her damp pussy on display.

Then she waited for a reaction—but got none. And when she finally looked up, she found his full attention on his own ball—he was obviously planning his next shot. For crying out loud.

Rolling her eyes in annoyance—since she hadn't expected

this to be so hard—she rose upright, returned to withdraw the putter from her rented golf bag, and took her shot. The ball curved more dramatically than she'd anticipated, but still stopped near the hole, which sported a bright red flag.

"Nice shot, bunny," Brandon said. "Go ahead and hit it in."

After removing the flag, she did so, surprised the putt actually resulted in success since she was thinking much more about sex than golf. Like she wished Brandon was.

So she decided it was time for drastic measures. *No hesitation.*

As Brandon carefully sized up his putt, she scanned the area once more to make sure they were totally alone—then she took her top off and tossed it on the grass. Her bra followed, leaving her bared from the waist up in the hot sun.

This Brandon finally noticed. She'd never seen his eyes go so wide—as big and round as . . . golf balls. "What the *hell*?" he asked.

Wendy felt utterly wanton in a whole new way to be topless in broad daylight, wearing only a tiny skirt and tennis shoes—especially in a venue often viewed as being serious and sophisticated. A glance down revealed her nipples to be fully erect, pink and stiff in the bright sun. Before answering Brandon, she walked calmly to the hole and sat down—her legs spread around it in a wide V. "Thought I'd give you something fun to aim for."

Finally, she saw the light of lust in his eyes. "I'm supposed to be able to focus with you sitting there looking so fucking naughty?"

She blinked innocently, playfully, feeling all the more shameless. "Well, if you can't focus on your game, try focusing on *this*." Then she reached down to lift her skirt, knowing she surely created the most obscene sight ever to be witnessed on this course.

"Jesus God," he murmured, his eyes dropping between her legs, and she knew she finally had him where she wanted him. He stood gaping at her, his putter dangling limply from one hand. "Where on earth are your panties?"

"I took them off in the dressing room."

His jaw dropped. "So you've been naked under your skirt the whole time we've been out here?"

She simply nodded, appreciating the escalating heat in his expression. "Now," she said, smiling, "aim for my pussy."

His mouth went slack. "It looks wet."

She licked her lips. "It's drenched for you."

"Shit," he muttered.

And again she said, "Make your putt. Aim for *my* hole."

They were both perspiring already, but she could have sworn he started to sweat more heavily.

Giving her another look laced with hunger, Brandon positioned his club, then putted the ball. Both watched as it rolled across the green, curving less than hers had, heading straight for the hole—and falling neatly in, directly between her legs.

"Damn," he whispered, shaking his head in clear disbelief. But his eyes stayed trained on the juncture of her thighs.

"Come get it," she said, her voice raspy with desire—and not specifying whether she meant his ball or her cunt.

And he didn't ask. Just dropped his putter and strode toward her.

A second later, he went to his knees and then all the way down onto his stomach, bending low across hole seven to drag his tongue up her pink center.

She moaned and leaned back on her elbows, lifting slightly and watching as Brandon licked her again, and again, then used his tongue to simply massage her clit.

"Oh—oh God!" she cried out, but tried to keep it down in case anyone was within hearing distance. "Oh baby, that's so good," she told him. "Lick me."

Arching her back, she cupped her breasts in both hands and kneaded them, overwhelmed by how exciting it was to be mostly naked and having her pussy eaten right out under the clear blue sky. The beaming sun seemed to shine a spotlight on their sex—making it all the more raw and animalistic, and leaving her to realize that the dark of night, even in a lit room, somehow turned the act more shadowy and secretive. But there was nothing secret about *this*.

Within moments she was on the edge of ecstasy, soon toppling over, sobbing as the hot pulses of orgasm echoed through her blood, her muscles, her skin.

When it passed, Brandon rose back up to his knees, but everything in his demeanor had changed—he had suddenly transformed back to the more sexually commanding Brandon she'd come to know. "Get up," he told her, pushing to his feet himself.

After which he grabbed her wrist to pull her toward the golf cart, and for a second she wondered if they were going to leave without her top, which remained back on the green—but then he positioned her where he wanted her. He faced her toward the cart's side and placed her hands on the bars that connected to its roof. "Hold on," he said. And without preamble, he planted his hands on her hips and plunged his cock inside her.

"Ohhh!" she moaned at the deep impact.

God, she hadn't even known he'd unzipped his pants yet!

But apparently he'd managed it one-handed on the way across the green. Now, this quickly, he was filling her with his tremendous erection, so big and hard that when she closed her eyes she saw a kaleidoscope of colors dancing in her head.

He rammed into her in unforgiving strokes, and now she couldn't *help* crying out, regardless of anyone hearing. "Unh! Unh!" Each rough stroke battered her whole body in a most exquisite way. Her tits bounced and her flesh quivered. She arched her ass toward him, thinking, *Yes, oh yes.* This was more than she could have hoped for a nasty golf excursion. It had been difficult to get him here, but now he seemed committed to fucking her like crazy.

Soon enough, he resumed one of their favorite little games, smacking her ass as he pounded into her tender flesh. Oh God, she loved it—it took the most pleasurable sensations of sex and . . . somehow added to them.

"Oh yes, spank me," she said. "I've been a very naughty girl today."

"Hell yeah, you have," he growled, and brought his palm down still harder on her ass.

It went on until Wendy could no longer think straight, until her legs nearly collapsed beneath her—until finally Brandon rasped, "God, *now*," and drove into her with four brutal strokes that made her feel positively impaled.

When it was over, his arms closed around her bare waist and she could hear nothing but the sound of their heavy breathing.

Finally, she turned in his arms, amazed at how comfortable she'd become with nudity. "Did you like that?" she whispered up to him with a hopeful smile.

He nodded and gave her his wicked Brandon grin. "I can't wait to see what you've got planned for holes eight and nine."

. . .

Later that afternoon, after changing back into her more practical shorts—*with* panties—Wendy rented a bike, deciding that
would be a good way to check out some of the resort's other
sport facilities. It was even hotter than this morning, but she
was diligent about her work—usually much more diligent than
she'd been on this trip so far, given certain distractions—and
she considered herself tough enough to stand up to a little
heat. So she wore sunscreen, drank lots of water, and stopped
from time to time to pull her journal from her purse to make
notes.

*Tennis courts are pristine, but basketball courts look a little
run-down. Some landscaping around the court would make it
more appealing, from both inside and out.*

*The mini-golf course looks fun and unique—but some
greens are littered with leaves and other debris. Must keep
clean! At $10 a pop, people don't want to have to clear leaves
off the green before they can putt.*

Of course, it was hard to explore the mini-golf greens without being reminded that just a few hours ago, she'd been mostly
naked on a real golf green. Now, back in her more practical
work mode, it seemed unbelievable, like something she might
have dreamed, one of her naughty nighttime fantasies.

After her last official stop, she did some thinking and made
another work note in her journal.

*What if we included some freebies with a three-night stay or
longer? Free bike rentals, a free hour of tennis.*

She knew it was too hot to be playing tennis or basketball right now, but she still couldn't help thinking the facilities appeared underused.

> *If someone has a chance to try something for free, they might enjoy it and be willing to <u>pay</u> for it the next day. They might tell their friends that such perks make this a great place to stay, worth the upscale price.*
>
> *And if other patrons see the facilities being used, it will naturally spur them to consider a round of tennis or shuffleboard, too.*
>
> *There are a million places for people to go on vacation, and this one is fairly unique, but we have to give people <u>perks</u>, too—extra incentives to choose Emerald Shores.*

It was only as she read back over the note that she realized she'd started saying "we," as if she, or Walter, had already invested in the resort.

Which meant she must be planning to recommend that Walter invest.

The truth was, despite the flaws she kept finding, she did consider the resort a self-contained paradise. Brandon had once called it Disney World at the beach and she thought the description apt. She couldn't think of any reason *not* to give Emerald Shores her endorsement.

And *that* meant . . . Well, it meant Brandon would now become a fixture in her life. A *distant* fixture, but a fixture just the same.

All the more reason to persist in living out her sex fantasies with him and *nothing more*. After all, she couldn't take back the riotous sex they'd had. But she could make sure that was *all* they shared, which would make leaving in a couple of days easier. If they had occasion to deal with each other on work in the future, it would make that easier, too.

As she rode along the winding, well-manicured bike path, feeling stuck somewhere between "normal her" and "wild her," she couldn't believe what a difference a few days had made. A few days ago, it had taken all her courage to buy a sexy bikini. Now she was taking her clothes off on a golf course like she'd been doing it her whole life.

Familiar questions ran through her mind. *At what point do you become the person you're pretending to be? When is it real? Where is the line between the old you and the you you've become?*

The lines between good girl and bad girl had grown more and more blurred because she felt so nasty bad with Brandon, like she could be an utter slut if that was what moved her, and yet when it was done, she was still *her.* She was still a person who enjoyed crunching numbers and going to her nieces' ballet recitals and watching gooey chick flicks.

How was it even conceivable that the same person had begged to have one man's cock in her cunt and another in her mouth at the same time? She shook her head at the sheer inanity of it.

And for the first time it occurred to her, maybe White Bikini Babe was the same way.

Maybe she could fuck indiscriminately and at the same time enjoy children and work hard at her job.

Maybe the only difference between her and Wendy was that White Bikini Babe was so comfortable with herself that she didn't even *think* about all this stuff, didn't bother to analyze it—and that made Wendy decide maybe she should quit analyzing it, too . . . and just live.

She wore more yellow lingerie—tonight's selection had come from her first Emerald Shores shopping trip, at the Beach Bazaar, and consisted of a sexy yellow demi-bra and matching thong with scalloped edging and lacy trim. It was delicate and pretty and possibly too flimsy to qualify as real underwear—but given that she knew she'd eventually end up having sex with Brandon tonight, that hardly mattered.

Over it, she dressed simply: dark jeans and an embroidered, formfitting tank. She'd chosen the clothes with Pete's date in mind—she wanted to look stylish, but not overtly sexy, just in case the guys were wrong about the girl's reaction to her presence. Especially since she also had no idea if Pete would tell the girl what had happened last night. He probably wouldn't, but they'd said she was a party girl and that she and Pete were totally casual, so who knew? All in all, she felt uneasy, like she was entering a situation with a lot of unknowns, so she didn't want to be *too* anything: too sexy or too threatening—too boring or too dowdy.

Mostly she just hoped she was overworrying it. And since she'd told herself earlier that she should quit analyzing everything, she tried to stop. She tried to think about afterward, when she would be alone with Brandon. When she counted it up, she realized it would be their fourth amazing night together.

When Brandon picked her up, this time it wasn't in a golf cart but a shiny black Mercedes-Benz convertible that nearly made her heart stop when she saw it. She still wasn't used to quite how rich her lover was.

The breeze felt good as they drove, yet as they turned out onto the crowded, busy highway that ran parallel to the ocean, she realized this was the first time she'd left the Emerald Shores property since arriving—and it felt strange to suddenly see things she'd temporarily forgotten existed: quickie marts, fast food, billboards. It somehow made her time with Brandon seem all the more *real*—and *shocking*. This wasn't just some incredible and really *long* dream about paradise—they were in the real world together, now navigating the traffic to Pete's house in nearby beach town Destin.

The truth was, the return to real life—gas stations, strip malls, red lights—was downright jarring. *But you'd better get used to reality, babe, because it's coming.* She was going home the day after tomorrow. Which she and Brandon had not discussed, but surely he knew since they had another business meeting scheduled to wrap up their talks on the morning of her departure. She saw no *point* in discussing it, either. Because this was *fun, sex*, and it was *easy*—and she intended to keep it that way.

Despite her internal warning about getting ready for real life again, she felt her whole body relax when Brandon turned left at a light—into the most pristine seaside community she'd ever seen. The streets were paved with red bricks in a zigzag design, and on either side set perfect little two-story homes painted shell pink, sunshine yellow, and sea green. White picket fences framed each small, well-tended yard, each blooming with bright flowers and sporting small palm trees.

"Did I just die and go to subdivision heaven?" she asked.

Brandon slanted a smile in her direction. "I'm sure that's exactly what the developers had in mind."

"I bet these houses cost a mint."

"I told you—Pete's place is a mini-mansion. These aren't huge homes, but they have every amenity you could want, right down to the marble floors and beveled glass doors." Then he pointed ahead down the long street. "And the beach is right there, close enough to walk."

Of course, by the time they parked in Pete's driveway before a peach-colored house with gables and lots of white trim, she was nervous again. About the whole thing. It was one thing to have a three way with your lover's friend; it was another to have dinner with him and his date the next night like everything was perfectly normal.

But stop this, she scolded herself as they walked to the door. *Be White Bikini Babe. Quit the damn worrying and analyzing. Get back to the fantasy.* Maybe that brisk drive back through the real world had *shaken* her from the fantasy. Or maybe it was the natural result of spending so much time with her fantasy *man.* How long could you live the fantasy before it ceased *feeling* like a fantasy?

When Pete opened the door, his smile held a hint of flirtation, but no more than usual. He said, "Hey, bud—come on in," to Brandon, then placed his hand warmly at Wendy's waist to give her a kiss on the cheek. Despite herself, her pussy surged with moisture. But maybe that was good—if her cunt tingled, maybe it meant she was getting over her jitters.

Wendy noticed immediately that neither guy acted remotely weird toward the other over what had happened last night—she supposed guys could do that. Or maybe it was just part of this whole casual-sex lifestyle that she'd never been a part of before.

"I just started the grill," Pete said, "and Stacy's out back. We're drinking chardonnay, but I've got about anything you want."

Both assured Pete that chardonnay was fine, and he ushered them through the house toward the French doors in back—as Wendy caught glimpses of the home's interior which struck her as fresh and bright and surprisingly tidy for a "beach bum."

The double doors opened onto a vast patio sporting a slat-roofed tiki-hut bar, a kidney-shaped pool, and a hot tub, all circled by a tall white privacy fence. Low music vied with the sizzle of the elaborate grill, and a salty sea breeze wafted through the air. Dusk was falling, but tiki torches lined the perimeter of the pool, their glow making the area feel somehow primitive but luxurious.

Note to self: Add suggestion of tiki torches in key resort areas. Her evenings with Brandon were the only time she didn't keep her journal with her, so she'd have to write that down later.

"Hey, Stace, what's up?" Brandon asked, drawing Wendy's attention to the dark-haired beauty exiting the shadows of the tiki hut to greet them.

And as the shapely girl gave Brandon a hug, Wendy realized that this wasn't just any girl—this was the girl she'd met at the Beach Bazaar! They recognized each other at the same time, but Wendy knew she was the more shocked of the two.

"Wait a minute," Stacy said to her, pulling out of Brandon's embrace. "You bought some great stuff from me a few days ago, didn't you?" She plastered on a pretty smile, reminding Wendy of how sexy she'd thought Stacy was. And possibly flirtatious?

"That's me," was all Wendy managed to say.

"Let me see if I remember. A sexy tangerine dress, some naughty lingerie, and that *hot* bikini that looked so killer on you."

"Right again." Wendy succeeded in smiling back now, but

still struggled to get over the surprise. And the memory: She'd wondered if the girl was subtly inviting her to fool around, and she'd briefly wondered what that would be like.

Stacy looked back and forth between Wendy and Brandon, her expression sly. "It looks like that bikini did its job."

"You could, um, say that," Wendy replied, and when Brandon cast a questioning look, she saw no reason not to be honest. "The first time I met Stacy, I was shopping for some things that might, uh, garner some interest from guys. Like you."

"Ah," he said, leaning his head back in understanding. "Well, she's right—they definitely worked. And that orange dress . . . mmm, bunny. The moment I saw you, I wanted you out of it."

Wendy's breasts tingled with fresh lust as Stacy nodded knowingly. "I *knew* that dress was fabulous on you."

"Although it's . . . seen better days now," Wendy confessed.

"Oh?" Stacy asked.

"It, uh, got a little sandy the night I met Brandon."

Apparently it was obvious *how* it had gotten sandy, since Stacy broke out into a laugh and Wendy and Brandon joined her. And that quickly, Wendy really *did* quit being nervous. Stacy clearly liked her, and Wendy could feel how truly easygoing she was, just as the guys had promised.

It was then that Stacy took her hand. "Come with me and I'll get you some wine. We can dish while the guys man the grill."

"All right," Wendy said—not that she had much of a choice since Stacy was already pulling her away from Brandon. She simply waved bye to him with a grin, then let her new friend lead her into the tiki hut.

As promised, Stacy poured Wendy a glass of chardonnay

from an open bottle, then said, wide-eyed and cheerful, "So you went fishing for a guy and reeled in Brandon Worth. What a catch."

The phrase instantly sent Wendy into defensive mode. "Well, I wouldn't say I *caught* him. Not to keep anyway. But we've certainly had fun the past few nights."

"In the sand," Stacy confirmed. "And lots of other places, too, I'm betting."

Again, Wendy wondered if Stacy knew about their three way with Pete. "It's been . . . the most sexually liberating week of my life."

Stacy bit her lip and leaned closer, giving Wendy a clear shot of cleavage down her low-cut cami. "Tell me everything."

Nope, no way. Wendy needed to do a *different* kind of fishing first. "I'd . . . rather hear about you and Pete. You've known each other a long time?"

Stacy nodded, sipping her wine. "Practically forever. He's hot as hell, and a great fuck, so we were talking a week or so ago and decided maybe we should actually try going on a date or two *before* fucking to see if we really like each other or something.

"But Pete's a pretty confirmed bachelor, and I'm only twenty-six, so I'm not looking for anything serious, either—especially since I happen to live in a smorgasbord of hot, rich men, you know? So . . . we're trying out the dating thing for fun—but mostly, I think it'll still be about fucking."

She laughed when she was done, then added, "You probably think I'm awful. You don't even know me, and all I can talk about is sex. I hold *this* responsible." She pointed to the nearly empty bottle of chardonnay on the rustic wooden bar.

"No," Wendy quickly assured her. "I actually . . . think

you're great." And she did. She'd never be as open about sex as Stacy, especially not with strangers, but given the sensual freedom she'd experienced this week, she could appreciate Stacy's bluntness. "And . . . Pete's great, too." She wasn't sure why she added that last part. She mainly needed something else to say. So she looked away, toward the grill, where the guys stood—and then dropped her gaze to the patio.

Stacy still stood close in the shadowy air and Wendy could smell her flowery perfume, the scent light and pretty. Stacy's small hand closed gently around her wrist. "Wait," she whispered, as if she'd just figured something out. "Did you do them *both*?"

Oh God, how had she given it away? Just by mentioning Pete's name? Wendy felt her eyes go wide, but had no idea how to answer.

Obviously seeing her alarm, Stacy said, "Hey, no worries if you fucked Pete. We're totally free agents, and I'm well aware that he and Brandon share sometimes."

At this, Wendy managed to spit out an "Oh." She wasn't surprised to hear about the "sharing" between the two guys. But she *was* surprised that hearing it made her stomach pinch—just a little.

Because she couldn't be jealous of anything Brandon had done before her. Or would do after her. She was living in the moment here—that was all. He was a catch, but she'd have to toss him back very soon.

"So was it good?" Stacy asked, leaning even closer. The back of her hand, where she still clutched Wendy's wrist, brushed Wendy's breast, bringing her mind—and her body—back to the present conversation. Her chest tingled.

She sucked in her breath—then admitted the truth. "It was

mind-blowing. I'd never done anything like that before, and it was . . . amazing."

Stacy replied matter-of-factly. "Yeah, two cocks can really rock your world."

And something in Wendy tensed, although she tried to sound natural. "Have you . . . with Pete and Brandon?"

Stacy shook her head. "Oh—no. Not that I wouldn't. But things just haven't gone that way. And just between you and me, if I was gonna have a three way with Pete, well . . . I've kind of been more into girls lately." Then she glanced down at the wine bottle. "I'm gonna go get some more chardonnay."

With that, she picked up her wineglass and strode from the tiki hut, leaving Wendy to watch the sway of her round ass within a snug pair of jeans as she headed inside.

As the door closed behind her, Wendy's pussy quivered.

Dinner was grilled salmon with a side salad, green beans, and herb-roasted potatoes that convinced Wendy that Pete had been a chef in a former life. "If the parasailing gig ever fizzles, you've got a great fallback position," Wendy assured him from across the patio table.

He shrugged. "My mom is a great cook, so it comes kinda natural. But I could never work in a restaurant—unless maybe it was on the beach," he added with his usual hot beach-bum grin.

Dinner also came with lots of wine. Wendy lost count of how many bottles they opened, but she knew they were going through it fast. The chardonnay went down easy with the fish— and it also relieved her uneasiness about her physical reaction to what Stacy had said about being into girls.

Besides, that doesn't mean she's into you. It just means whatever vibe you picked up on when you first met was correct. No biggie. Especially in this world where everyone seemed to be fucking everyone else without a care.

So Wendy forgot all about it as they ate and talked and laughed. They explained to the guys about their previous meeting, and that led everyone at the table to sharing how *they* had met.

Pete had first gotten acquainted with Stacy when she was waiting tables at a local restaurant; now she managed the Beach Bazaar and hoped to have her own boutique someday. Brandon had met Stacy when Pete had brought her to a party at Brandon's penthouse condo a few years ago. And Pete and Brandon both relayed the story of *their* very first meeting while working on the beach in college, although they both remembered it differently—mainly, Brandon said Pete was a lot cleaner cut in those days, just then getting out from under his father's military thumb, and Pete claimed the opposite, that Brandon had been *less* clean cut, with longer hair. To wrap up the conversation, Wendy explained how she'd met Brandon at Volcano's when he'd offered her that elevator ride. The elevator ride that had changed her life. Although she left that part out.

As Pete drained another bottle by emptying the last of the wine into the two girls' glasses, he said, "Bad news. That's it. We've gone through every bottle of chardonnay in the house. But we can switch to red if you want. Or mixed drinks."

Wendy decided to use it as an opportunity to hint at ending the evening. It had been fun, but . . . "Remember, some of us have to work tomorrow. As it is, I'll be lucky if I don't have a hangover."

"Good point," Brandon said, then motioned to their dinner companions. "These two don't have early-morning jobs, so they get to sleep in. Then again"—he grinned toward Wendy— "maybe you should sleep in, too. The later you get up, the less you can find to pick on at the resort."

Wendy's reason for being at Emerald Shores had come up earlier, so she replied simply by casting a teasing smirk in his direction.

"I say we all get in the hot tub," Stacy suggested merrily.

Wendy felt her eyes widen at the unexpected suggestion— before declining. "I can't—I didn't bring a swimsuit."

Yet it was just as the words left her lips that she remembered who she was with here—two guys who'd already seen her naked and a girl who probably wouldn't mind. Undaunted, Stacy said, "Me neither—we'll just strip down to our underwear."

Wendy hid her sigh. There were so many reasons to say no. For some reason—maybe Stacy's youth, her exuberance— Wendy had reverted back to feeling mature and responsible here, remembering she had a job to finish. And maybe she'd had so many new sexual experiences that it felt like enough now. All she really wanted to do was go back to the resort and get into Brandon's pants. She wanted to have hot-but-easy sex with a guy she'd grown comfortable with.

But then she remembered.

In a couple of days this week would be over, along with all the sex.

It would be like waking up from a dream you couldn't go back to.

And Stacy was so young and pretty that, despite herself, Wendy didn't want to feel like the boring grown-up who ended everyone's fun.

So she asked herself one simple question: What would White Bikini Babe do? Then she said, "All right. Sounds fun."

And once she'd said it, once she'd allowed herself to slip back into that I-want-all-the-new-experiences-I-can-get mindset, it *did* sound fun. Sexy. Naughty. And she was pretty sure her nipples were already hard as she stood up and crossed her arms over her body, easily removing her tank top over her head to reveal the delicate pastel bra underneath.

*I*f you close your eyes and someone touches you, they could be a boy or a girl, fat or thin, black or white, ugly or beautiful, and you would never know. The pleasure would be the same. Pleasure is pleasure is pleasure.

Chapter 11

Wendy had just started wondering if her nipples were poking through her bra for all to see when, to her left, Stacy let out a sexy sigh of awe. "So pretty," she said, and Wendy found Stacy's gaze resting on her boobs. "That bra was *made* for you."

She couldn't help glancing down at herself, and being reminded that despite being thin the bra provided good support, lifting her ample breasts high and leaving the top half on proud, curvy display.

"I have to agree," Brandon said with a sly grin—although when Wendy met his gaze, she couldn't quite read it. *Has he noticed Stacy flirting with me? Does it turn him on? Does it turn* me *on?*

The truth was, she already knew the answer to the last question. But was she going to act on it? Was Stacy?

The questions made her glad she'd drunk so much wine. As was often the case, standing up made her feel much more intoxicated than she had sitting down. Pleasantly so. Like maybe the questions weren't all that important. Like maybe she would just go with the flow. Like she kept telling herself to do. Like White Bikini Babe would.

"Your turn," she said to Stacy. Yikes—where had *that* come from? The wine, obviously. And—yes, the sudden anticipation.

The sudden *go with the flow* feeling that had just washed back over her like a wild ocean wave.

Stacy smiled sexily in response, then removed her lace-trimmed cami over her head to reveal a tight leopard-print bra underneath.

"Nice," Wendy said. She'd known the gorgeous Asian girl would have spectacular breasts, and she did—as big or bigger than Wendy's, they arced enticingly upward from the clingy fabric.

Biting her lip, Wendy then unbuttoned and unzipped her jeans. Kicking off her beaded flip-flops, she didn't hesitate to push the jeans down and step out of them, showing off her flimsy matching thong, so small it barely covered the patch of pubic hair that remained above her slit.

"Shit, honey," Pete said in admiration, and she realized that both guys still sat, fully clothed at the table, watching the show.

"Aren't you boys getting undressed, too?" she prodded flirtatiously.

Brandon's eyes gleamed, his chin propped arrogantly atop his fist. "It's more fun watching *you two* get undressed."

Wendy pointed at him playfully. "Get that shirt off, buddy. Pants, too. Show me those silk boxers."

Meanwhile, Stacy was slinking out of her jeans, as well. "Oooh, silk boxers. I can't wait."

Pete looked teasingly affronted. "Don't tell me you don't like my plain white undies, babe?" Wendy had noticed last night that he was a boxer-brief man, which suited him well.

Stacy smiled. "I love your undies, Pete. And I love what's inside of them even more."

"That's better," Pete said, pushing to his feet and starting to shed his clothes. Brandon followed.

But Wendy's attention was drawn back to Stacy when she said, "God, I can't get over how incredible your tits are."

The compliment warmed Wendy's pussy—and made her gaze drop to see what kind of panties Stacy wore. Black lace boy shorts that hugged her slender hips perfectly. "*Your* body is pretty freaking hot, too," she heard herself say, and realized she was studying it unabashedly, the same way a guy would.

Raising her gaze back to Stacy's face, Wendy found her looking mischievous, and sexy as hell—until she grabbed Wendy's hand. "Come on—let's get in. I'm tired of waiting for these guys."

And like that, they scampered hand in hand across the patio toward the hot tub—but of course, they had to slow down in order to ease into the hot, bubbling water.

Once they sat next to each other in the big round tub, the first thing Wendy noticed was that the water, lapping and frothing around her tits, left the pale yellow fabric transparent—the dark peaks of her pointed nipples shone clearly through. Given that she was already aroused, the tumultuous water buffeting her breasts instantly made them tingle.

The second thing she noticed was how close she'd ended up to Stacy—despite ample room in the hot tub, their thighs pressed together beneath the water's surface. They were wearing so little that it made her cunt feel heavy, swollen.

Almost as if reading Wendy's mind, Stacy turned to her in the hot tub, easing her palm across Wendy's stomach beneath the bubbling waves until it curved around her waist—then she slid her small hand smoothly up to the side of Wendy's wet, oh-so-sensitive breast.

Wendy sucked in her breath but didn't protest.

And Stacy smiled into her eyes. "Play with me," she said, soft, naughty, inviting.

The touch of another woman was so startlingly gentle, even in the roiling hot tub, that Wendy's pussy wept uncontrollably and she never even thought of saying no. Maybe she'd wanted to experiment with another girl since that first moment she'd met Stacy. Or maybe she'd been methodically seduced tonight by a pretty young girl. But either way, she felt drunk on more than the wine and suddenly wanted to experience more of this female softness—so she answered by easing her hand onto Stacy's thigh, then following her instincts, sliding it smoothly inward, where her legs met.

Stacy sighed, then smiled again, her eyes gone a little glassy now. "Sit on my lap," she said. "Straddle me."

Wendy thought about admitting that she'd never fooled around with a girl before, but she stopped herself. She was tired of it being so clear to her partners that she was new at particular sex acts—she just wanted to do this, without talking about it, without weighing it, without thinking. She just wanted to experience Stacy's sexy body, and she wanted Stacy to experience hers.

So, carefully pushing up on her knees, she lifted one leg over Stacy's lap, until she settled on her new girlfriend's thighs. The move crushed their bodies together; their tits met instantly and both emitted small sounds of pleasure.

Oh God, so soft. Soft like her. Wendy bit her lip and swayed her boobs against Stacy's once more, deliberately. Even through their bras, Stacy's hardened nipples abraded Wendy's flesh, practically making Wendy shiver despite the warmth of the hot tub.

"*Mmm*, I have to touch these gorgeous tits," Stacy practically purred, then lifted her hands from Wendy's hips to her breasts, beginning to massage her in the water.

Wendy followed suit, unable to help herself—the move came naturally. Her hands closed around Stacy's large breasts, and she stroked her thumbs over the turgid peaks, then found herself lightly pinching, squeezing them between forefinger and thumb.

"Oooh, you're such a bad girl," Stacy cooed. "Aren't you, baby?"

Wendy sighed, getting lost in the strange, soft, new pleasure of being with another girl. "Oh, yes, so bad." Finally, someone who wasn't so difficult to convince.

"That's so fucking hot, girls."

Wendy looked up at the sound of Pete's voice to find both guys, now stripped down to their underwear, but they each perched on the edge of nearby lounge chairs, still looking far more interested in watching than in coming into the hot tub. Every inch of Wendy's flesh hummed with this new, strange, he-donistic pleasure, but she found herself going still—in order to meet Brandon's gaze. She supposed she just wanted to make sure he liked what he saw. Because "playing" with Stacy had her body wired, excited, and ready for more—but if Brandon wasn't as turned on by it as she was, that would somehow ruin it for her.

His blue eyes glimmered darkly in the torchlight. His expression was serious, but his focus on the two girls intense. "Keep going, bunny," he said, low, deep. And then she could feel it. His arousal. It was almost as if it now oozed off him over the patio and seeped into her.

And it fueled her. It fueled her like she couldn't have imagined. Finding out—*feeling*—that Brandon took pleasure from watching her with Stacy made her bolder, hungrier, ready to truly, *truly*, go with the flow.

She kept her eyes on him only a few seconds more until her own voice came just as low. "Watch me," she said. Then she turned back to Stacy and gave her a long, slow tongue kiss.

The move was spontaneous—simply what her body told her to do. But Stacy responded in kind, and Wendy had never experienced anything like kissing a woman before. It was—again—like kissing . . . herself. Soft, light, delicate, sweet. As their lips and tongues played together, her cunt pulsed, and stark pleasure echoed through her breasts as Stacy continued squeezing, kneading, toying with her beaded nipples.

Both girls breathed heavy, and like so many times before on this trip, Wendy ceased thinking and simply basked in the joy of being a free spirit who soaked up pleasure like a sponge.

"I need more of these sweet tits, baby," Stacy rasped. Then, after a prolonged pinch of Wendy's nipples that made her hiss with the pleasure-pain of it, Stacy reached up to push Wendy's bra straps off her shoulders, which made her heavy breasts tumble free.

Wendy groaned with the rush of moisture that resulted from having her tits put on display for all of them, and Stacy moaned at the sight—just before bending to rake her tongue over one already wet, shiny nipple.

Wendy sucked in her breath—oh God, *yes*! Despite the temperature of the water, she *did* shiver in delight now, watching excitedly as Stacy drew the full tip of her breast into her mouth.

That was when things ceased being entirely soft—everything that came after was a strange mix of female softness and hard passion. Stacy's intense suckling shot straight between Wendy's legs and made her begin to undulate, rubbing her pussy against Stacy under the water.

"Ooooh," Stacy moaned, releasing Wendy's tit for only a second to shut her eyes in pleasure—but then she began sucking on the other one and at the same time parted her legs, just enough that Wendy sank down slightly between them.

Oh God, she immediately understood the move—the shift brought their clits directly together. Pressing, grinding instinctively, she thought Stacy's pussy felt as swollen as her own. Was it possible, even in the bubbling hot tub, that their cunts could be a few degrees hotter than anything else around them?

As they moved together, both girls panted and sighed. At moments, Wendy almost forgot Pete and Brandon were watching, but then one of them would groan or say how hot they were together, and she would bask anew in the pleasure of arousing Brandon with one more hedonistic exhibition.

Wendy was breathing heavily when she managed to say to Stacy, "Need *your* bra off, too."

Stacy leaned up just enough to reach behind her and undo the hook. A second later, she flung the animal-print bra up on the patio behind her, and Wendy's hungry gaze dropped to the pair of big, beautiful breasts that seemed to almost float on the surface of the rolling water.

She took reckless joy in capturing Stacy's bared tits in both hands—exploring their softness, their weight, the beaded nipples darker in color than her own. She pinched them, twirled them, then caressed and kneaded with abandon, no longer shy. And even though it brought her face down almost to the water's surface, she lifted one gorgeous tit in her hand and flicked her tongue across the beautifully hard peak and loved Stacy's little whimper of pleasure.

Then she did it again, again, relishing the strange new feel of another girl's engorged nipple on her tongue—somehow soft but amazingly hard at the same time. Finally, she sucked on it, drawing deep, not being gentle, making sure Stacy felt it all the way through her. Her girlfriend's mewls of pleasure were more satisfying than she could easily understand.

Finally, she sat back upright, her body urging her to resume the glorious thrusting of their pussies. They moved together, flesh pressing into flesh, both of them getting hotter and hotter. The presence of their panties didn't get in the way—if anything, it only heightened the friction. They panted as they writhed like sensual serpents rising from the water, and their bared breasts bumped and swayed together, delivering still more naughty delight.

"Oh God, oh God," she heard herself say as the pulsing pleasure built within her cunt—and beneath her, Stacy was practically sobbing.

"Such a nasty little slut," Stacy started saying with an unmistakably lust-filled smile. "Rub that dirty pussy on me."

For half a second, Wendy was stunned. But then, to her surprise, she was excited. She wasn't sure she'd have been into it if a *guy* had said that to her, but with a *girl*, it was instantly different. They were being sluts for each other, and for the guys, and they knew it, and it only made the sex hotter.

"*Mmm*, God," Wendy said, then, "Yes, baby, oh yeah. You're a hot little slut, too, with such a soft, sweet pussy."

She almost couldn't believe such words had left her, but she had no time to think about it because that was when Stacy said,

"Oh God, I'm gonna come! I'm coming!" and she pumped hard against Wendy's cunt, and Wendy continued to move against her—*yes, yes*—until hearing Stacy's cries of orgasm took her there, too.

Wendy moaned her pleasure up into the night, her body still rocking against Stacy's, their curves meeting, colliding, both of them sobbing in ecstasy. Even to her own ears, she found it more exciting to hear two feminine voices climaxing than just one.

Still straddling Stacy, she began to come down, to catch her breath. A quick glance at the guys found Pete with his long, stiff cock out—he stroked it in his hand as he watched them. Brandon's stayed inside his underwear, but she could see even in the shadowy night that he sported a full erection that appeared ready to burst free at any moment.

And she thought—vaguely, for she was still in that in-between place of recovery—that maybe she would go to him now, because his hard-on beckoned her, and now that she'd had the utter softness of a woman, she wanted the demanding hardness of a man. Yet then Stacy said, "I want to lick your pussy so bad."

In a mere second, it was almost as if she had never even come, since she was already excited again. More with the idea than anything else. More with the vision in her head: Stacy's head between her parted legs while Brandon watched.

No hesitation. She rose up on the hot tub's seat, then reached for one of the big, plush rolled-up towels in a basket nearby. She spread the thick white towel out at the tub's edge, sitting down on it, her feet still immersed—then she lay back, propping herself slightly on her elbows.

Stacy remained in the water and when their eyes met, Wendy

licked her upper lip: an invitation—which Stacy took. Rising to her knees on the seat, she bent forward and reached for Wendy's soaked panties, slipping her soft fingers in the elastic at Wendy's hips. Wendy lifted her ass and let Stacy peel them down, over her thighs, knees—until finally she tossed them aside, near where her bra had landed.

Stacy didn't have to ask Wendy to part her bent knees—and when she did, pretty Stacy appeared between them, the ends of her dark hair wet now, her almond-shaped eyes shaded with anticipation.

Wendy spread wider, wider, pleased to put her cunt on display. "Pretty pussy," Stacy said, then stroked her middle finger across Wendy's swollen clit, as if petting it.

The pleasure made Wendy lie back completely, too weak to stay propped up. But she could still glance down and see Stacy's head dipping, lower, lower, until her tongue raked firmly over the hot, swollen nub, moisture meeting moisture.

Wendy gasped—both at the sight and the sensation. It felt the same as usual, but it looked so different—wild, arousing, forbidden—to see gorgeous female eyes between her thighs staring back. "Yes," she whispered. "Lick me."

After which Stacy began dragging her tongue upward through Wendy's open cunt—long, thorough licks—again and again.

Wendy moaned at each prolonged stroke, and her hands found their way to her tits, her bra still framing them. She massaged them in rhythm with Stacy's ministrations, and she listened to the guys sigh and groan almost as if it was *them* being pleasured.

At some point, Wendy closed her eyes. The visuals were exciting, but the sensations themselves defied description. The sensation of having her pussy eaten by a girl while the guys watched every second of it. Again she felt like Brandon's naughty porn star, every bit a bad girl, every iota of what she'd wanted to be when she'd first seen and envied the girl in the white bikini. And then some. Because in the beginning the ideas had been vague, the aspirations foggy. But this was real, real, real.

So real that the blood was gathering again in her clit.

So real that she was lifting her ass from the towel against Stacy's face.

So real that she was beginning to feel that hard, dirty feeling—that strange disregard for the person licking her, she only wanted to fuck Stacy's mouth until she came, regardless of whether Stacy wanted those hard pumps against her lips, her tongue.

But Stacy *met* Wendy's thrusts, and when Wendy began to moan, she realized hers were not the only hot sounds filling the air—her female lover was whimpering excitedly against her pussy.

I should have known Stacy would like it hard, would love having me drive my crotch into her face. That very thought—dirty and raw—was what pushed her over the abyss into another orgasm, this one longer, harder, harsher, making her crush the terry cloth at her sides in her fists, making her scream out into the night. She thrust, thrust, thrust at Stacy, the pleasure swirling through her like a hurricane—until finally it passed, and she could breathe again, she could rest again. She went still on the towel.

Then she came back to herself and, raising her head, bit her lip and gave Stacy a weakened smile through her still parted legs. Stacy's face was wet with Wendy's juices as she smiled back, then said, with some arrogance, "I made you come *hard*."

Wendy could barely speak. "Yes," she whispered.

And she was just on the verge of wondering: Was she supposed to return the favor? Was she supposed to eat Stacy now? And did she want to?—when Brandon rose from his chair and came to her. Standing over her, he said, his voice deep—and bossy again—"I have to fuck you." Then he bent and literally scooped her into his arms.

She forgot all about Stacy. Maybe that was wrong, horrible, but she did—because all she wanted now was Brandon.

He laid her—not particularly gently—in the lounge chair where he'd been sitting. She became vaguely aware that Pete was no longer in her line of vision—he must have gone to Stacy. Which suited her fine. Suddenly she wanted to be alone with her man. Well, as alone as possible given the circumstances. She didn't care if Pete and Stacy were still nearby, but suddenly, all she could think about was Brandon and his blue, blue eyes.

Of course, when he pushed down his underwear, she started thinking about his majestic cock, too. It stood ever-amazing and oh-so-rigid before her, and part of her still couldn't believe she managed to get *that* inside her, but another part of her wanted it so bad that she stopped thinking at all.

Except for spreading her legs wide for him.

Over the arms of the lounge chair.

It was a most inelegant position—but Brandon had taught her the joys of being sexually inelegant at times. Visions of spankings and sand-covered dresses and cucumbers wafted through her mind. Until, that is, her man straddled the chair and she saw his hard-on coming closer.

The position allowed them both to look down and see Brandon's sturdy shaft slide into her—and so smoothly now, too, as if her body had transformed to be the perfect glove for him. They both groaned at the slow, even entry, but neither said a word.

Both continued to watch the astounding way he slid in and out of her wetness, slow, steady, deep—until she grew aware of sounds besides their own, the sounds of Pete and Stacy fucking somewhere else on the patio.

When Wendy looked up to find Brandon's gaze on hers, it heightened her pleasure immeasurably. "You have the most beautiful blue eyes," she heard herself say.

A slow grin stole over his face as he continued gliding in and out, in and out. He spoke softly. "You're not supposed to be thinking about my eyes right now."

She smiled, too. "All right. You have the biggest, most amazing cock I've ever had."

"That's more like it," he said with a solemn nod.

She giggled softly and at some point simply closed her eyes, just like back on the towel, and soaked in the simple sexual joy and pleasure of the night. "Oh God, this is good," she told him, eyes still shut. "Fuck me. Keep fucking me."

Her pleas made him drive into her more roughly, and the hard pleasure forced her to bite her lip. When he did it, again, again, she couldn't stop a wicked grin from forming on her face. "I love being dirty for you," she purred up at him.

Then she opened her eyes long enough to see his eyes shining on her darkly. "You do it well, bunny. You get me so fucking hard. Keep massaging your tits for me. And tell me again what you want, baby. Tell me."

"*Fuck me,*" she said harshly. "Fuck me hard."

And then there were no more words, only the hard, fast, brutal plunges of Brandon's shaft into her ever-hungry cunt. His fists gripped the arms of the chair, near her thighs, and she continued to rub her breasts for him—and also for her.

He rammed into her, rocking her body, shaking her world—until finally he let out a groan that she knew signaled his orgasm. She braced for it, for those extra-hard thrusts, and met them even when they felt like his cock had rammed clear through her. "Yes, yes," she said, breathless, even though she hadn't come, because the way he fucked her brought enough rough pleasure regardless of orgasm.

Then he collapsed softly upon her, and her arms curled around his shoulders and his warmth encased her as she peered upward into the stars overhead.

I belong here.

She wasn't sure where those words came from, but they came. And she felt them.

Although she knew she *couldn't* feel them, knew it was *crazy*. She knew that in a little while she'd be okay again, her stronger self, the self that kept the emotions out of it. And it would all be fine—back to normal.

But for just a moment, she let herself keep exploring the heavens, let herself cling to him a little too tightly as his undeniable warmth cocooned her.

*I*n our culture, we are taught that it is wrong to have sex in public, to bring it out in public at all. It makes sense, because most of the time, in most circumstances, I don't care to be walking down the street forced to watch strangers indulging in sexual behavior, nor do I want my nieces to be exposed to such. Yet in learning that social value comes an associated sense of shame, the idea that sex is wrong. In a way either great or small, we are all taught to feel that. It seems an unavoidable consequence of our societal mores, a thing impossible to unlearn.

And yet, since I stepped onto these "emerald shores," that stigma has been lifted—it seems not to exist.

Possibly because I've not been caught having sex someplace I shouldn't.

Possibly because I've been so swept away in lust that I've chosen not to think about it.

But it has provided me some of the most glorious moments in my life.

When Brandon knelt over me on that patio, sliding in and out of me, nothing existed but pure pleasure. Nothing else. <u>Nothing else</u>. Not often in life does such magic come along.

So I held on to it too tightly for a moment. Both the unsullied pleasure part and the . . . well, the Brandon part. The *fact that I'm not sure I could be doing all these things with just any other guy. The fact that he has given me such liberating freedom, all without judgment, with nothing but respect.*

I held on to all that for a long moment—but it's okay. The moment ended, just as it had to, and I have my head on straight again. I know this has to end.

Chapter 12

As Brandon's convertible traveled Emerald Shores Boulevard, winding toward the ocean, he winked and said, "My place or yours, bunny?" After their ultra-arousing evening at Pete's place, he wasn't sure there'd be more sex, since it was late and they did both have work to do tomorrow, but he found himself wanting to sleep next to her. He was still adjusting to the strange new phenomenon, but he'd mostly given up fighting it, since he never exactly succeeded at that anyway.

Next to him, she hesitated. "I'm not sure."

His chest tightened just a little, but since he'd reached the turn-off to her building and had to make a decision, he swung the car onto Shellside Way, heading toward the collection of pink stucco buildings not far from his own. "What's wrong?" he asked. He sensed there was something she wasn't saying.

She turned to him, the breeze whipping through her hair and making her all the more beautiful. "It's not that anything's wrong—it's that . . . well, I'm leaving in a couple of days."

He was well aware of that. They hadn't discussed it, but he'd seen paperwork with her arrival and departure dates, and once he'd discovered the girl he was fucking was Gwendolyn Carnes, he'd found himself checking it again. "I know. And . . . ?"

She let out a sigh, her lips pursed uncomfortably as the car came to a stop in front of Shellside Tower I. "And . . . if you get in the habit of sleeping next to someone, when they're suddenly not there anymore, the bed can feel empty. If you don't get into that habit, though, you don't have to worry about it."

He leaned his head back in understanding. He didn't explain that he'd never actually shared a bed with a woman for more than a night, and that even the staying-over part was rare for him, but what she'd said made sense. "Good point," he said, trying to sound easy about it, like it was fine with him.

Then he gave her thigh a casual squeeze and changed the subject. "So what have you got going on tomorrow?"

"There are some outlying parts of the resort I still haven't seen, so I thought I'd visit some of those to wrap up my analysis of the place."

"If you need a golf cart to make getting around easier, I can put one at your disposal."

She smiled. "Thanks, but I think I'll bike. I did that this afternoon, and despite the heat, I enjoyed it."

He shrugged, grinned. "Whatever you like."

"Then, if you'll be in your office, I'll call you with my final suggestions on improvements."

"I'll be there," he said. "I have some meetings in the morning, but I'll be catching up on paperwork after that, and I'll let Joanna know I'm expecting your call. And then . . . well, tomorrow night's your last one here, so I'm hoping you'll spend it with *me*." He couldn't imagine not being with her again, one more time, before she left.

The smile that lit her face warmed his heart. "I think I could arrange that, Mr. CEO."

"Good," he said—but then it hit him. "Oh, shit."

"What?" She looked alarmed—and he *felt* alarmed.

"I just remembered I have a business dinner I can't get out of. I totally forgot about it until now, but it's with a major investor—he's coming into town specifically to meet with me and Charles over steaks." He stopped, sighed. "But . . . well, how about if we meet at the Shellside pool at ten? Is that too late?"

She looked doubtful. "It's not too late for *me*, but I happen to know the pool is *closed* at ten."

He raised his eyebrows playfully, devilishly. "That's the point."

"But we'll be breaking the rules."

"Bunny, I *make* the rules around here. Wear your bikini and come hungry."

With that, he leaned over, lifted his hand to her face, and gave her a warm, slow kiss good night. "By the way," he whispered, their faces close, "you and Stacy—that was fucking amazing." And he meant it. He'd known a lot of women in his years, but still, there was something about Wendy—her innocence, her wildness, the way they meshed—that made him crazy for her. Watching her go at it in the hot tub with Stacy had been everything from softly sensuous to deeply erotic to insanely nasty. He was getting hard again now, just thinking about it.

"I'm glad you liked it," she whispered back. "I wanted to excite you."

He felt the sentiment in his gut, supremely satisfied by it. But then he asked, "You liked it, too, though—right?"

She nodded, a slightly lascivious expression in her eyes. "Don't worry—I did it for me. But at the same time, I did it for you, too."

A small groan left him. "Baby, that's *so* hot. I love it."

They kissed again, their tongues twining, and Brandon was trying not to get too carried away, but that didn't keep his hand from creeping onto her lovely breast to squeeze and massage as the kisses deepened further.

When finally the kissing ended and they eased apart, their eyes stayed locked as she said, "Well . . . good night."

" 'Night, bunny," he said, giving her a little wink.

He watched her exit the car, shut the door, and walk toward the building, her ass swaying in those sexy blue jeans.

Letting out a sigh, he put the Mercedes in gear and started toward home.

And he'd just started picking up speed—when something inside him made him put on the brakes. An instinct, a need, something he couldn't quite define—but he didn't waste too much time trying. Instead, he threw the car in reverse and backed up the drive, pleased to see she'd just now reached the door and wasn't yet inside.

"Hey, bunny!" he called.

She looked up, clearly surprised, but then she smiled and started back up the stone pathway toward the car. "What is it?" she asked, getting closer.

He didn't beat around the bush, just smiled suavely. "I changed my mind."

"About?"

"Sleeping with you tonight. That stuff about the bed feeling empty is for the birds. I'll take my chances. Get in. I want to wrap around you and fall asleep together."

Was he mistaken or did her eyes light with romantic joy? He didn't know a lot about romance, but that was what he felt from her in that moment, and he supposed it pretty accurately described what had brought him backing his Benz up the drive.

She didn't answer—merely bit her lip, gave him a sensuous look that turned his dick still harder, then got back in the car.

I shouldn't have done it. I must be losing my mind. Or at least my grip on this situation.

Wendy berated herself silently as she biked across Emerald Shores the next day. She still couldn't believe she'd let Brandon talk her into going back to his place last night. After all, she'd been so strong, so rational—and she'd actually made it out of the car and all the way to the door, ignoring the way his heated kisses had burned through her and how those gorgeous blue eyes had borne down into her very soul.

Of course, sleeping next to him had been wonderful. They'd ended up having sex again, just natural, normal sex in his bed—she'd put on one of his T-shirts to sleep in, sans panties since hers were still wet, and more good night kisses had led to good night fucking and good night orgasms.

She sighed now as she steered her bicycle through a picturesque tunnel that led beneath the main boulevard to keep bikers from having to cross traffic. Her pussy warmed at the recollection, which made her both happy and sad. She was happy because it had been wonderful, and *he* was wonderful. But she was sad because she still couldn't let herself feel all lovey-dovey about him. She was leaving tomorrow and this would be over and tonight would be her last night with him—forever. She let out another sigh.

Oh, for God's sake, stop this. Don't be such a girl. Be White Bikini Babe—your inspiration, your idol. White Bikini Babe doesn't care about the last night with any guy, because for her sex is a lifestyle, and there will be more of it, and she will be in control of it. White Bikini Babe lives for pleasure and power. And this week, so do you.

To her surprise, the little pep talk actually helped. Maybe all it took was a reminder—okay, *constant* reminders—of what she'd wanted from this experiment in the first place. Once she refocused on that, she felt stronger, tougher, more like she had earlier in the week. She pedaled onward in her practical shorts and tennis shoes feeling, once again, like a woman with a secret. *Lots* of secrets. About cucumbers, and threesomes, and beach sex, and being with another girl.

There, that's better.

And when she passed a cute guy—probably in his late twenties, also on a bike—she followed her natural instinct to smile flirtatiously and earned a similar response. Even in her practical shorts.

Yes, that's much better.

Now, you have one more night with Brandon. Don't forget who you are. You are woman, hear you roar. You are a sex machine, a pleasure seeker, a hedonist. You are . . . Black Bikini Babe.

"Hey, bunny."

The warm voice on the phone nearly turned her knees to jelly, despite the fact that she was sitting down, relaxing barefoot on the sofa in her studio condo.

"Hey," she said when Brandon picked up her call, "but shouldn't that be Ms. Carnes in this instance?" She was teasing, yet also thought it was smart to keep some walls erected between business and pleasure, especially given their potential future business association.

"All right, *Ms. Carnes*," he said, though his voice still sounded outrageously sexy. "And by the way, I'm still battling a hard-on from visions of you sucking Stacy's tits last night, *Ms. Carnes*."

Okay, now her pussy was practically humming. She had to get them back on track here. "So are we gonna have phone sex or are we gonna talk about the future of Emerald Shores?"

He chuckled. "I like when you're authoritative, Ms. Carnes. That's hot."

She let out a sigh, having her *own* battle—between talking business with him or talking pleasure. "I'm glad you feel that way," she said, "since I have some more . . . suggested improvements for the resort."

That turned him slightly more serious. "Oh boy. Do I need to brace myself?"

"Depends. I feel everything I'm asking for is reasonable and practical—but who knows if you'll feel the same way?"

On the other end of the phone, he sighed. "Okay. Let's have 'em."

Again, by paging through her journal to find the business notes in between her more personal ones, Wendy had put together a new list and now began reading it to him, ticking off items as she went. After the ones she'd given him at their meeting a couple of days ago, she supposed it was adding up to a lot, but she had no choice—she had to be objective when it came to investing millions of dollars of Walter's money. In fact, if Walter invested in Emerald Shores, it would become a substantial percentage of his holdings. She had to ensure that the resort was the best it could be before she could recommend her boss sink that kind of money into it.

She concluded with, "Some of the rental bikes seem to be

in disrepair—I've seen a few people biking around with bent handlebars. And the guy running the rental could be more attentive—he needs to help people get the bikes adjusted correctly before they leave, since I saw several people wrestling with raising and lowering their seats on the bike path. Finally, some of the older swimming pools need to be refurbished or maybe even replaced. Particularly the pools at the Sea Cottages and the Dunes. They simply don't compare with others built since then and the pool at the Sea Cottages seems not very well cared for."

When she at last went quiet, he said, "Is that all?"

"Yep."

On the other end of the phone, he only sighed again, pointedly, and she thought he sounded annoyed. And too quiet for the Brandon she'd come to know.

She bit her lip, then said, "Remember, I'm just doing my job. I have to think of Walter's best interests."

He hesitated before replying. "No offense, Wendy, but . . . I'm not sure you realize how much these things cost. You're suggesting lowering prices on activities and drinks, and giving *some* things away for free, but at the same time you want us to shell out considerable funds on improvements. I have other investors besides Walter—who will wonder where their annual profits went."

"Well, I'm sure they know that sometimes you have to spend money to make money. You're selling luxury here—and the product needs to fit the advertisement."

"Point taken, but some of my investors are large corporations. All they care about is the bottom line. If it drops, they could walk. Then I'll be right back in the same boat I'm in now—out looking for someone new to put substantial money into the resort."

"Not if they have an ounce of business sense. Look, I know it's more complex than I make it sound, but if you don't keep your luxury resort in tip-top shape, it's no longer a luxury resort. And I realize that keeping a place this size and scope in tip-top shape is monumentally more challenging than it would be to keep any *other* resort that way, but I'm afraid that's the task you set before you when you conceived Emerald Shores."

In response, he only sighed yet again, in obvious irritation.

Prompting her to say, "You're mad."

How strange, she thought, to be doing big business with her lover. If he were any other guy in the world, this conversation would go differently; mainly, she wouldn't give a rat's *ass* if he were mad. But with Brandon, she did.

"No, not mad," he said then, sounding more like himself to her. "Maybe I'm just pissed off at myself for not seeing how many flaws have slipped past me. I view this place as a paradise and I didn't realize so much was wrong. Guess I'm a glass-half-full kinda guy."

"Let me be clear," Wendy said. "If I've failed to mention it, this place *is* paradise. It's . . . made me feel like I'm in another world." *Where I can do anything I want without any consequences.* "But ultimately . . . I guess *I'm* a glass-half-empty kinda girl."

"Why?" he asked. The concern coloring his voice told her it was more of a personal question than a business one.

What was the answer? *Maybe because guys like you have never looked twice at me? Maybe because I had to transform myself, turn myself into a mad seductress, to get your attention? Maybe because had none of that happened, and I'd walked in here to meet with you a few days ago, I'd have been totally intimidated by you. I'd have felt dread-*

fully average in your presence. Beautiful people don't know what it is to be average; success follows beautiful people wherever they go.

God, where had all *that* come from? Finally, she caught her breath and said, "I don't know. But given what I was sent here to do, I think it's probably a good attribute to possess. I'll plan on meeting with you and Charles tomorrow morning before I leave to get your feedback on my . . . requests."

For a second, she wondered if he was still angry, if the business part of their relationship was going to put a serious damper on the pleasure part. But then he said, very professionally, "All right then. Charles and I will plan on seeing you at ten a.m. as scheduled. And, of course, I'll be meeting with you tonight, Ms. Carnes, to fuck your brains out."

Her pussy rippled as she responded in her best corporate tone, as well. "Looking forward to it, Mr. Worth. Goodbye now."

Then she hung up the phone and decided to hit the beach for a couple of hours one last time. To sort of . . . say goodbye to it, and to get a little sun so her tan lines would be fresh and sharp and sexy when Brandon took her bikini off later tonight.

The beach excursion was good for her, in more ways than one. Besides the relaxation of soaking up some rays and listening to the calming sounds of the surf, she was reminded of who she was now. Since she really *had* changed—the things she'd experienced since arriving here had progressed from being a pretense to being a true part of her. She was now a woman who could wear a sexy bikini with confidence; she was a woman who could flirt with—and fuck—even the hottest man. The male stares she garnered as she strolled up the beach had brought that home to her. And it would make tonight, with Brandon, easier.

Because she would *remember* who she was now. That simple. The woman who could fuck for mere pleasure and then wave goodbye without looking back. She liked Brandon—*a lot*—and sometimes she felt downright close to him. But she saw those as "weak moments"—which had all hopefully passed now. In the end, she expected to have fond memories of the time they'd spent together, and *passionate* memories of the sex—and that was all.

When she went downstairs and entered the pool area at ten on the dot that night, indeed, the gate was unlocked and the scene dark, quiet.

Except for Brandon, who had spread out a checked table-cloth on the concrete near the pool's waterfall, and lay lounging comfortably across it in swim trunks, next to a picnic basket. Her heart swelled in her chest, but she tried not to feel it as she approached.

"A poolside picnic, Mr. Worth?"

He looked up with a grin. "Consider it foreplay, Miss Carnes."

"We can go back to 'bunny' for tonight."

His grin widened. "Come here, bunny—you look hot, and I need to kiss you."

Words like that never failed to entice Wendy, so she wasted no time letting him take her in his arms. The lights in the pool illuminated the water to a bright aqua glow, and the palm trees and tropical flora that dotted the luxurious lagoon-style pool made the scene much more seductive than Wendy had imagined. She'd checked out the pool in the daytime—and had even taken a quick dip one afternoon—but at night the mood was much more enveloping, and as they kissed, she came to understand why Brandon had wanted to spend their last evening together here.

Over grapes and cheese and wine from the basket, they talked—mostly about the intimacies they'd shared this week. It was a naughty conversation, Brandon insisting she tell him what parts she'd like best, prodding her to describe them in detail—almost like phone sex without the phone.

"If you could have only one of those experiences—if you had to choose—which one would you keep?" he asked.

She thought about it for a minute and instantly knew the answer. It was the very first night, with him, on the beach. It had spanned the gamut from flirty to dirty, it had been both freeing and intimate, and she'd left feeling amazed by *herself* and thoroughly satisfied by *him*.

But that just seemed like too boring an answer, given all that had come after. So she very purposefully lied. "The ménage à trois."

A knowing grin unfurled on his handsome face. "I knew you loved having two cocks at once."

"Guilty," she replied smoothly, still quite astounded that she could be so cool and blasé about such forbidden acts.

But that was what Brandon gave her—the respect that encouraged that kind of freedom.

"Come into the water with me," he said then, taking her hand to pull her to her feet. He slid one arm warmly around her bare waist and whispered low and wicked, "I don't have two cocks, but I can still make you scream."

Her whole body tingled at the promise—until she remembered, "Um, what if I do? Scream, I mean. Someone will hear." It was one thing to scream at the beach, but another to scream right outside the Shellside Towers. And since it wasn't all that late, people would still be coming and going from Bayside Village.

Brandon simply grinned, then pointed to the waterfall tumbling over a man-made precipice a few feet above them. "Listen," he said.

Then she realized the rush of water was fairly thunderous, and in fact, they had to talk loudly just to hear each other. "Ah," she said. Perhaps another good reason he'd wanted to come here.

After that, he led her into the water, down the steps that curved around one "tributary" of the expansive pool, holding both her hands in his. As a warm sea breeze tickled the nape of her neck—since she'd swept her hair up on top of her head—she felt as if he was leading her down into *pleasure* instead of just water. The pool seemed their private outdoor sanctuary, and she was suddenly thankful she *could* scream if she wanted to. Because of the words that suddenly rolled through her head: *This is the last time. The last time.*

But no—*no!*—she couldn't dwell on that; it broke her own sensible, necessary rule. Brandon might make the rules at Emerald Shores, but *she* had control here. *It's only sex. It's only sex. It's only sex. Nothing more.*

And like earlier today, she remembered who she had become here—a woman of strength, a woman who could fuck without emotion—and she became that once more as they swam sensually around each other, beginning to kiss, touch. Somehow, the water heightened each sensation as Brandon's hands brushed over her ass, her smooth stomach, her breasts.

When the urge struck, she didn't hesitate to wrap her arms around his neck and deliver a hot tongue kiss, pressing her pussy to the hard column of stone that had risen between his legs. "Mmm," she moaned, then issued a naughty demand. "Suck my tits."

He cast an utterly wicked smile that said he liked when she talked dirty. With one arm wrapped around her waist, he dropped his hand to her ass, hoisting her slightly higher in the water—and with the other, he pushed the fabric of her bikini top aside to bare one breast, the tip pink and beaded.

When he sucked it into his mouth, she moaned, the sensation stretching all through her, all the way to her cunt. "Mmm, yes," she said. "Suck it, baby."

He did as she asked, suckling deep, making it feel as if he somehow added more length to her nipple with each pull. It almost hurt, he sucked so hard, but at the same time, she felt it *everywhere*—a buffeting, dirty pleasure that forced her to drop her head back in abandon.

Soon, however, he softened the ministrations—now that he'd made the peak ultrahard, he backed off to flick his tongue over it, to lick, again, again, as if truly tasting it, testing the feel and rigidity in a way that had her practically purring.

As her breath came heavier, she couldn't resist untwining one arm from around his neck to pull aside the other panel of fabric, revealing her other aching tit. She bit her lip as a surge of pleasure sizzled up the small of her back, urging her to arch her breasts higher toward him.

He didn't hesitate to bend down once more and latch on to the newly bared flesh, this time using his teeth to lightly catch the distended nipple.

"Unh," she sobbed softly.

His eyes rose to hers, filled with unadulterated heat.

Then he *pulled* on the turgid tip, soft but potent, using his teeth to harden it further.

She heard her own panting—even against the sound of the rushing water nearby—as he began to lick and suckle that breast as well. Her flesh shone wet and shiny in the glow of light beneath them and she found herself thrusting her tit deeper, deeper into his mouth, making him take as much of it in as he could.

Under the water, she grinded slowly against him, cunt to cock, hungry for more. She issued another demand. "Make me scream."

A hot, ready smile transformed Brandon's face as he turned them both in the water, leaning her back against one wall. A small shelf, less than an inch below water level, ran around the entire edge of the pool, so she balanced her elbows there, which lifted her wet tits from the water for him to see.

"Float your legs out in front of you," he instructed.

When she did, he smoothly drew down her bikini bottoms until he was tossing them up on the side of the pool. Instead of putting her legs back down right away, though, she kept them lifted, floating near the surface, because she wanted Brandon to see her denuded pussy through the water.

Running her tongue sensually across her upper lip, she slowly parted her legs. She could sense his excitement as he moved between her spread thighs, slid one hand under her bare ass to help keep her afloat, then with the other hand, thrust two fingers inside her.

"Oh!" she cried out, not expecting the naughty intrusion—

but then her voice went deeper, sultrier, as she added, "Oh . . . *yes*." Because he was driving them in and out, fucking her, and the simple rawness of it made her cast her lover a dirty little smile.

Soon, though, he withdrew his fingers and, reaching between her legs to her ass, he lifted her bottom up onto the pool's shelf. She felt wantonly beautiful there—dirty and hot. She loved having her breasts on display, selfishly, arrogantly loved that they were big and round and pretty. Just as much, she loved having the pink folds of her cunt open for his eyes—and also for his tongue, since it put her pussy at the perfect height for licking.

And that's exactly what Brandon did. He went down on her as if he were a man who hadn't eaten in a week and she was a gourmet meal. His ministrations were at once rough but sensual, rhythmic, and she felt her whole body begin to undulate with the motions. "Oh baby, yeah, just like that," she told him.

He lifted his mouth only to say, "Play with your tits for me," and she happily obliged, loving his eyes on her as she took the two globes in her hands, let their weight rest there, then began to tease her nipples as he watched, as he licked.

She got lost in it all—the wet, soft stimulation between her thighs, the pleasure she derived from caressing her own breasts, the added pleasure that came from having his eyes on her. Blood engorged her clit—her pussy felt like the heaviest part of her body—and Brandon sank his face into her open slit with a hungry abandon that made her even crazier about him. He had the ability to turn everything raw and raunchy, yet at the same time, he somehow turned the raw and raunchy into simple good, hot fun—merely by acting as if it were all totally normal.

And maybe it was; maybe for the beautiful people there'd never been any reason to worry about what anyone thought afterward because no matter what happened, they were still the beautiful people. But it didn't matter why—all that mattered was that Brandon made her feel just as beautiful as *he* was.

He suckled her clit and she pinched her nipples. "A little more," she heard herself whimper down to him. "Oh God, yeah." She was breathless, panting, as the pleasure grew, mounted, hotter, hotter—until finally the orgasm crashed over her hard and she thrust at his mouth and had to hold on to the edge of the pool with both hands to keep from flying off the shelf. She moaned and groaned up into the night, safe in knowing the sound of the waterfall hid her cries of pleasure.

And when it was over, she was reminded once more: *This is the last night.* But instead of letting herself feel any emotion, she instead thought of what she needed more of before it ended—and she said, "I need to suck your cock—bad."

Between her legs, his face wet with her juices, he looked nearly dumbstruck with passion. "Ah, bunny—baby, I need that, too. I need to watch it slide in and out of your pretty mouth."

She lowered herself back into the pool and kissed him ravenously, at the same time struggling to get him out of his trunks, after which she wrapped both hands around his erection beneath the water. Meanwhile, he reached behind her neck and untied her top, tossing it aside, too, leaving them both completely naked, completely natural.

Brandon lifted himself up onto the same shelf where she'd been moments before, and the angle—being face-to-face with his cock—left her in awe. "My God, you're *so* huge," she nearly moaned.

His smile was adequately nasty. "The better to fuck your mouth with, my bad little bunny."

A week ago, talk like that might have paralyzed her or, at the very least, made her feel objectified. But with Brandon, all that changed. With Brandon, it was simply another part of hot, down-and-dirty sex. More than that, she took it as a promise—that she wanted him to keep.

Stepping up between his legs, she started by licking his balls, which rested in the small depth of water on the shelf. He moaned, obviously liking it, but she moved upward to what she *really* wanted—she let her tongue glide from the root of his shaft all the way to the tip, although that required pushing up on her tiptoes. Once there, she again curled both fists around his spectacular length, twisting, squeezing, massaging, as she lowered her mouth over the rounded head.

"Fuck," he whispered softly, then as she eased deeper down onto him, "Yeah. Oh yeah."

She angled his dick outward slightly so she could get to it easier, and then she began to move up and down on it, taking in as much as she could with each descent. Above her, he groaned, and she felt his gaze as she worked, and she wanted to be a badder bunny for him than ever before.

So she pressed herself, pushed her own limits, tried to take him deeper, deeper. He filled her mouth so full already, but she tried to relax her throat, go down on him a little farther with each slide of her lips. She could tell he noticed, felt it, for he'd gone very still, but his breath came heavier, harder. He whispered his encouragement as he threaded his fingers back through her hair. "Ah, baby, that's so good . . . so nice . . . yeah, oh yeah . . . so deep in your mouth, bunny . . . that's right, swallow me."

Soon Wendy's mouth tired; her throat muscles, too—but she felt filled with Brandon's enormous cock in a whole new dirty way. She'd gone down on him deeper than before, deeper than she bet most girls had. It filled her with a strange, nasty satisfaction she'd never felt even as she eased back into her usual mode of sucking him.

Now he began to do as he'd promised, to fuck her mouth. He held her head in his hands and thrust his cock between her waiting lips, and again, she felt truly fucked by him in a different way than ever before. And, oddly, she sensed the very subservience of it giving her an unexpected *power* over him—it showed him the full measure of her lust, the full measure of what a bad girl she really was, to welcome another such raw form of sex.

Finally, she released him from her mouth—oh God, it was stretched and sore now—to smile lasciviously up at him. "Do you like to watch me suck you?"

His soft laugh echoed with more awe than humor. "So, so much." He reached out, ran his thumb over her lips. "You do it so damn good, bunny." And the compliment caused a strange little ball of warmth to gather in her stomach, almost the same as if a man she loved told her she was beautiful.

But quit thinking about love here, for heaven's sake. Get back to fucking.

The thought made her step back in close to his majestically jutting cock, rise back up on her toes again, and press her tits wet and warm around it.

"Ah, God," he moaned, then instantly began to slide, up and down, in the deep valley her breasts created.

"Oh . . . oh . . . *mmm*." She loved it, too, and still couldn't explain why. Just another way to fuck him, she supposed. And . . .

maybe another way to fuck him that not every girl could employ since her breasts were more sizable than many. Despite herself, she'd found that it mattered to her—being able to leave impressions on him or make him feel things that no one else could.

So she fucked him with her tits as vigorously as she'd fucked him with her mouth, and they moved that way together, moaning and groaning, until she lowered her lips back over the tip of his shaft as he thrust, and she sucked the gathering pre-come away and tasted the light saltiness and let every sensation fill her—from the taste of him to the feel of him to the way the water seemed to wrap around her like cool velvet in this strange, heady moment of strange, heady sex. He had taught her to be kinky. He'd taught her to be kinky and to love it. He'd taught her to be so kinky that at times it didn't even feel kinky—it just felt normal, one more way to give and receive pleasure.

Finally, Brandon eased down off the shelf and took her in his arms. They didn't speak, but their eyes met in the shadowy light and the aqua glow from beneath them made it feel ethereal and dreamlike when he kissed her swollen lips, slow, deep.

Easing her back against the wall once more, he splayed his hands across her ass, lifted her into his grasp, and pushed his cock inside her. The deep entry forced a long, low sob from her throat. Instinctually, she wrapped her legs around him, locking her ankles when they met in back, and he began to move in a slow, thorough rhythm that echoed through every inch of her.

Together, they panted, moaned. Her breasts brushed his chest, water lapping gently around them. He pushed deeper, deeper, and at moments went totally still, making her feel how completely he penetrated her very core. She suffered the sensation that he was so deep inside her that he was becoming a part of her in those slow, intense moments.

They traded sweet kisses, and she held to him tight—and though neither spoke a word, there was no denying that this was a different sort of sex than they'd ever shared. And she tried not to feel that, but it was impossible not to.

A heavy moan from her lover told her he was nearing the brink, and she found herself running her hands through his hair, kissing him more, suddenly aware, frightened, terrified, that she'd never kiss him again. It was strange—a desperation she hadn't anticipated and couldn't fight.

But thankfully she pushed it aside as he murmured in her ear, "Coming in you now. Coming in you." And he thrust hard, again, again, and they held tight that way for a long moment, until he finally stilled.

Small waves continued to ripple around them as he lifted his head from her shoulder, where it had come to rest after his climax, and he whispered in her ear, his voice raspy. "Tell me you've never done the things you've done with *me*. Tell me you've never been this way with another guy."

She tensed within his embrace and felt a blush rise to her cheeks. She knew it had been clear that she'd never been fucked in the ass before, or been with two guys before—but she also felt his question going deeper than that, deeper in a way she didn't want to talk about. Because she was . . . Black Bikini Babe. She *had* to be. She *had* to hold on to that. She didn't want to ruin what little may remain of her mystique.

"Tell me," he said.

She let out a breath. He remained inside her. "Fine. No, I

haven't. But I don't know why you care. I mean, you've done these things with *millions* of girls."

He pulled back slightly to look at her. "First of all, millions is a big number."

She rolled her eyes. "Dozens then."

"And second . . . no, I haven't."

"Liar," she said.

He hesitated, his eyes seeming far away for a second, but then coming back to her, back to the moment. "Yes, I've done these things. But not like this. What I mean is"—he shook his head as if in disbelief—"you're the first woman since college that I've spent more than one night with."

She blinked, rather disbelieving herself. "Why?"

"I don't like attachments. Obligation. One night just always kept that part simple."

Something in her stomach curled as she asked the next question. "Then why did *I* get more than the standard one night?"

Again, he shook his head, looked down for a moment, but then met her gaze anew. "I've been asking myself the same thing. But you're just . . . special, bunny." He paused, and her chest tightened from the emotion brimming in his blue, blue eyes. "I guess I just wanted to tell you that before you go."

Wendy weighed the situation, the moment. She felt trapped in a way. A way that touched her soul. She couldn't help but respond in kind—with the truth. "You've been . . . really special to me, too, Brandon. You've made me feel . . . free. And liberated. And beautiful." She knew this completed the ruination of the image she'd tried to build with him of the aloof, purely sexual animal. But maybe, just maybe, even White Bikini Babe had moments of weakness, moments of romance, moments that tugged at her heart and soul.

His expression softened—a gentle smile playing about his mouth. "I've got some bad news for you, bunny. You're *not* really a bad girl."

"Yes, I am," she insisted. "You *know* the things I've done with you. I'm *very* bad."

Yet he simply shook his head. "You're . . . adventurous and hot and sexy as hell. But you're also smart and sweet and fun, too."

His voice had softened along with his look, turning downright tender—and she couldn't let herself feel that, respond to that. She couldn't. Or she'd be lost. "Brandon, I'm leaving tomorrow after our meeting. We can't suddenly be saying things that—"

"*Shhh.*" He cut her off, lifting one wet finger to her lips to quiet her. "Don't. Just take me back to your room. I want to sleep next to you again."

*M*ission complete. <u>So</u> complete. <u>Amazingly</u> complete. I have lived the dream. I have fucked a man, over and over, without letting emotions get in the way—well, not <u>too</u> much. There for a few minutes tonight, yeah, they were there—no point in saying they weren't. But they're gone now. Because they have to be.

He is sleeping in my bed and I can look over at him and feel strong, knowing that I have taken what I wanted here. I have followed my every whim and desire. I have become that girl on the beach, that one you always see and envy, that one who draws the stares because she's beautiful and confident and sexually open in a way that radiates from her. She is no longer a mystery to me. I <u>am</u> her.

The only question now is—will I continue to be her when I leave this place?

Chapter 13

She'd told him to shower first, so now he sat, dressed and waiting for her. He'd actually brought a suit and tie in a garment bag to the pool with him, because he'd had every intention of whisking her up to her room for more sex after they fucked in the pool, and that was exactly what he'd done. Fucked her again. Then slept with her again. And got that warm, cozy feeling again. The one that should be scaring the shit out of him but wasn't. Ever since he met her. She made it shockingly easy to care for someone. Whether or not she advised Carlisle to invest with them . . . well, he hoped to hell she would, but this was about way more than money and business.

He stared at the rumpled sheets, letting a small smile steal over his face—but it faded when his gaze drifted beyond the bed to the table where her suitcase sat open, in the process of being filled for the trip home. His chest tightened when he caught glimpses of things he recognized: those killer shoes she'd been wearing the night they met, those sexy-as-sin pink panties she'd worn the night he'd shared her with Pete. The fact was, he didn't like that she was leaving. He was afraid she was going to be right about the bed feeling empty.

Letting out a sigh, he dropped his gaze to the coffee table in front of him, littered with a pad of paper and pen, a half-full glass of soda apparently left from a previous day, her cell phone, and a small hardcover book with vintage hula girls decorating it in lieu of any words. Amused by the hula babes, he absently picked it up and thumbed through it—surprised to see it was filled with handwriting. He wasn't sure what he'd expected, but not that.

And he knew he should probably put it down in case it was something personal—and hell, even if it was professional, it was none of his business. But the truth was, he could tell this was some kind of diary or journal. And the further truth was, he instantly wanted to know if maybe she'd written about him. If maybe, just maybe, she didn't want to go home, either.

So, even though he felt like a jerk to be doing it, he let his gaze skim across the page it was open to.

Maybe on some level I wanted to find out that sex meant more to me than just the physical pleasure of it. I wanted, deep down, to discover it was about the connection, the emotion. But that's not what happened—that's not what happened at all.

Whoa.

Despite himself, his stomach churned. Was that about *him*? Or . . . could this be something old? The entries weren't dated, and they looked sort of randomly placed, so it was hard to tell. Maybe she used this book to write about everything she *ever* did with guys. Maybe she'd written that about someone else.

But he flipped around a little more and saw notes about the resort, notes to herself about the way things were run. So . . . no, every word she'd written, it appeared, was about this week.

He couldn't help it—he flipped around some more, just letting his eyes grab on to snippets of feminine handwriting.

Hard to believe it was just over twenty-four hours ago that I began this hedonistic little game.

I want some hot man to make me feel like the white bikini girl, like the personification of sex, like nothing else matters, like sensible Wendy Carnes doesn't even exist. I want to be the hunter, the one who takes, the one who feels nothing but pleasure and walks away satisfied in the end.

I began this game in pursuit of pleasure, power, control. Don't I need to grab as much of those things as possible before the sand empties and the game comes to an end?

He is sleeping in my bed and I can look over at him and feel strong, knowing that I have taken what I wanted here.

It didn't take long before he didn't want to see any more. He closed the book, aching inside, despite himself.

Clearly, what had happened between them was only some . . . grand experiment, only sex. She'd just wanted to snag some guy she thought was hot, and it had been him. The journal also made it clear she was quite pleased that it had all meant *nothing* to her.

He sighed, ran a hand back through his hair. The fact was—he couldn't be mad at her. She'd done nothing wrong. They'd indulged in casual sex together—and that was what it had been: *casual.*

He was the only idiot here who'd started to care, started to get attached. It wasn't her fault she didn't feel the same way. He was only some weird sort of game to her.

And that was okay—he was just glad he knew now.

So that he could *dis*attach, starting now. Hell, what did it matter? She was leaving in a couple of hours anyway. Maybe it was just as well.

Still, his heart physically plummeted. It didn't make sense. When they were together—talking, playing, fucking, whatever— didn't they have a good time? *More* than a good time? He'd held her while they'd slept. He'd helped her experience things she never had before. Deep down inside, he'd been sure—*sure*—that she felt at least a *little* something for him. Some of the moments between them had seemed downright *profound*.

Well, at least to him.

Apparently not to her.

This is what you get, buddy, for letting your guard down, letting yourself care for someone.

Obviously, it had been smarter to play his life the way he had before she'd come along. One-night stands. Nothing meaningful. No one to worry about hurting—and no one who could hurt *him*.

He swallowed back the emotions assaulting him even though his whole body tightened with the effort. Maybe this was what people meant about it being bad to keep stuff bottled up inside. He'd just never honestly experienced that before. But he'd have to experience it *now*, at least for the next couple of hours until she was gone. And maybe then he'd feel better.

Hell, maybe he'd get Pete and some of the guys to go back to the village with him tonight—maybe he'd find some *other* willing chick to take his mind off Ms. Gwendolyn Carnes. And this time, he'd be smart enough to keep it to one night—and smart enough not to give a fuck.

They'd gotten up late and didn't have time for breakfast before heading to their meeting with Charles. Where Wendy would sit on the opposite side of the table from Brandon and bargain with them about Emerald Shores' future. That was the only reason she could come up with as to why Brandon suddenly seemed so . . . chilly, despite the heat.

As they walked together toward the Emerald Shores offices, he was perfectly cordial, but . . . something had changed. And it was actually hard to believe he'd just suddenly popped into business mode, because when they had shared that business call yesterday, he'd seemed perfectly able to discuss business without his entire personality changing. He'd seemed irritated, but it hadn't lasted this long.

Was it . . . because she was leaving, because their affair was over? Last night, after all, things between them had gotten . . . intense. And she'd tried to pretend to herself later that it hadn't happened, or hadn't mattered, but it *had* happened.

"Is something wrong?" she asked as they wended their way past a small palm tree that arced over their path.

"No. Why?" He didn't even look at her as he answered.

"I don't know. You just seem . . . in a hurry."

"Because we're late." Not a playful 'Because we're late, bunny,' but just a stiff, cold 'Because we're late.'

She tried to lighten the mood with a smile. "You're the CEO. And I'm the person you're meeting. I think it'll all work out okay."

He simply shrugged. "Charles is meeting with us, too—his time is valuable and I respect that. And I'm never late—just a rule I live by. I take my work seriously, Wendy."

She felt affronted by his tone. "I know you do. I wasn't implying otherwise. You just seem . . . not yourself this morning."

"Maybe it's because I'm hungry. Hopefully Joanna will have some pastries. Or maybe it's because the future of my resort could ride on this meeting."

She didn't know what to say, how to answer. She trudged along beside him in another summer suit and a pair of wedge heels that made it hard to keep up with him—and she remained dumbfounded by his attitude.

When they reached the building, Brandon put on his usual, friendly smile for the receptionist in the lobby, transforming instantly as he said good morning. "Do me a favor, will you, Anita? Call up and ask Joanna to let Charles know that Ms. Carnes and I are on the way. And tell her if she can make some donuts or pastries magically appear that I'll give her a huge raise," he added with a wink. Back to his old self. It left Wendy all the more confused. When had she become the enemy?

Likewise, when they stepped off the elevator and into his expansive office where Joanna stood talking with Charles, he greeted them both with big smiles. "Sorry I'm late, gang."

"Um—me, too," Wendy added, feeling a bit like a puppy trailing after him.

A big tray of scrumptious-looking danishes sat in the center of the conference table, clearly prompting Brandon to say, "Joanna, you're perfect. Will you marry me?"

The older woman laughed good-naturedly, and said, "Oh,

now, you know my Hank would be jealous," and Wendy could tell this wasn't the first time he'd teased her this way.

He shook hands with Charles and, all in all, seemed delighted with everyone—except her. Her stomach tightened with what felt like a sudden, strange rejection. Which made no sense. You couldn't be rejected by a guy you didn't want to keep—right?

But still, they'd . . . they'd shared things. Good things, intimate things. So this sudden, rude about-face simply hurt.

When the meeting started, however, he began behaving more pleasantly to her. In a professional way. Same as he had at their last meeting. Indeed, just as no one would know he'd fucked her, no one would know he'd spent the last fifteen minutes being cold and distant to her, either.

One by one, Charles went over the demands she'd made for improvements, and both he and Brandon addressed the issues thoroughly. On most they conceded and agreed. A few they suggested be postponed for a year or two to prevent having so many expenditures at once. A few more they declined, explaining to her why they didn't feel they were important or feasible.

Wendy listened, made notes, and weighed the situation. She'd pretty much decided to give Emerald Shores a thumbs-up to Walter, but *they* didn't know that, and *she* was willing to drive a hard bargain if she had to—for Walter's sake. She truly felt Emerald Shores had to be nearly flawless for her to advise Walter to risk so much money here.

"Gentlemen, we'll need a commitment in writing as to when the deferred items will be completed," she told them. "And we'll also need to reach an agreement about the items you're declining. I feel strongly about them, and if you will simply add them to the list of deferred items, put on the schedule for no later than two years from now, I can gladly give Mr. Carlisle my recommendation that he invest in Emerald Shores."

Both guys wore poker faces and she could see they were skilled at such games. She, conversely, had little experience, but maybe her other "games" earlier in the week had helped prepare her for this.

"Ms. Carnes," Brandon said, meeting her gaze with smooth professionalism, as if nothing of note had ever passed between them, "what I think you fail to understand is that money doesn't grow on trees and even a tropical paradise has bills to pay. We've been very reasonable in meeting your demands and we would ask that you show us the same courtesy."

Okay, now he was just being condescending. Which plain pissed her off, regardless of the fact that they'd been curled up in bed together a little while ago, kissing, snuggling, and touching each other. "And perhaps what *you* fail to understand, Mr. Worth, is that it will be a lot easier for this tropical paradise to pay its bills if it has Mr. Carlisle's money to do it with. I'm not sure you're in a bargaining position here," she added. Two could play at being cold and rude.

Brandon's eyes on hers were shaded with anger now—pure and clear. He didn't like being pushed around or having her point out that she had the ability to do it. The sad truth was, if he'd continued acting normal this morning, maybe she would have given in on those last items, or at least discussed them in a more flexible manner. But she didn't like being treated poorly, either, so he'd brought this on himself.

Across the table, she watched Brandon and Charles exchange glances and knew she had them between a rock and a hard place. She pushed the issue. "Do we have a deal, gentlemen?" They all knew that her "recommendation" to Walter was mostly just a formality—if she agreed to give it, the deal was as good as done.

She was pretty sure Brandon's teeth were clenched when he finally said, "Fine. It's done."

A sure but cold satisfaction ran through Wendy's veins as she said, "Very good. I'm glad we could work it out. I'm on my way to the airport within the hour, but you can draw up the aforementioned document and fax it to the Carlisle offices. After which I'll talk with Walter, and if all is in order, we'll be in touch to finalize the investment."

With that, she stood up and reached across the table to shake first Charles' hand, then Brandon's. "A pleasure doing business with you, gentlemen," she said, trying not to feel the word *pleasure* at her core, trying to forget what the word had meant to her when it came to Brandon.

"We're happy we can do business together, too. Can I walk you down?" Charles asked politely.

Wendy waited for Brandon to intercede, to say *he'd* walk her down. After all, despite the animosity that had just passed between them, this was *it*—this was *goodbye*.

When he didn't, her heart dropped. But she said to Charles, "Would you mind if Mr. Worth escorted me down? I need to speak to him in private." It was clear that Brandon still hadn't told Charles about their relationship, but she didn't care if this seemed odd—Brandon could answer Charles' questions later.

"Um, sure," Charles said, then looked to his business partner, still seated at the conference table. "Brandon?"

"All right," Brandon said in a tone she couldn't read, then pushed to his feet and followed her to the elevator as Wendy struggled to understand what had just happened, what was *still* happening. She had to *ask* him to say goodbye to her? She'd never imagined things ending this way.

As soon as the elevator doors closed, locking them together in privacy, she said, "You weren't even going to say goodbye?"

He looked solemn, paler than usual, as he raised his eyes to hers. "I guess I thought we'd already said everything we needed to say."

She felt her eyes widen in shock. *"Brandon."* Was he serious? What had she missed? When had he gone from being her lover to being her adversary? "Is this because of the way the meeting went? Because I know I was kind of a hardass, but you were, too. Besides which, I thought we'd agreed to keep business out of . . . *us.*"

"The fact is, even if I think your demands are . . . *uninformed,* I'm relieved you're going to give Walter your recommendation and I appreciate your confidence in the resort. But as for *us,* well . . . it was a casual fling, a few nights of fucking. I didn't see any reason to make a big deal out of you leaving. It was fun, but now it's over."

Wendy simply blinked in disbelief. What had happened to the man who'd been saying such sweet things to her in the pool last night? "This isn't you," she said simply. "I realize we haven't known each other long, but . . . this just isn't you. What's wrong, Brandon? What did I do?"

Brandon drew in a deep breath in reply, then answered, still speaking in a calm, professional voice. "You didn't do anything wrong."

"Then what happened? What's going on?"

Next to her, he sighed, looked put-upon. "All right—here it

is. While you were in the shower, I found your diary. And I know I shouldn't have read it, but I did. So now I *get* that the stuff we did together was some kind of game to you. And that's fine—it's your prerogative—like I said, it was casual fun. But I'm not accustomed to being used, so you'll have to forgive me if it makes me feel a little less warmly toward you."

Wendy felt like she'd been punched in the gut. He'd read her journal.

Oh God, what had she written? She couldn't even remember. Just arbitrary—and perhaps brutally honest—thoughts about the things that were happening to her. Some about "the game" she was playing with herself, but surely other, deeper thoughts, too—about the intimacies they'd shared, about the world he'd opened to her, the amazing freedom he'd shown her.

"Well, you couldn't have read *all* of it or you'd know it was *way* more than a game."

"Didn't sound that way," he said, his voice going cold.

Just then the elevator *ding*ed, indicating they'd reached the lobby. The doors parted and they were no longer alone. Two men stood outside, waiting to get on, so she and Brandon were forced to step out.

When the elevator doors closed again, they stood by themselves in the airy lobby—the receptionist's desk sat a good distance away and she was on the phone anyway.

"Brandon," Wendy said softly, "I don't want things to end this way."

"From what I read, you already *got* what you wanted. How it ends doesn't really matter."

She gasped. "How can you say that? We had an amazing time together."

He looked incredulous. "And then you went back to your room and wrote about how meaningless it was. And like I said, that's your choice—it's not like we were making promises to each other. But don't expect me to act heartbroken to see you go."

She remained dumbfounded, unable to believe this. His voice still sounded calm, analytical—but underneath it she felt the anger just seething from him. She tried to rationalize, be calm *herself*. "Can we go somewhere and talk?"

"You have a plane to catch," he reminded her. "And I have documents to draw up for Mr. Carlisle."

When a second elevator arrived just then, Brandon stunned her further by stepping onto it. She simply stood staring at him, dumbfounded. And just before the doors closed, separating them forever, his expression shifted to one of . . . sadness. "Bye, bunny," he said. Then he was gone. And she was all alone.

Oh God. That was all she kept thinking, the only words that floated through her brain. *Oh God.*

Even as her plane lifted off from Okaloosa Regional Airport, Wendy still couldn't quite fathom how things had turned out. She hadn't seen it coming, and when it had, she could barely gather her wits enough to react.

That jerk. Reading words that she'd spilled recklessly onto the page, words never meant for any eyes but her own.

Sitting in the airport waiting to board, she'd dug the journal from her carry-on bag to thumb through it, wondering which parts he'd read. Much of it, she supposed, was damning—if read by a guy who thought they were developing a caring relationship. She'd just never thought Brandon was that sort of guy or that that's what they were developing. She'd worked so hard *not* to develop that.

Now that she was in the air, though, flying away from him, able to start putting the past few hours in a little perspective, she couldn't help but wonder how much of his anger related to ego. After all, a guy like Brandon Worth didn't have to fight for women. And it wasn't until that moment in the pool last night that she'd had much indication from him that he *did* care for her in any sort of romantic way. By writing the things she wrote in her journal, she'd only been protecting her heart.

So even if she could understand someone being hurt by the things she'd written, what she *couldn't* abide was his cold reticence, his unwillingness to let her explain—that was something that *hadn't* changed in retrospect. Again, she could only chalk it up to his wounded ego. Beautiful people like him didn't get wounded very often, she'd bet—all this meant was that Brandon had never had his feelings hurt before, and he didn't like it. Nothing more. She was sure of it. Because if he truly felt something for her, wouldn't he have cared enough to let her explain the journal, the whole "experiment," from beginning to end?

The worst part of this, she couldn't deny, peering out the window into the fluffy white clouds passing by, was that this whole upsetting event had forced her to realize how she *really* felt. *She cared for him.*

She was crazy about him.

She'd tried and tried to lie to herself about it all week, but now she couldn't anymore.

The way he'd treated her this morning hurt way too much— it made her feel, even now, like her heart was crumbling in her chest. At the moment, it was all she could do not to cry. She had to shut her eyes, in fact, to keep from it, and she only hoped the older woman sitting next to her wouldn't realize she was upset.

So she *still* hadn't succeeded in having sex without emotion. She'd been so bent on living that particular dream that she'd lied to herself about it, over and over, just to make it okay, just to feel strong, just to protect herself because she'd known the affair was temporary.

Proving that her experiment, in the end, was actually an abysmal failure.

Two weeks later, Wendy stood in a busy, popular downtown Chicago bar watching a cute guy across the room. Early thirties, she'd bet—no tie, but a nice shirt and jacket that told her he probably worked in a business-casual office nearby. She'd come for an after-work drink with her friend, Kayla, but Kayla had had to leave to meet her husband for dinner. She'd invited Wendy along with them, but Wendy had declined, deciding to stay here instead. Deciding to . . . see if she could resurrect her experiment, figure out how to make it a success.

She'd had some time to think through what had happened with Brandon, to get over that initial crush of heartbreak, to analyze it all. In Florida, she'd tried so hard *not* to analyze the situation, but now she'd faced the facts: She was a person who analyzed, plain and simple. That was why she'd done well working with stocks and bonds, and it was why Walter had sent her to Emerald Shores. She hadn't succeeded in stopping it *there*, so she'd given up on stopping it here, too.

It still felt like someone had flung a spear through her heart every time she thought of Brandon, but the passing weeks had made her realize it simply wasn't meant to be. They were, at heart, two different kinds of people. He was naturally gorgeous and successful, inside and out—whereas she had to work at it, hard. And she still didn't believe he could have cared for her very much, given the way he'd ended things.

So now the paperwork had been finalized and Walter had officially invested a major chunk of money in Emerald Shores. Brandon's name was all over documents that littered her desk these days. And she was trying to think of him that way—as just a name, just a . . . ghost of sorts. What she'd experienced with him hadn't been real, which she'd known from the beginning— he'd simply given her . . . well, a vacation from her real life, in the truest sense of the word.

However, she'd also thought a lot about her personal revelations in Florida. About that sexual box she'd broken out of. She wondered if she *could* remain that new, aggressive, confident woman upon returning home. And she still didn't know. She'd been too busy—and too hurt and upset—to find out. But tonight she was going to change all that. Because she was tired of hurting.

When she'd first fucked Brandon, she'd concluded that sex with a stranger hadn't been empty. She knew *now* that it hadn't been empty because of the spark between her and Brandon— the spark that had soon caught fire. But if she'd never seen him again after that first night, maybe things would have been fine— maybe it was giving it time to catch fire that had been her mistake. And maybe *that* meant . . . well, that she could be just as satisfied with any other guy, just for a night.

Like Mr. No Tie sitting over there at the bar with his other semi-professional buddies.

So she took off her suit jacket and tugged at the sleeveless sweater she wore, enough to create ample cleavage. Then she subtly adjusted her skirt, hiking it up to show a bit more leg than at the office.

This was going to be harder than it had been in Florida, where she hadn't actually *approached* a guy. But her experiences at the beach had felt like sufficient training. And *one* thing definitely *had* lasted since returning home: She had continued to find herself simply enjoying other people more—feeling more confident and friendly, taking a more sincere interest in those who crossed her path, both personally and professionally. Like it or not, she had to credit Brandon with bringing about that change.

Traversing the floor with purpose, she tried to feel the way she had at Emerald Shores—like an outgoing, sexually confident woman who knew men wanted her. She tried to smile into men's eyes. She couldn't tell if it was working because it simply didn't feel the same—but maybe that was because she was on her home turf, because she'd been in a fantasyland in Florida, and making herself into someone new there had been easier.

Still, she felt her guy's eyes upon her as she drew up to the bar next to him with the pretense of needing a drink. She "accidentally" bumped his arm, then said, "Oh, sorry," lowering her chin slightly and trying to look pretty and willing to flirt.

Mr. No Tie smiled. "No problem at all. My name's Matt," he said. "And you are?"

"Wendy."

He grinned. "Now I can tell my friends I met a girl named Wendy in the Windy City."

She smiled back. "Not from here?"

"New in town. On a temporary assignment for my software

company. I'll be here about six months and then it's headed back to D.C. So . . . can I buy you a drink, Wendy in the Windy City?"

Bingo!

Wendy climbed up onto the stool next to him and spent the next half hour talking, drinking, and flirting with cute Matt from D.C. Turned out that besides being attractive, he was smart, funny, and likable. Maybe not in the same killer way Brandon was, but that was okay—a limited number of guys in the universe could be that hot.

I can do this. I can fuck this guy and have a good time with him and be perfectly satisfied when it's over. Although, again, she'd decided that maybe Brandon had the right idea about *one* thing—she'd make this a one-night fling. That way nobody got hurt.

"Listen," Matt said as they finished their drinks, "you want to get out of here? Have dinner, take a walk—whatever?"

She wanted to have sex with him. She'd gotten so used to daily sex with Brandon that not having it for the past two weeks had been almost physically painful. Her body ached for a man's touch, for a hard cock. So she giggled flirtatiously and said, "Let's go with whatever."

"Works for me," Matt said, and they left the bar hand in hand.

They walked leisurely along the city street, warm now that it was June, and he ran his thumb caressingly over the back of her hand, causing her pussy to flutter. Oh God, she needed sex; she needed it bad.

Again, she promised herself she could make it just like it had been with Brandon that first night. No muss, no fuss. A nice, hot, sexy tumble and a kiss good night—that was all she needed.

She could make herself into a city version of White Bikini Babe yet.

"My place is just a few blocks that way," Matt said, pointing. "If you want to go there. We could . . . I don't know, order a pizza . . . or whatever."

She smiled, warming to the idea of sex with him even more. He was a nice guy. But he wanted to fuck her, too—she could feel it. She smiled and said, "Sure. And I still vote for whatever."

On the way, though, Wendy realized that maybe she didn't want to go to his apartment. Because he could be an ax murderer. Unlikely, but possible. So when they passed by a small park—a place where an old building had been demolished and replaced with green space—she drew him off the sidewalk, saying, "Come here."

He willingly followed as she led him to the most secluded corner of the empty park. Darkness had just fallen, so the setting felt private enough—especially given some of the places she'd fooled around with Brandon.

"Are you trying to put the moves on me, Wendy?" Matt asked teasingly as she drew him back against a brick wall behind a small potted tree.

She smiled up at him. "Too forward?"

His voice deepened. "Not at all. I like a woman who lets a guy know what she wants."

With that, he slid his arms around her waist and she looped hers around his neck. His subtle cologne mixed with the natural musky scent of a guy. Yes, yes, she could do this. She could live the fantasy—the right way this time, without getting hurt.

The first kiss felt . . . dry and slightly awkward, which she hadn't expected. They both bent their heads in the same direction and bumped noses, but laughed and tried to go on. Then they kissed in earnest—a longer, slower kiss. His hands splayed at her waist, beginning to caress through her clothes, and her body responded the right way—but her mind did not.

She sucked in her breath. *No. You can do this. You can.*

When he kissed her again, she tried harder. To feel what she wanted to feel. That sense of lust and shameless abandon she'd experienced with Brandon on the beach. That sense that she could do anything with him that she wanted and it would be all right.

But—oh God—she still didn't feel it. In fact, something in her chest shriveled.

"Hey, you okay?" Matt drew back to ask.

"Um . . ." God, she felt like a loser. She'd pulled him off the sidewalk into the park, after all. "I'm not sure."

He looked understandably confused, then said, "Are you . . . sick or something? Need to sit down?"

She lied. It seemed simpler. "Yeah—maybe."

Fortunately, a park bench sat nearby, so Matt led her to it. And after they rested there for a minute, him being a perfect gentleman and the guy she thought she should *probably* be crazy about, she heard herself admit the truth. "You should hate me. Because I can't do this. I thought I could, but I can't. I'm . . . trying to get over someone. I'm . . . trying to learn to have casual sex."

Matt looked dumbfounded by her rank honesty. "Wow." But he was also kind, for which she was grateful. "It's, uh, nice you picked me, but I'm getting the idea you're not really in to it."

She looked into his eyes, which were brown, and sweet. "I wish I was. You seem like a great guy."

He laughed softly. "I wish you were, too. And I *am* a great guy. But hey, if you're not over the other dude yet, then you're not over the other dude yet. It's okay."

Matt walked her home—just a few blocks beyond his own place. By the time they parted ways, she wanted to kick herself. He was so nice and so cute—she was crazy not to be in to him.

But the cold, harsh reality was—sometimes passion didn't make sense; it wasn't logical, a thing you could manipulate or create. And as much as she'd wanted to feel true passion for Matt, she hadn't. Once she'd gotten in the position to have sex with him—it had felt . . . empty.

And as she rode the elevator up to her apartment, a horrible, shocking, stunning revelation hit her—hard. Oh God. *Oh God.*

What she'd had with Brandon had been real.

From the very beginning.

It had never *been* "just sex."

That was why the sex had been so intense and good—from the very *start*. Why it *hadn't* felt empty.

It hadn't been about letting it catch fire—it had been about that *very first spark*, those very first moments with him. He'd simply been *right* for her. So very *right*.

And she'd been so, so wrong—about so much.

Breaking out of that box hadn't been about sex—it had been about the connection she'd experienced with another human being, about the stark, heart-wrenching intimacy. It had been about honesty and respect and shared lust and chemistry—but all of that had been there, clear and easy, because they'd connected, almost instantly.

When she'd walked into Volcano's that night, she had just

happened to stumble, amazingly, upon the perfect guy for her to be intimate and wild *with*. And now she knew that she'd fallen for him that very night, that very *hour*. And that because of him, she wasn't sure she'd ever be satisfied or truly connected with another man again.

*T*here is some sex that you thoroughly enjoy in every way—it's hot, it's powerful, it's pleasurable, it's dirty, and it leaves you totally satiated in ways both mental and physical.

Then there is sex that holds all of those same attributes, but somehow it happens <u>harder</u>, so hard that you cease thinking—couldn't if you tried. It's mind-numbing, thought-stealing—it turns you into nothing but a pleasure-seeking being; in those moments, no other part of you exists. Just your body. Just your nerve endings. Pleasure, pleasure, pleasure.

I thought maybe I could have more of that second kind—it sounds so easy. But the irony is—for me to have that kind, where I cease thinking, it has to be with someone I trust enough to completely let go.

The <u>ultimate</u> catch-22: To have mindless sex where all that matters is pleasure, I have to do it with someone I love.

Lately, now, I keep thinking about the way a woman sounds when she's getting excited, coming—how the sounds of pleasure so closely resemble the sounds of pain. How could something so exquisite and so horrid be so closely related? Perhaps because they lie a mere heartbeat away from each other?

Chapter 14

$\mathcal{A}$ warm, salty breeze lifted the hair from Wendy's neck as she strolled through Bayside Village in search of dinner. She couldn't believe she was here, back at Emerald Shores. And she hoped it wasn't a mistake.

The very morning after her blunder with Matt and her revelation about Brandon, Walter had summoned her into his office. "Sit down, Wendy," he'd said. "I have a proposition for you, and I'd like for you to listen to it all the way through before you say anything, all right?"

It was standard Walter-speak—he often felt people asked too many questions and jumped to too many conclusions because they reacted to things too quickly. And when she thought about her life lately, she couldn't argue the point.

"The more I look at our new association with Emerald Shores, the more complex I find it. And just like when we acquired The Lofts properties in Seattle, I've decided I need someone on site to manage our holdings. I'm sure you're aware that our agreement with Emerald Shores states that I reserve the right to place someone on their board of directors, and I've decided to exercise that right—there's simply too much money involved not to. And I'd like that person to be you.

"That said, your duties may stretch beyond the resort itself. I may ask you to scout out other potential investment opportunities in the area now that more of that particular coast is being so aggressively developed and, in some areas, refurbished. I may send you to other areas of Florida from time to time for the same purpose. But starting out, you will be there primarily to protect my investment and make sure my money's being well spent. I know from my talks with their CEOs that you stood your ground with them, and that gives me a lot of faith in you.

"Now, I know relocating is a big deal, and that you were born and raised in this area, so I'm willing to make it worth your while. You'll have on-site housing, cost free, and the job also comes with a twenty percent raise.

"So if you have any questions now, feel free to ask them. Otherwise, I won't rush you for a decision—take a few days, think about it, and let me know. I'd miss having you around here, but you're a smart young woman and I'd feel confident having you represent the Carlisle interests in Florida."

Wendy *hadn't* asked any questions. She *had* sat across from Walter dumbfounded, her mouth hanging open.

The downsides of the move were many. She would miss her family, particularly her sister and nieces. And she was also leaving some friends behind—but the truth was, most of them were married now and busy doing married-people things like decorating new houses and having babies. She had also quickly realized that free housing plus more money meant she could fly home for weekends whenever she felt like it without worrying about the cost. Her new locale would provide a good vacation destination to bring her parents and sister south, and she could help pay for that, too.

So the only real obstacle to accepting had been worries over

Brandon. Given how things had ended between them, could they work together? And how the hell would she ever get over him if she had to see him across a meeting table all the time? And what if she saw him with other girls—how much would that hurt?

Now that she'd discovered, once and for all, that she simply couldn't fuck someone without emotion, she didn't think she could move to the beach and become White Bikini Babe, either. That truly *had* been a fantasy, a person who she simply . . . wasn't.

But despite all those worries, she just didn't feel she could pass up the opportunity. Walter was advancing her career, making her more than the glorified secretary she'd been up to now. This was a chance to learn about running a resort from the inside out, a chance to serve on a board of directors. It was, when she broke it down, choosing to do something bigger with her career or . . . choosing to be a secretary, albeit a good one, for the rest of her days. It seemed like an offer she couldn't refuse.

So now she was here. She'd arrived just today and moved into a temporary studio condo back at the Shellside Towers until she selected a larger one somewhere on the property to make into her new home. Most of her stuff was being shipped later, but she'd still had a busy day unpacking her entire warm-weather wardrobe and other personal items: a few favorite books, her laptop and printer, and some framed photos of her family.

She'd decided it would be a good idea to go out to dinner, to simply get reacclimated to being back here. She'd purposely arrived on a Friday so she'd have the weekend to get settled before going into the Emerald Shores offices, but she had the strange feeling that if she didn't get out *now, tonight*, she might turn into

some kind of hermit who was afraid of men and bars and anything that could end up being even remotely related to sex. So
she'd thrown on a simple cotton sundress with a pair of pretty
cork wedge slip-ons and hopped on the shuttle.

It was early in the evening yet, so the village teemed with
young families—handsome husbands and their fashionable
wives, little girls in pretty dresses and little boys in khaki shorts
that made them look like miniature golfers.

She wanted something easy, quick—she wasn't in the mood
to wait for a table somewhere—so when she saw an easel on
the brick walkway outside Volcano's promising fish and chips
for $8.99, she stepped inside and took a seat at the bar. She didn't
look around or size up the men; this wasn't like that first night.
But she did try to enjoy the lively pianos, already dueling with
their version of "Only the Good Die Young," hoping the cheerful atmosphere would make her feel . . . well, more like she fit
here. More like the *real* her fit here. The her who, yes, could
have crazy, uninhibited, screaming sex with the right man. But
also the her who was usually an average, normal woman who
already missed her nieces, who hoped she'd maybe be able to
find some good sitcom reruns on cable later, and who was the
newest member of the Emerald Shores corporation board of
directors.

As she sat eating the casual meal, it dawned on her that one
thing Emerald Shores *was* lacking was a variety of quick, easy
foods. *A pizza place,* she decided—the village needed a pizza
place. Not part of a chain, but something fun and unique with
an Italian feel—and also a place where you could pop in for a
quick slice without having to wait, and maybe they could even
deliver to properties within the resort.

Then she rolled her eyes, thinking, *Oh boy, Brandon's going to love* this.

But she was here to help improve the place, to keep the money flowing in, so he'd just have to live with her ideas.

"What are you drinking?"

The question, the voice, nearly made her heart stop. *Brandon.*

She drew in her breath and lifted her gaze to find the blue, blue eyes that had first held her captive in this very room.

Oh God, he was *so* freaking hot, *so* freaking beautiful—the very sight of him made her scalp tingle as a frisson of heat rippled down her spine. His expression was lustful, passionate—and so, so familiar. All the blood drained from her face; she felt vulnerable, and instantly aroused. She wasn't ready for this—she wasn't ready for this at all.

Remembering their first conversation—only two short months ago, although it felt like a lifetime—she nodded briefly toward her soda and said, "Nothing—yet. Just Coke. What do you recommend?"

His voice echoed deep, raspy, as fully sexual as she'd ever heard it, and his eyes continued to burn through her as he said, "A sloe-screw-against-the-wall."

Despite herself, her pussy surged. When she spoke, it came in a breathy whisper. "The drink? Or the act?"

"The act," he answered slowly.

Her heart fluttered, along with other key parts of her body—and when Brandon took her hand and drew her down from the stool, she didn't protest. When he led her up a set of stairs next to the elevator where they'd had their first fateful encounter, she simply followed. Her heart beat like a drum in her chest.

The Lava Room was quiet this early, empty—no band, not even a bartender. Leaning her up against a wall across from the bar, Brandon molded his hands to her hips, pressed his cock to her crotch. The sensation—like a lost memory that comes back with startling clarity—rushed through her entire body. The small of her back ached with desire and her knees went weak.

Looking into her eyes, Brandon slowly lifted her arms up over her head, then skimmed his fingertips slowly down them, then over her sensitive breasts and stomach until they molded firmly to her ass through her dress. She shuddered, peering back at him through heavily lidded eyes. Oh God, he still knew, more than any other man she'd ever been with, exactly how to touch her. Everything about him made her crazy with want.

As he began to kiss her—slow, deep, lingering kisses that melted all through her and made her drop her arms around his neck—he gathered the back of her dress in his fists, bit by bit. In front, they grinded together, naturally—she couldn't *not* respond—and she yearned for his big, beautiful cock like never before.

Beneath her dress, she wore the same sexy pink boy-short panties she'd had on the night of their ménage à trois with Pete, and he seemed to recognize them by feel—he groaned as he massaged her ass and it made her thrust her cunt against him harder. God—*oh God*.

A moment later, with his help, the panties fell at her ankles and she stepped out of them as she reached for Brandon's belt. She could barely make sense of this, but she felt drunk on him, that quick, swept up in a desire she couldn't fight.

Soon she wrapped her hand around his hard-on and they both moaned. Oh, how she'd missed this. The rawness of sex with him. The uncontrollable passion that welled up in her like a tidal wave ready to crash. He was so hard and smooth in her grip—she instinctively squeezed and caressed and let the feel of him ooze all through her chest and stomach, making her hotter, hotter.

"Lift up your dress," he rasped, already sounding as breathless as she felt.

Releasing him from her fist, she slowly gathered the fabric in her hands, raising it, higher, higher, until her pussy was on display. Knowing he liked it bare, she felt thankful she'd fallen into the habit of keeping it that way.

Without preamble, Brandon dropped to his knees, leaned in, and buried his face in her slit. She whimpered and parted her legs, peering down at him and hoping she didn't collapse from the sensation.

He licked her vigorously, like a wild man, and then sucked her clit deep into his mouth, nearly making her come, that fast. Her whole body pulsed with urgent pleasure and she had to bite her lower lip to keep from crying out.

When he stood up, she was trembling. She could smell her sex on his face. Stepping in close, he gripped her ass, positioned himself against her, and plunged his cock up into her pussy.

Now she *did* cry out at the rough impact—it couldn't be helped—but he went still against her, letting her adjust to having him inside her again.

"So big," she whispered desperately.

"So wet." Their faces were a mere inch apart.

As he began to fuck her in earnest, she found herself lifting one foot, curling it around his thigh—for balance. Oh God, he was so huge in her. Every slow, thorough stroke he delivered made her moan. He looked in her eyes the whole time, and she peered back, feeling his gaze as much as his cock.

"So good," she breathed. "I missed this. You *in* me."

"I know," he whispered back, eyes half shut in lust. "Me, too, bunny—me, too."

He continued moving in her in that same slow rhythm. A slow screw against the wall—mmm, God, that was exactly what he was giving her.

Together they groaned their pleasure as he impaled her on his long shaft, the position nearly too much for her to handle, given his size—and yet handle it she did. She craved him like she'd never craved anything in her life.

In front, her clit met his body with each deep plunge, and she bit her lip as the blood gathered there, as her pleasure intensified. "Oh God," she whispered. "Don't stop."

"Don't worry," he murmured. "I'm gonna make you come so fucking hard."

The words excited her, made her thrust her cunt more roughly against him in slow, jerky movements. He kneaded her ass in his hands, up under the dress—and just when she least expected it, he reached inward, stroking the tip of his middle finger across the fissure of her ass.

And then she tumbled—deep—into a tumultuous orgasm that vibrated through her like sonic booms, making her lightheaded, weak, crazed with pleasure. She heard herself sobbing, felt herself clinging to him—and then she heard him say, "Ah, fuck, me too. Here I come," and he thrust deep, deep, painfully deep, but she didn't mind, still coming down from her climax and wanting him to come just as fiercely.

A moment later they stood, embraced, their foreheads

touching, both breathing so hard that the sound nearly blotted out the piano music from below.

Finally, she looked up at him. "Wh-what was that?"

He looked solemn, a little sad. "What you wanted. Just sex. Just a fuck."

She drew in her breath, her stomach plummeting. "That's not all I wanted."

"Look," he said, still holding her, their bodies still agonizingly close, "I apologize for the way I acted on the day you left. I was caught off guard and . . . hell, I was a jerk. But I understand what you were after—just a good time—and that's okay."

"Only, Brandon, you truly *don't* understand. I need to explain."

"*Shh,*" he said, seeming serious, agitated. "Please listen to me, Wendy, because I need to say this." He ran his hands back through his hair. "I . . . I can't do this."

She remained as dumbfounded as she'd been since he'd approached her. "You can't do *what?*"

"Work with you and fuck you. I know they do it on TV all the time, but I can't."

She was still confused—for God's sake, ever since the morning she'd left, everything *about* him confused her. She shook her head, trying to clear it. "Why?"

"I'm sorry, bunny," he said. "I'm just . . . sorry." Then he zipped up his pants and walked out, leaving her there, panties at her feet, in the Lava Room. Her heart beat a mile a minute—and she began to wonder if she'd made a very big mistake coming here.

Brandon walked on the beach in the dark, trying to let the surf, rushing coolly up over his feet, wash his troubles away.

Shit, he'd made a mess of things. Repeatedly.

First the way he'd treated her on the day she'd left. And now maybe he'd accidentally treated her even *worse* on the day she'd come back. He was acting like some immature asshole who had no hold on his emotions.

Maybe the problem was . . . he had no hold on his emotions.

Before Wendy, he'd just never dealt with stuff like this. Caring for a woman. Wanting her in some deep way he really couldn't understand or describe. It was damn confusing. Not to mention painful. He almost wished he'd never met her. Except he couldn't imagine *not* having met her, because she'd sort of . . . changed every second of his life since then.

He thought about her all the time. He wondered what she was doing, if she was happy. He hoped she wasn't fucking other guys because the very idea made him want to strangle somebody—mainly the other guys.

He'd confided the whole pathetic story to Pete last Saturday when they'd taken one of Pete's boats fishing in the bay, and his buddy had formed the theory that Brandon was in love. "That's why you're acting like an immature idiot. Most guys fall in love for the first time when they *are* still an immature idiot. I was eighteen. You're what—thirty-six? No wonder you're so fucked up about it."

Brandon's initial response had been denial.

But the reality was—Pete was probably right. Brandon was in love with Wendy, the best fuck of his life, his new board member, and the woman who'd made it clear in her diary that she didn't care for him in any significant way.

Even though Brandon had seen them only for a few minutes, the words he'd read there played in his head over and again. They'd made him feel so . . . incidental. Like he could be any guy. Any cock would do.

He didn't hate her, and he wasn't mad at her, despite what he'd probably given her reason to believe—but hell, the truth was that he simply didn't know how to handle the hurt, a far deeper hurt than he'd known he could even feel.

It made him angry at himself—successful CEO and resort magnate Brandon Worth was acting like a baby because the girl he wanted didn't want him back. Well, at least not the way *he* wanted *her*.

Maybe in the end, what it came down to was: Wendy really *was* a bad girl, exactly the kind of girl who could fuck a guy's brains out and not give a damn when it was over.

Which was usually fine with him—but with her, things were different. She'd had him so fooled—until he'd happened to pick up that damn diary.

He tried to look on the bright side. Despite what had happened, Emerald Shores had ended up with a huge influx of cash thanks to Wendy's recommendation to Walter Carlisle. It had saved his fiscal ass and allowed his dream, and his career, to continue. The resort was now in good financial shape, lifting a world of professional worries off his mind.

So he thought he should feel better, given that Emerald Shores was his main concern in life.

But maybe that had been before Wendy Carnes had come along.

He didn't know what to do, how to fix this. It was like he'd woken up in some foreign land where everything was different, where he didn't understand the language or the customs and just kept making mistake after mistake. He felt lost. And that was the problem—he'd never felt lost in his life, and he didn't know how to find his way back to where he'd come from.

Wendy strolled out onto the beach in shorts and a tank late Saturday afternoon. She hadn't quite been in the mood to don her bikini and soak up rays, even though maybe that would have relaxed her. But she'd decided to come out now that the day was waning and most of the beachgoers were gone and the boys who worked on the beach were busy taking down umbrellas and chairs like Brandon once had.

The soft sand felt warm, somehow comforting, beneath her feet, and the sea breeze refreshing. She walked up the shoreline, watching the water, the sand, the last few families and couples who were packing up their sand buckets and towels, ready to call it a day. She saw a little boy with a sunburn and felt sad for him, knowing he'd be crying later. She thought about all the people who flocked here for so many reasons: relaxation, fun, a getaway, a tan . . . and sex.

Just then—oh God—Wendy spotted her, walking up the beach! *White Bikini Babe*. Again in her stunning, sexy white bikini, heading straight in Wendy's direction. They would pass at the water's edge in just a few moments.

The girl was as gorgeous as Wendy remembered, and just as wholly sexual, her breasts bulging from those slender white triangles, her hair blowing in the breeze, her beautiful face filled with confident arrogance.

And God help her, Wendy *still* wanted to be her. Even after all of this.

But maybe for a different reason now. If she were that

woman—that idealized woman in her mind who could fuck and not care—she wouldn't be hurting so badly over Brandon.

Wendy considered saying hello when they passed, maybe even trying to start a conversation, trying to get a window into the other woman's world to see what was happening there, what her life was really like . . . but just as quickly, she realized she didn't want to know. She didn't want to lose that almost magical image White Bikini Babe had held in her mind for so long now.

There remained some part of Wendy that still wanted to believe a woman existed who could live that life, who could soak up the physical pleasure without experiencing any of the emotion from being that close to a man.

Even so, as they passed each other, leaving two sets of footprints headed in opposite directions, she was forced to recognize the *real* truth—magical image or not. The real truth was that no matter how perfect that woman looked or what message she sent out, no one had a perfect life. Even White Bikini Babe had problems. Possibly big ones. Possibly she was in love with someone right now who didn't love her back.

And that quickly, Wendy stopped feeling envious.

Well, mostly. She still wouldn't mind having that ass and those firm, perky boobs, but it was official—she was perfectly happy with who she was and she didn't want to be anyone else.

Walking farther, Wendy noticed an older but striking woman, probably in her fifties. She sat on a beach blanket wearing summery white pants and a roomy white tunic with metallic gold trim, her dark hair pulled up onto her head in a bun. She wasn't beautiful, but there was something about her, an understated elegance that Wendy found instantly compelling. She looked happy and content to be by herself at the beach, not even remotely intimidated by anyone in a racy bikini.

And Wendy amended her last thought just a little—because *that* was who she wanted to be: someone who was that comfortable in her own skin.

A quiet wisdom radiated from the dark-haired woman and Wendy almost wanted to go talk to her, share her troubles, seek her advice.

But maybe she didn't want to risk disillusionment there, either.

Or maybe she just thought she was a big enough girl to solve her own problems. She was on the board of directors of a major vacation resort, after all—she needed to start acting like a woman in control of her own destiny.

And maybe that woman, that woman she wanted to be— that powerful, in-control woman—needed to be the bigger person here.

She was still hurt by the way Brandon had handled this, and she still wasn't certain whether his reaction had to do with ego or truly caring for her. But she needed to take the situation in hand and find out once and for all, even if it put her at risk, both personally and professionally.

I'm starting to think Brandon is a obstinate idiot.

Because I care for him, so freaking much, but he won't listen or give me a chance to explain. He read something I spilled recklessly into this book, something <u>private</u>, meant only to allow me to purge my thoughts during a highly intense time of my life, and he acts as if those words are <u>all</u> that matters.

Doesn't he remember the great talks we had? Doesn't he remember the times we held hands or just kissed and kissed and kissed, or the way we looked into each other's eyes? Doesn't he know I couldn't have done any of those wild things if he hadn't been there with me, encouraging me to experience it all, treating me with kindness and respect?

Isn't he a smart enough guy to look back on all that and realize it adds up to a hell of a lot more than a few journal entries where I was trying to convince myself I didn't care?

Isn't he a compassionate enough person to look past that and see how much more we shared?

Isn't he a wise enough man to realize that I LOVE him?

Chapter 15

Wendy quietly stuck a ribbon in the journal, marking the page she'd just filled. Then she left the Shellside Towers and walked to the nearby building that held Brandon's penthouse.

She thought of all the ways this could turn out. He could never mention it and she'd never know what he thought. He could continue being belligerent and confusing. He could have his ego repaired and it could make way for more cordial working conditions—but nothing more. Or . . . well, she wouldn't let her mind go to the best possible scenario. Glass-half-empty girls tended to work with *worst*-case scenarios instead, because how often in life did the best possible outcome occur?

She thought she would be nervous about this, but she felt weirdly calm. Like it was a thing that simply had to be done, regardless of the result. Like she *had* to tell him, *had* to let him know—even if he *was* acting like a jerk. She had to put this on the table once and for all. If she didn't, she'd never feel a sense of closure, and she was a person who *needed* closure.

Approaching the grand double doors to his condo, she quietly laid her journal outside, then turned and walked away.

On Sunday, Wendy rented a bike and went shopping at some of the resort shops. She needed more "beach wear." Or at least she hoped she did. She hadn't heard from Brandon, and she only prayed what she'd done wouldn't somehow worsen the situation and make it downright impossible to work together.

As she shopped, she made a point to steer clear of the Beach Bazaar. Just for now. She simply felt compelled to keep a low profile until she and Brandon got things resolved one way or another, and she didn't want to have to fake her way through a conversation with Stacy should Brandon's name come up. Besides which, what if Stacy wanted to fool around again? Wendy couldn't deny the sensual pleasures she'd shared with the pretty girl, and she might not mind sharing them again sometime—but she was pretty sure that if Brandon hadn't been there, involved on the periphery, her hot tub encounter with Stacy would have felt as empty as her kisses with Matt back in Chicago. She was still finding her way through all the new recipes for sex in her life, but she was pretty sure Brandon was a required ingredient.

By dinnertime Sunday evening, she'd still had no contact from Brandon and it hit her that she would have to go into the Emerald Shores office tomorrow, her first official day on the job, and face him having no idea what he'd thought of her journal entry. Sheesh. It had seemed like such a bold, take-charge, forward step at the time—but if he didn't respond, that made it kind of useless, and possibly problematic, since it left her having no idea where they stood. Not that she'd exactly grasped where they stood *before* yesterday, either—that was the whole point of putting her cards on the table and telling him how she felt.

After a light dinner of soup and salad at a café near her building, she decided to go for another walk on the beach. It was either that or hole up in her condo and cry. She believed strong women cried, too, sometimes, but she just didn't want to give in to her girlish emotions yet. She truly was a tougher, more confident woman since her week with Brandon, and she wanted to keep it that way. Even if her heart was breaking a little more with each passing minute she didn't hear from him.

Maybe you were right in the first place and this was all about his ego. Maybe, when all is said and done, he just doesn't love you back. Maybe seeing those words on the page freaked him out and sent him running in the other direction.

She sighed at those sobering thoughts as she descended the same steps to the beach that she and Brandon had taken together that first night.

It was later than she'd arrived yesterday, so the wide white beach was mostly empty, the umbrellas packed up for the night—although a few beachcombers walked along with metal detectors, and the occasional young family played near the water.

In the distance, she spotted the cabanas in front of Brandon's building—they were heavy enough that no one could steal them, so she supposed that was why they weren't put away at day's end, why they'd remained there to be fucked upon that first night and why they were there now.

Her skin sizzled at the memory of that very first penetration. She sighed, bit her lip, her pussy aching for more of what, apparently, only Brandon could give her.

That was when she saw him, stretched out on the very same padded cabana chair on which he'd delivered those glorious strokes with that glorious cock. Oh God, he was just as beautiful as ever, his pale hair messier than usual—from the sea breeze, she supposed. He wore a white linen button-down shirt over light beach pants, rolled up around his legs—she guessed he'd been walking in the surf.

His eyes met hers then, but she couldn't read them—so she walked toward him, albeit cautiously.

"Hey," he said softly when she reached the cabana.

"Hey."

After that, they both went silent and her heart beat so hard that it hurt. Clearly, they had things to say to each other, but no one was saying them. And given what she'd told him via her journal, she definitely thought the next move was his.

Finally, he pushed to his feet and said, "Let's walk."

Side by side they strolled through the soft sand down toward the water, and Wendy had the feeling that he was going to tell her he didn't love her, since if he did, wouldn't he be telling her *now*? And wouldn't he at least look *happy*? Her stomach sank as they neared the water's edge, but she resolved to stay strong—at least until she was alone.

Once at the shoreline, Brandon seemed hesitant, looking out over the horizon, then picking up a broken seashell to throw out into the ocean. "You keep asking me to let you explain," he said without looking at her, "but I haven't done that. So please— explain to me what you were doing, what you were after, when you met me."

Oh boy. Wendy sighed. She had wanted *desperately* to explain, but it was so complex that, now that she had the chance, she wasn't sure how to.

Finally, she decided to sink deep into the heart of the matter, for the honest truth of it. "You don't realize this," she began, "but there are . . . different planes of existence out there."

He looked understandably confused. "What?" But maybe that was good, since it was the first time he'd really looked her in the eye since meeting up with her a few minutes ago.

"There are . . . different types of people living in this world," she said. "There are beautiful people, like you, who are living a charmed life with other beautiful people, always being confident and always feeling desirable. And then there are . . . more average people, like me."

He couldn't have appeared more stunned. "I'll never understand what on earth makes you think you're average."

The response flattered her, just like the last time she'd referred to herself that way, but she couldn't be sidetracked if she had any chance of making him understand. "Before I got here, before I started dressing a certain way, trying to project a certain sexual image, I *was* average. So maybe it's all about attitude—who knows? But what I *do* know is—before you, I never knew what it was like to be on the beautiful side. And I just wanted to experience that. But then I also wanted to . . . not need it. I wanted to *beat* it. I wanted to use it, the same way guys use girls for sex."

He protested. "I've never used a girl for sex."

She narrowed her gaze on him. "You've never slept with a girl knowing that when it was over she might want more than you did?"

Brandon pulled in his breath, let it back out. "Well, I never set out to hurt anyone."

"My point is . . . usually guys get to run the show. And usually beautiful people get to make the decisions and get what they want without having to work as hard for it as other people. And just this once, I wanted to have that sort of power."

She slowed down then, since she was getting to the important part. "But I didn't count on caring about you. And I kept telling myself I didn't, because that went against everything I wanted when I started this whole thing. To care about you seemed . . . almost like I'd defeated myself. I hadn't gotten what I was seeking, which was the power to have meaning-less sex. I'd never had meaningless sex before you—and I still haven't.

"I thought it was meaningless at first, just because I felt so good afterward, even though I didn't know you very well. But all that meant, in the end, was that I liked you so much, so quickly, that it didn't *feel* meaningless—it felt like I could be open with you, like I could let you see parts of myself I'd never shown anyone before."

He raised his gaze to her again, his brows knit, his expression earnest. "I never thought of what we were doing as a game, Wendy—but clearly, you did."

"It's the only time in my life I've *ever* treated sex like a game. And in the end, I lost. Because you found out about it . . . and it was your horrible reaction that made me realize I'd fallen in love with you."

His eyes changed then, but she couldn't read them. His voice dropped to barely a whisper as the tide washed in around their feet. "So you meant what you wrote. You're . . . in love with me."

She glanced down, feeling more exposed than she ever had in her bikini, but then looked back up. She had to face this. "Sad but true."

"Why sad?"

"Because you seem to hate me now, because of the *other* things I wrote."

He shook his head, looked tired. "I don't hate you. I was . . . confused. Hurt. For the first time in my adult life I was starting to care for somebody. I was having a relationship that . . . went beyond sex, *way* beyond sex. I thought . . ." He stopped, sighed, looked to the horizon as if it held the answers he needed. "I can't believe I'm telling you this, but what the hell. I thought I'd found this perfect woman—this woman who had everything: beauty, brains, personality, and enough passion to make me crazy with lust every day of my life. And then . . . I found out you weren't real."

Oh, wow. He'd been crazy about her, and her journal had really, truly hurt him. This *was* about more than just his ego. Ouch.

"I *wasn't* real—at first. Except that . . . I *was*," she tried to explain. "Don't you see? I changed after I got here. I had this image I wanted to portray, but somewhere along the way it became real—it blended with the rest of me and became who I really am. *You* changed me. *I* changed me. But I'm real now. I'm that woman . . . the one you thought I was. Except for the perfect part—I'm *not* perfect. I'm extremely flawed, in fact. I fucked up, and so now . . . I guess you know how it feels. . . ."

He blinked, looked her pointedly in the eye. "To be on the losing end? To be one of the *average people* you keep talking about, the ones who don't have everything so easy?"

"Yes," she whispered. "And I'm sorry. But . . . you should forgive me. Because I don't think what I did was *that* horrible. I think you're taking it harder than you should because you're not used to getting hurt." There. Wow. She'd been totally, brutally honest—but she had to be. She'd deceived him in ways before—so she had to lay it all on the line now, for better or worse.

"Hell, maybe you're right about that—it *is* new for me, and

I'm not proud of how I've handled it. But maybe I'm also taking it hard because I . . . cared for you so much."

She pulled in her breath. "Cared?" *As in past tense?*

But he didn't hear it that way; he thought she was still questioning how he felt for her after all he'd just admitted. "Yes, for God's sake, bunny—*cared!*" He shook his head, seemed exasperated. "I'm not good at saying this sort of stuff—I never have before. But of course I cared. Why the hell else would I get upset about your little game? Any other girl, any other time in my life, if I'd found that book, it wouldn't have mattered. But with you . . . it mattered."

There it was again—past tense. "Are you saying, Brandon, that it's too late for us?"

"No, that's not what I'm saying at all." Again, he looked tired, frustrated, as he stooped down in the wet sand and began doodling in it with a piece of shell as he talked. "Wendy, I'm good at business, I'm good at socializing, I'm good at sex . . . but I'm not that good at feelings, which is why I tried to shut them off when I thought I meant nothing to you. But it backfired and I ended up saying horrible things.

"Same thing at Volcano's the other night. I saw you at the bar and I wanted you so fucking bad, and I thought maybe I could do this, just fuck you for fun—nothing more. But I figured out I couldn't, and so . . . I just shut down, just had to get away from the situation. As the CEO of this place"—he motioned behind him with one hand, still drawing lines in the sand with the other—"I'm a pretty damn good communicator. But as a guy who's trying to tell a girl how he feels . . ." He shook his head yet again. "I'm just no good at finding those kinds of words."

Wendy swallowed. She'd been wrong. He really *did* feel what she felt. But he was right—he was pretty bad at explaining it. Which meant . . . "*What* kind of words, Brandon? I need you to say it."

He rose up and looked into her eyes, his expression passionate, pensive, and maybe even a little nervous—then he pointed down to the sand where he'd been doodling. He'd written:

$$\mathscr{I} \; \heartsuit \; \mathscr{U}$$

And Wendy could barely breathe.

"I should have told you before now," he said, "but when you're a guy like me, a guy who's never . . . loved anybody before, and then you do, and it hurts, it's hard to . . . put yourself out there again. And *I'm* the one who needs to be forgiven. Can you forgive me, bunny?"

"Yes," she said immediately, her eyes still glued to the note in the sand. He still hadn't said it out loud, but maybe this was better. Like her, he'd put it in writing. And maybe that explained why her journal hurt him so very much—because seeing something in writing somehow made it seem more real.

Brandon looked surprised that she was suddenly being so easy about this. "You do?"

She nodded vigorously, then pointed back down at the sand. "If you really mean that."

"I do," he said softly but surely.

At this, Wendy threw her arms around him and kissed him. He wrapped around her in a full embrace and as his tongue snaked into her mouth, things felt right again, with him, and in her heart, for the first time since she'd taken that ill-fated shower seven long weeks ago, leaving him alone with her journal. "I really love you, Brandon," she said, peering into those blue eyes that had captivated her at first sight. "I really do."

He gazed back at her and spoke slowly, carefully. "I . . . I love you, too, Wendy. I really want *this, us*. I'm sorry for being a jerk. You're just . . . the first girl I've ever loved and it threw me for a total loop."

"I told you, I forgive you," she said, "as long as you don't make a habit of it and you go back to being the hot, sweet, sexy guy I fell for."

He smiled the handsome, winning smile she'd fallen in love with and said, "Consider it done, bunny." Then he chuckled. "And consider me lucky that you're sweeter on the beach than you are in the boardroom."

They laughed about that and talked about how fun and strange it was going to be to work together by day and be a couple by night. Wendy asked, "Will we tell people? Or will we keep it a secret?" and they decided they'd figure that out later.

"Right now," Brandon said, "all I want to do is wait for it to get dark out here, then take you back to our beach cabana and have my way with you."

Wendy couldn't wait for that, either—her pussy hummed with anticipation already. "I've been a bad girl," she said, "so I think I deserve a spanking."

A lecherous grin unfurled on his face. "Don't worry, bunny. Good girl or bad, I see lots of spankings in your future."

Just then, a particularly high wave rolled in, crashed over their ankles, and Brandon glanced down at the sand behind him to say, "It washed away my message to you."

She liked that he was a soft enough guy, deep inside, to sound sad about that. But she looked into those sexy, sparkling blue eyes of his and promised him, "Nothing will wash this away, Brandon. It's scary for me, too. But I want this, I trust in this. Nothing will wash it away."

Epilogue

A year after Wendy had first come to Emerald Shores, she was as happy as a woman could be.

Okay, so maybe she and Brandon occasionally knocked heads in the boardroom, but they'd learned how to leave work at work, and mostly, he seemed to respect her ideas—even if he still claimed the resort would be out of business if they approved every money-spending idea she came up with. Overall, though, a year after Carlisle Enterprises had invested in Emerald Shores, most of Wendy's "suggested improvements" were in place, business was booming, and everyone was happy.

Wendy did miss her family, but as she'd hoped, they visited often, and she went home on occasion, too. She'd even taken Brandon for Thanksgiving, and made it up to his mother by going to Alabama for Christmas, where she'd finally gotten to hear his accent, since he seemed to slip back into it there.

Of course, the nights and weekends were her favorite parts of life these days. She enjoyed her work immensely, but she enjoyed her pleasure even more. She still maintained her home at the larger condo she'd selected in the Shellside Towers, even if most nights found her at Brandon's place. Sex with Brandon never got old; she still wanted as much as she could get, and she still let her every inhibition run free with him. He'd continued encouraging her to spread her sexual wings—there'd been a few more hot, steamy evenings with Pete, and one particularly scintillating night when Stacy had joined the three of them. But those encounters had taken place early in their relationship, and since then, they'd pretty much made it a two-person show, having decided that experimentation was fun, but being alone was even hotter.

Wendy loved living at the beach, having weekends and the occasional weekday afternoon to hit the sand and soak up the sun in her sexy bikini, but she and Brandon actually spent more time there in the evenings, holding hands and watching sunsets. Of course, White Bikini Babe was there, too—although spring had brought out a new metallic silver and even skimpier bikini. To this day, Wendy had never exchanged a word with the woman who had changed her life, and she still thought it best to keep it that way.

Now the sun hung low in the west as she and Brandon walked hand in hand up the shore. She wore a flowy cotton skirt and cami, he wore khaki shorts and a golf shirt; both were barefoot.

"Did you know," he said, "that it's been exactly a year ago this week since we first met?"

She looked up, surprised he realized. "As a matter of fact, I *did* know."

He squeezed her hand, lifting his eyes slightly to hers. "It's been a good year, bunny. Best of my life."

She bit her lip, warmed by the words. "Mine, too," she admitted softly.

Brandon had grown skilled—as he was at most things he tried—at sharing his emotions and telling her how he felt, so the conversation was no longer an unusual one, but it still touched her as they walked along the water's edge.

Just then she glanced down to see, carved out in the wet sand ahead of them, the words:

Will U Marry Me?

"Oh, wow," she said, "look what someone wrote in the sand." She couldn't help thinking what a romantic way it was for someone to propose.

And it was just when it occurred to her that Brandon had first told her how he felt about her in a very similar way that he said, "Not just someone, bunny."

She stopped and turned, peering up into his eyes, amazed. Was he saying what she thought he was saying? *Oh God*.

Brandon dropped down on one knee and drew from his pocket a black velvet box, opening it to reveal the gorgeous diamond ring inside. "Will you, bunny?" he asked, taking her hand in his free one. "Marry me?"

Wendy pretty much tackled him in the sand, saying, "Yes, yes, yes!" And they laughed together and kissed like maniacs, and Brandon slid the most beautiful ring she'd ever seen onto her finger.

And then, as was often the case, they waited for it to get dark so they could visit their favorite cabana.

About the Author

Lacey Alexander's books have been called deliciously decadent, unbelievably erotic, exceptionally arousing, blazingly sexual, and downright sinful. In each book, Lacey strives to take her readers on the ultimate erotic adventure, and she hopes her stories will encourage women to embrace their sexual fantasies.

Lacey resides in the Midwest with her husband, and when not penning romantic erotica, she enjoys studying history and traveling, often incorporating favorite destinations into her work.